Books by Tom Hoffman

The Eleventh Ring

The Thirteenth Monk

The Seventh Medallion

Orville Mouse and the Puzzle
of the Clockwork Glowbirds

Orville Mouse and the Puzzle
of the Shattered Abacus

Orville Mouse and the Puzzle
of the Capricious Shadows

Orville Mouse and the Puzzle
of the Last Metaphonium

Orville Mouse and the Puzzle
of the Sagacious Sapling

Available online at Amazon and Barnes & Noble

An Orville Wellington Mouse Adventure

ORVILLE MOUSE

and the Puzzle of the Clockwork Glowbirds

by Tom Hoffman

Tom Hoffman
Visit my website at thoffmanak.wordpress.com
Email: BartholomewtheAdventurer@gmail.com

Printed in the United States of America

Second Printing: 2018
ISBN 978-0-9971952-4-8

With lots of love for
Molly, Alex, Sophie, and Oliver

A very special thanks to my
wonderful editors
Beth, Debbie, Sophie,
Alex, and Amanda
for their invaluable assistance
and excellent advice.

Table of Contents

"The cave you fear to enter holds the treasure you seek."

–Joseph Campbell

"Our truest life is when we are in dreams awake."

–Henry David Thoreau

An Orville Wellington Mouse Adventure

ORVILLE MOUSE

and the Puzzle of the
Clockwork Glowbirds

Chapter 1

The Orange

A gentle breeze carried the delicate fragrance of ten thousand newly bloomed orange blossoms across the balmy summer air. It was far too early in the season for the trees to be bearing fruit, but the intoxicating scent of the blossoms floating through the grove was more than enough to satisfy Orville Wellington Mouse. Besides, strolling alongside Orville beneath a gloriously radiant summer sun was his best friend in the world, Sophia Mouse, and that alone made him supremely happy.

Sophia had moved to Muridaan Falls only one year ago, dropping like a bossy know-it-all gift from above into Orville's life. He was drawn to her immediately, even though at first blush it would seem the two mice had little or nothing in common.

"Isn't this an amazing place, Sophia? I could sit under this lovely orange tree for a hundred years."

"I wish there were oranges on the trees. The blossoms smell nice, but I'm hungry, and we only get oranges in Muridaan Falls in the summertime when the

train can get through the mountain pass."

"That's quite true of course, but doesn't this seem like an exquisitely magical world to you? You know, enchanting and the like?"

"And the like? Are you trying to sound smart? I guess it's kind of enchanting. Hey, look at that monster tree over there. That is huge, and it has bright blue leaves. I've never seen a tree that big, not even back on Quintari, and they have some colossal trees there."

Sophia was always comparing Muridaan Falls to her former home on the planet Quintari. Most of the time Orville didn't mind, but he liked Muridaan Falls just as it was and sometimes the things Sophia said bothered him just a little bit. Of course he never said anything to her because Sophia was his best friend in the world and the very last thing he wanted to do was hurt her feelings. Besides, when he thought about it there was nothing wrong with being proud of where you came from.

"Creekers, I never noticed that tree before. Look at the size of it! It has to be at least a thousand feet tall and five hundred feet wide. Look at all the glowbirds, chirping and tweeting. There must be a hundred of them just on that one branch."

Orville and Sophia made their way out of the picturesque orange grove and over to the enormous tree.

"What kind of tree do you think it is?"

"I don't know. I don't recognize the leaves. It doesn't look like anything I'm familiar with on Earth or on Quintari. The leaves are sky blue and form perfect circles. I've never seen a tree like this before, and I know a lot about trees."

Sophia plucked one of the leaves from the tree and

examined it, then held it out for Orville to inspect. She gazed at Orville for a moment, then grinned and said, "Hey, I bet you can't do this." There was a blink of light and a fat juicy orange appeared in her paw.

"Creekers! How did you do that? You made an orange pop out of nowhere! That's incredible!"

Sophia laughed and gave him the orange. "It's just a little gift from the universe for my best friend in the world."

"Thanks, we can share it. It looks delicious. Really though, how did you do that?" Orville glanced up at Sophia. He could see her mouth moving, but instead of hearing her answer he was hearing a loud, irritating rattling noise. "What is that noise? Do you hear it? It's driving me crazy."

And then, in less than a blink Orville Wellington Mouse was back in his bed listening to his window rattle wildly in the roaring north wind that screamed down from the towering snow-covered peaks surrounding Muridaan Falls.

Chapter 2

Sophia's Gift

"Unnhh. So cold. Why did that dream have to end?" Orville peered out from under his covers into the darkened room. A tiny sliver of dawn had found its way over the top of the mountains and into his bedroom, enough light that Orville knew if he didn't get up now he would be late for school. He gingerly poked one paw out from under the covers and felt around on his bedside table for the box of matches, quickly pulling them back into his little cocoon of blankets. Then, with a loud groan he flung off the covers, sat up in bed and scratched a match on the side of the box. It flared brightly, causing him to squint as he reached over to light his bedside lantern.

"School. Unnhh. Thank goodness I only have one more–" Orville never finished his thought. He never finished it because his eyes were frozen on something that should not be.

"Oh, no. No, no, no!" He glanced furtively around his room, searching for any skulking nocturnal intruders, but found only the darting shadows from his flickering lantern. His insides had turned to ice, but it had nothing to do with the frigid north wind roaring down from the mountains. It did however, have everything to do with the fat juicy glistening orange resting comfortably on his bedside table.

"Oh, no. How did that orange get here? It's not possible. It *can't* be real. First there were the bird feathers, then the round blue leaves, and now this. I feel sick. I think I'm going to throw up. Wait, maybe it's not really there. It could just be my imagination." Orville reached over and tentatively tapped the orange. "Urggh. It's real. Just like the leaves and the feathers." He climbed out of bed, reaching for his clothes, then stopped, his gaze returning to the orange.

"I wonder if it's tasty?" He plucked the orange off the table and proceeded to peel it, the skin practically falling off in his paw.

"Mmm... it smells good." He separated one of the juicy segments and popped it into his mouth.

"Whoa, this is delicious! So sweet. This might be the best orange I've ever had, not to mention the scariest one I've ever had."

With a long sigh he began to get dressed, finishing off the very tasty but terrifying orange along the way.

"I'd better dispose of this peel on the way to school. We haven't had an orange in Muridaan Falls since last summer. I'd have a difficult time explaining to Mum how it got here, especially since I don't have the slightest idea where it came from." He stuffed the orange peel into his pocket and headed downstairs to breakfast.

"Morning, Mum."

"Good morning. Are you all set for your last day of school? Are you excited? It's going to be a new world for you now that you've finished your schooling. When do you start working full time at the Book Emporium?"

"Oh, it will be a couple of months until the store opens again. Master Marloh said things are slow now, but business will get back to normal once they finish adding the new rooms. The store will be twice as big as it was before. Master Marloh said I only need to work a few hours a day until they're done with all the building."

"Well, it sounds like you'll have a nice break between school and your new work. Better finish your breakfast, Sophia will be here soon. She's quite a lovely young mouse isn't she?" Orville's Mum watched closely, gauging his reaction to her comment about Sophia.

"I guess so. She's just a friend."

"Oh, I know that, I was just chattering on. I think it's wonderful that she wants to attend the Symocan Institute of Mechanistic Studies. I'm certain she'll be accepted. She's quite a brilliant mouse."

Orville nodded. "She's the smartest mouse I know."

Orville was not entirely thrilled with Sophia's plan to attend the Symocan Institute, located fifty miles north of Muridaan Falls on the other side of the mountain range. In fact, he didn't like the idea of her going away at all. She was his very best friend, and he didn't have friends to spare.

With breakfast finished and the table cleared, Orville threw on his heavy winter coat and grabbed his backpack as he dashed for the front door.

"Bye, Mum!"

"Bye! Have a wonderful last day of school and say hello to Sophia for me."

Orville's mom grinned as Orville slammed the door

behind him. She had become quite fond of Sophia.

Orville immediately spotted Sophia trudging through the deep snow toward his house.

"Hi, Sophia!"

"Hi, Orville. Have any more strange dreams?"

Orville raced down the stairs toward Sophia. "Uhh... well, sort of. I dreamed you were from that planet called Quintari and you made a fat juicy orange appear in your paw and told me it was a gift from the universe."

Much to Orville's surprise, Sophia did not laugh the way she usually did at his odd dreams. Instead, she stared intently at him with a complicated look on her face.

Orville had always been extraordinarily good at gauging the feelings of other mice. When he looked at Sophia's face he saw a combination of surprise and concern, with a smidgeon of elation, bewilderment and fear tossed in. He could also see Sophia's brilliant and inventive mind was spinning at top speed. He could almost hear her brain clicking and clacking, and he hadn't even told her the part about the fat juicy orange appearing on his bedside table.

"What? Why are you looking at me like that? It was just another one of my crazy dreams."

"I know. It's just an odd thing to dream about, that your best friend is from another planet. Did anything else happen in the dream?"

"Well, there was a giant tree with round blue leaves."

Sophia's eyes narrowed slightly. "Really? What did it look like exactly?"

Orville was about to reply when he heard the voice.

He didn't want to hear it, but nonetheless, there it was, echoing in his mind.

"You may trust her. She is your eternal friend and you may trust her always."

Orville had heard the voice since he was a mouseling, but was still surprised every time it spoke. He had eventually come to believe that everything the voice said was true, even though sometimes it spoke in riddles or told him stories that didn't make much sense at the time. Later on they usually made sense, though. He had also come to believe that the source of the voice was not another mouse, but came from a deeper part of himself. It was a little like having his conscience talk to him. He thought about what the voice had just said. It was true, of course, Sophia was his best friend and he knew he could trust her always. He decided to tell her about the orange.

"If I tell you something, will you promise not to think I'm loopy? And promise not to laugh at me? You're my best friend and I don't want to have you not like me."

Sophia's face softened. "Of course I promise. You're my best friend too. I would never laugh at you."

"Well, the orange you gave me in my dream... when I woke up this morning it was sitting on my bedside table."

Orville couldn't help himself, he had to turn away so he wouldn't see the look on Sophia's face.

"What did you say?"

"There was a real orange sitting on my bedside table this morning. The fat juicy one you gave me in my dream."

"You're certain it was real?"

10

Orville reached into his pocket and pulled out the peel, holding it up for Sophia to see. "It's even worse than that. It's happened twice before. Once there were seven glowbird feathers on my dresser, and once there were thirteen of those round blue leaves scattered across my floor."

"Creekers. Double creekers." Sophia took the peel from Orville and held it to her nose, sniffing it.

Her eyes were fixed on Orville as she rubbed her furry chin with one paw. Finally she stopped and pursed her lips, studying Orville's face intently.

"Orville Wellington Mouse, you are my best friend in the world. If I share a deep secret with you, will you promise never to tell a soul and not think I'm weird and spooky? And not laugh at me or run away?"

"Huh? Of course I promise all that."

Sophia glanced around to see if any mice were watching them, then extended her arm toward Orville. There was a small flash of light and a fat juicy glistening orange appeared on her paw. She held the orange out for Orville to take. "Just a little gift from the universe for my best friend in the world. It's called shaping."

Chapter 3

The Clockwork Glowbirds

Two months had passed since Sophia's surprising revelation that not only was she from the planet Quintari, but she was also a proficient shaper. Orville had read a little about shaping in storybooks when he was small, but he always thought it was just a fanciful tale told to mouselings. He'd heard of Quintari, but Sophia was the first Quintarian mouse he'd ever met.

The frigid winter had transformed into glorious summer, and the warm afternoon sun found the two best friends hiking up the rocky trail that led to the falls, discovered over two hundred years ago by Muridaan Mouse, the original founder of Muridaan Falls. Sophia was sharing her abundance of knowledge with Orville as they wove their way through the dense spruce trees.

"You're not listening. I told you before, it's *not* magic. Shaping has nothing to do with magic. It's just plain science, based in the deep physics. If you weren't so busy dreaming about other worlds in science class you might have figured this out already. It's very simple. I learned all about it back on Quintari when I was just a mouseling. Now, please listen carefully. Everything in the world is made of energy. A table, a spoon, a planet, a galaxy, a mouse – they're all made of compressed energy. Physical matter doesn't really even exist, only energy does. Scientists on Quintari have known this for over a thousand years. When two objects collide it's just two energy fields repelling each other. The tricky bit about how shaping works is that a mouse is made up of two parts, its physical body and its mind. When I say 'mind' I don't mean the mouse's physical brain. The mind is the part of you that exists outside of space and time."

"What does that mean, outside of space and time?"

Sophia gave a sigh of exasperation, but the truth was she thoroughly enjoyed knowing more than other mice did and was quite willing to display the rather staggering depth of her knowledge.

"It means your mind, your true self, is not part of the physical world. It can exist without your physical body, but of course to interact in this world you need a physical body. Do you understand that?"

"I guess. So your mind is like a ghost living in your body?"

Sophia snorted. "Sort of, I guess, but it's not all spooky like a ghost, it's just physics. Anyway, every time you have a thought your mind creates an energy field. Shapers call it a thought cloud. A shaper takes one of their thought clouds, which is just an energy field, and compresses it into physical matter using the power of their mind."

"That sounds a little dramatic."

Sophia glared at Orville.

"Dramatic or not, it's true. They call the objects they create 'thought forms'. Every mouse has the potential to be a shaper. It's just a question of learning how to do it."

"You're not tricking me are you? All this is real?"

Sophia looked at Orville with a dark frown. "I'll prove it's not a trick. Orville Wellington Mouse, I want you to think of a big number, but don't tell me what it is."

"Umm, okay. I'm thinking of one right now, a really big one."

Sophia closed her eyes, then said, "Six million, three hundred and twenty-nine thousand, four hundred and seventeen."

Orville's legs got wobbly. "What? How did you do that? How did you know what I was thinking? That's impossible!"

Sophia gave a groan.

"If you had been listening to me you would under-stand why it is very possible indeed. Please listen carefully. When you have a thought, like thinking of a big number, your mind creates a thought cloud. When I look at you I see a puffy cloud floating out of your ear and I simply draw the thought cloud to me. When the cloud touches me, I hear your thought in my head, and I feel your emotions. If you're really angry, then I feel really angry or if you're really sad, then I feel really sad. I can also tell your mood by looking at the color of the thought cloud."

Orville stared at Sophia, his eyes blinking rapidly as he processed this new information. Finally he grasped the full implication of what she was saying. He moved back a step, a look of horror crossing his face. "You know everything I'm thinking? All my private thoughts?"

Sophia was appalled by his accusation.

"Of course not. That would be very, very rude of me. Shapers don't do that. Ever. That would be like me sneaking into your room in the middle of the night and reading your diary. It's just not done."

Orville relaxed. "Oh, well, that's good. Not that I have awful thoughts or anything. Just, umm, you know, some are kind of personal."

Sophia grinned. "Oooooh, like what *kind* of personal thoughts? Do they have anything to do with how beautiful I am?" She batted her eyes then burst out laughing.

Orville snorted. "Seriously, are you saying I could learn how to be a shaper?"

"Orville, pay close attention. Why do you think you had a dream that I was from Quintari? How did you know that?"

"I don't know. Wait, do you think I read one of those thought cloud things?"

"Precisely. Now you're getting it. You read one of my thought clouds without knowing it. Now you just have to learn to see them and read them anytime you want, and then you have to learn how to compress them into physical objects."

"Sooo... just to be clear, you could shape oatmeal cookies if you wanted to?"

Sophia held out her paw and two large oatmeal cookies blinked into existence. Orville plucked one from her paw.

"Creekers, I think I'm going to like being a shaper.

Mmmm... these cookies are really good."

"Look! There's the falls. We're here already. Are you certain you're not mistaken about the glowbirds? You do have quite a vivid imagination you know, and this doesn't seem like something that would actually happen."

"And making oatmeal cookies pop into your paw does?"

"That's a good point. Where do the glowbirds land?"

Orville looked up at the towering falls. They were magnificent, over four hundred feet from top to bottom, and made up of seven separate falls. The mist from the tons of falling water was transformed into brightly colored sparkling rainbows by the warm Symocan sun as it shone across the face of the mountain. The falls were a popular tourist attraction, mice coming from all over Symoca to see them. The High Counselor of Symoca himself had come to visit the falls when Orville was just a mouseling.

"See that big ledge on the third falls up? The glow-birds land there like clockwork every day at exactly twelve minutes after three, sit there for six minutes, and then all fly west at exactly the same moment."

"How many times have you actually seen them do it?"

"At least six or seven times. At first I thought I was imagining it. There's lots of other glowbirds flying around the falls, but these seven birds behave different-ly. They don't swoop and soar like the other glow-birds."

"What time is it now?"

"We still have an hour until they arrive."

"Let's sit on the benches and watch the falls."

Orville and Sophia strolled over to a long row of wooden benches built to accommodate the summertime tourists. Orville plopped himself down on one of the hard seats.

Sophia gazed upward. "The falls really are beautiful aren't they?"

"Do you ever hear a voice in your head that tells you things?"

Sophia turned to Orville with a curious expression. "Are you talking about your inner voice?"

"Uhh... I don't know. Just a voice that tells you stuff?"

Once again Sophia knew a great deal about it.

"It's called your inner voice. I don't really understand exactly how it works, but I can tell you what my shaping teacher said. She said the universe is infinite in size and infinite in depth. It's made up of dreams within dreams, worlds within worlds, and selves within selves. I think what she meant was that we have a bigger self that's deeper down and knows a lot more than we do. If we listen carefully we can hear what it says."

"Oh, that's kind of what I thought it was. Well, at least I know I'm not loopy. I was kind of worried."

Sophia looked at Orville in surprise. "Loopy? You're not loopy at all. I think you're brilliant. I had to go to school to learn everything I know about shaping. They told me I was a shaping prodigy, but I still had to study really hard to learn all the things I know. You heard your inner voice without even trying. Plus, you're good at finding puzzles."

"What do you mean?"

"You find puzzles, like these glowbirds that land like clockwork at the same time every day. Most mice

17

wouldn't have noticed them, but you did. You found a puzzle. If you never found puzzles then you wouldn't know they were there to be solved, and you'd never learn anything new about the world."

Orville grinned. "Thanks for saying that about me. You're the smartest mouse I know. "

Sophia grinned, raising one eyebrow dramatically while trying to make her voice sound deep and foreboding. "Now it's time for Sophia and Orville to solve... dun dun dun dun... *The Puzzle of the Clockwork Glowbirds*." She gave a loud guffaw.

Orville laughed. "I like that. It sounds really mysterious."

"It *is* mysterious. What time is it now?"

"Almost time. We should climb up the falls to get a better view."

Orville and Sophia hurried over to the right side of the falls and found the trail leading up the mountain. Not wanting to miss the arrival of Orville's mysterious glowbirds, they scrambled up the rocky path until they found a spot with a good view of the birds' landing area.

"Whew, that was steep. I need a rest."

"What time is it?"

Orville pulled out his pocket watch. "Ten minutes after three."

"Okay, keep still so we don't scare them."

Precisely two minutes later, exactly as Orville had predicted, Sophia spotted seven glowbirds flying toward the falls from the east and watched as they landed on the third ledge at exactly twelve minutes past three. The seven glowbirds sat motionless for precisely six minutes, then took to the air as one, heading west.

"See? I told you. Isn't that strange? Creekers, I just thought of something – there are seven glowbirds and I found seven glowbird feathers on my dresser! Do you think that means something?"

Orville turned to Sophia but froze when he saw her. She was hunched over with her paws pressed tightly against her ears, her eyes squeezed shut.

"What's wrong??"

Sophia was shaking. "My inner voice. It just told me something. Something scary. It said we have to discover the true purpose of the seven glowbirds or all of Symoca will be destroyed in a terrible war."

Chapter 4

The Blue Triangle

With the arrival of the startling message from Sophia's inner voice, the mysterious glowbirds who landed like clockwork on the falls had become far more than just a curious puzzle. Orville and Sophia spent the next few days discussing the glowbirds, Orville's orange grove dream, and the mysterious dream objects which had appeared in his room. They both agreed there must be a connection between his dream, the seven feathers, and the seven clockwork glowbirds. It was Orville who came up with idea of looking for clues on the ledge where the glowbirds landed.

"There might be something there. I don't know what exactly, but there might be something. If you think about it, the glowbirds are coming from somewhere and going to somewhere every day. We need to discover where they're going and what they're doing."

The next morning the two best friends headed back to the falls to search for clues on the third ledge.

"What's in your backpack?"

"Just a few scientific instruments I brought with me from Quintari. I can take lots of different measurements with them – you know, like radiation, cosmic rays, and electrical fields."

"Oh. I brought sandwiches and cookies."

The long hike to the falls was arduous, but Sophia and Orville finally reached the trail leading up the mountainside to the third ledge. After an exhausting scramble up the rugged rocky trail they arrived at the third falls.

Orville looked out with some dismay at the narrow outcropping running along the rock face. It hadn't looked quite so narrow when he didn't have to walk on it. His knees were feeling a little weak. He called out to Sophia, his voice barely audible over the deafening roar of the falls.

"It doesn't look very safe out there. It seems awfully high up and that ledge is really narrow. Maybe we could just look from here."

"It will be fine. I use to rock climb all the time back on Quintari."

Sophia stepped out onto the jagged mantle, pressing herself against the rock face.

"Just use the protruding rocks as grips and stay close to the rock face. Don't look down or you'll get dizzy."

A very anxious Orville Mouse followed behind Sophia. Fortunately the ledge grew significantly wider after the first fifteen feet and Orville was able to relax.

"They land next to that scrubby little tree."

"Hmm... I don't see anything. The ledge is covered with dirt and debris. I don't know what I'm looking for though."

"Maybe you should test for those cosmic ray things." Orville had no idea what cosmic rays were.

"Good idea." Sophia slipped off her backpack and dumped out an assortment of gleaming silver and brass devices, most with small blinking lights, colored tabs and round dials.

"You really know how to use all those things?"

"Of course I do. I learned all about them in my science classes on Quintari. I think I'll test for radiation first, to see if the birds have been exposed to it."

Sophia picked up a narrow brass cylinder and pressed two colored tabs. The device emitted a slow and steady beeping noise as she moved it across the ledge.

"Hmmm... nothing. No radiation signal. I'll test for electrical fields now. Maybe the glowbirds have some kind of electrical grid guidance system. When I think about it, it's quite obvious they're acting far more like machines than living creatures."

She grabbed a sparkling green sphere, pressed three tabs and twisted a small brass dial. The device began to make a shrill whining noise. Sophia turned to Orville with a victorious grin. "That's it! There's a powerful electrical field right here on the ledge. I don't see an obvious source for it though."

Orville kneeled down, using his paw to sweep away the rocks and dirt. "Creekers! I found something made of metal!" His efforts soon revealed a three foot long blue metallic triangle embedded deeply into the rocky ledge.

Sophia rubbed her furry chin. "There's a symbol on it – a square with a spiral inside it. I've seen that before. Somewhere. Now where did I–" She stopped in mid sentence, her eyes wide. "Oh, no. This can't be good."

"What is it? What does the symbol mean?"

"It's the symbol on the old Anarkkian flag. This is bad."

"Why is it bad?"

"It's the *old* Anarkkian flag, the one they had during the Anarkkian Wars."

Orville had a sheepish look. History was not his strong suit.

"Umm, I can't quite remember, what were those wars about?"

Sophia gave Orville a disapproving frown.

"Anarkkia was trying to expand its empire and invaded almost two hundred different worlds in several different dimensions. It was the worst war in history. Hundreds of civilizations were wiped out or set back thousands of years. Many civilizations never recovered and are still living in primitive conditions. Just look at Earth. It's nothing like it used to be."

"What do you mean, like it used to be?"

"When the Elders were here. Before they moved to Mandora."

"Who? Moved where?"

"Orville! What do they teach you here? Fifteen hundred years ago, before the Anarkkian Wars, there was a civilization of rabbits known as the Elders living here on Earth. Their technology was extremely advanced and they played a major role in the battle against the Anarkkians. After the war they created their own peaceful world called Mandora in a dimension outside of space and time. It was only a few years ago that the existence of one of their ancient underground cities was revealed by Bartholomew the Adventurer. Bartholomew and his friends discovered a vast subterranean transportation network of gravitor trains beneath the ancient Fortress of Elders, along with thousands of functioning indestructible robotic rabbits called Rabbitons. There was a rumor that some of Bartholomew's friends were involved in deposing Counselor Pravus on Quintari. I can tell you that everyone on the planet was happy to see him go, but I don't really know much about what happened."

"How come I've never heard about any of this?"

"I don't know, I thought you would have learned all this in school. To be honest, I guess Muridaan Falls is kind of... ummm... out of the way. You don't really get much news here. It's nice though. I like it. It's a pleasant change from a big bustling city full of a million mice and noise and traffic."

"Oh. I feel kind of like a dimmer not knowing all those things."

"You should look for history books at the Book Emporium. There are probably quite a few about the Anarkkian Wars, and you might even find some about the Elders' move to Mandora."

"That's a good idea. I'd never even heard of the Elders before." Orville stood up and gazed at the long blue triangle. "I just noticed something. It might be nothing, but the long triangle points in the same direction that the glowbirds were flying. Maybe they stop at other triangles along the way."

"That's it! You really are brilliant! Look at the ledge again, but this time tell me what you don't see."

"What I *don't* see? Well, I *do* see rocks and debris and dirt and the blue triangle, but I don't see... umm... I don't see... bird poop! There's no bird poop on the ledge!"

"Exactly! We know the birds arrive at the same time every day, just like a clockwork machine. There's no bird poop so we know they don't eat food like living birds do. I think they stop here to absorb energy from the powerful electrical field surrounding the blue triangle. They stop here to charge themselves so they can fly on to wherever they're going, and it takes exactly six minutes for them to recharge."

"That makes sense. But what do the Anarkkians have to do with this? You said that war ended fifteen hundred years ago. Why are the glowbirds still here?"

"I don't know. Those are good puzzles though. We need to follow the glowbirds and find out where they're going. Then we'll know what's going on, and maybe discover how to prevent Symoca from being destroyed in a terrible war.

Chapter 5

The Book Emporium

Orville gazed up at the newly installed sign hanging above the book store, a large red oval with crisp white letters reading:

MASTER MARLOH'S
BOOK EMPORIUM

"Here we go, my first day as a full-time employee."

Orville lifted the wrought iron latch and swung the door open. Master Marloh was standing at the long wooden counter examining a stack of paperwork.

"Good morning, Master Marloh. I like the new sign."

"Thank you, Orville. You're right on time, as I knew you would be. You have your work cut out for you today, my young friend. We have over a dozen large crates of new books to be unloaded and sorted."

"I'll get right to it. Oh, do you know if we're getting any new history books? I was looking for books about the Anarkkian Wars or the Elders' move to Mandora."

Master Marloh looked up from his paperwork, removing his glasses and gazing with new interest at Orville.

"Mandora? How in the world do you know about Mandora?"

Orville froze. Maybe nobody else knew about Mandora except Sophia, and she knew about it because she was from Quintari. He certainly couldn't tell Master Marloh that Sophia was–"

"Orville? Are you still with us?"

"Oh, sure, I was just trying to remember where I heard about Mandora. I guess it was in history class or something."

"Ah, history class, yes, that must have been it." Master Marloh nodded, but seemed less than satisfied by Orville's answer.

Orville darted off to the loading area and spent the next four hours opening long wooden crates packed with hundreds of new books. He then began the rather tedious task of carting them into the store and distributing each book to its proper place on the shelves.

While he was doing this he also kept an eye open for the mice he had come to call 'the strangers'. On a fairly regular basis unfamiliar mice would enter the shop and browse the aisles as though searching for a particular book. Orville, however, with his excellent powers of observation, had noticed on his first day of work that things were not as they appeared to be. He could tell the strangers had no real interest in the books, but they did keep sidling closer and closer to the dark blue door at the rear of the shop. Once they got close enough, they would casually stroll over to the door and enter the room, quickly closing the blue door behind them.

Orville had worked part time at the Book Emporium for almost three years and he had never caught a glimpse of what lay behind the blue door. He had tried to open it several times only to find it locked. There was a small sign on the door reading *STORAGE ROOM*, but Orville did not for a moment believe that was the true purpose of the room. Many of the strangers had a rough and tumble look about them, and a few of them had even been carrying weapons. Just this morning he had spotted three strangers enter the store and meander back to the blue door.

Orville had no idea who the strangers were or what they were doing, their identity one more puzzle in a long line of puzzles he had uncovered. He doubted there was anything unscrupulous going on, but he was curious. Some mice would call Master Marloh eccentric, but he was quite proper, and by all accounts appeared to be a kind and generous mouse. Orville sensed there was far more to Master Marloh than he let on.

The following morning Orville discovered a history book containing a few paragraphs about the Elders. Sophia was right, they were technologically advanced rabbits who had helped bring an end to the Anarkkian War, although the book did mention that the Anarkkians had never been defeated. For no apparent reason they had abruptly withdrawn all their forces and the war came to an abrupt and unexpected end.

Orville was searching for any mention of Mandora when a voice from behind made him jump.

"Find any mention of Mandora?"

"Oh, sorry, Master Marloh, you startled me. It's my break time and I was just looking. No, nothing there about Mandora, I'm afraid."

"Hmmm... that's undoubtedly because only a hundred or so mice and rabbits on the entire planet have ever heard of Mandora. You're certain you can't remember who told you about it?"

Orville gave sigh of resignation.

"I remember now where I heard about it. A friend of mine mentioned something about Mandora and the Elders, but I have no idea how she knew about them."

"I see. I'd like to speak with you in my office if you wouldn't mind."

"Am I going to get fired? Did I do something?"

Master Marloh looked sincerely puzzled.

"Fired? Why would I fire you? To the contrary, you might even say I'm giving you a promotion." He gave a low chuckle, then motioned for Orville to follow him. "Come along, we'll talk in my office."

Filled with growing apprehension, Orville followed Master Marloh down the hallway. It didn't feel anything at all like he was getting a promotion.

Chapter 6

The Blue Door

Master Marloh leaned back in his chair, his eyes coming to rest on a very anxious Orville Wellington Mouse.

"Let me ask you this. Would you say you're fond of oranges?"

These were the very last words Orville had expected to come out of Master Marloh's mouth. Orville's body froze, but his mind was spinning a thousand miles an hour trying to come up with a satisfactory answer while simultaneously deciding exactly how much, if anything, Master Marloh knew about the orange he'd found on his bedside table.

"I… uhh... oranges, let's see... well, yes, now that you mention it, I am quite fond of them. It's a shame we only get them in the summer though, when the train can make it over the mountain pass."

Master Marloh nodded, his expression unreadable even to Orville.

"Indeed. An excellent answer. You know, I couldn't help but notice you were so busy unpacking the new books that you didn't even take time for lunch. You must be famished. Would you care for something to eat? Perhaps a fresh juicy orange?"

Orville's mind was a whirlwind. What game was Master Marloh playing? Why did he keep talking about oranges? Maybe he was far more eccentric than Orville had suspected. Or maybe Master Marloh was as nutty as Aunt Molly's fruitcake. Orville decided to play along with his peculiar game.

"A fresh orange does sound quite delicious."

Master Marloh flicked his right paw, and with a flash of blue light a fat juicy orange appeared on the desk in front of Orville. Before Orville even realized what he was doing he had skittered his chair away from Master Marloh's desk. He gaped at the orange, then at Master Marloh.

"You're a shaper?"

Master Marloh smiled pleasantly, quite amused by Orville's reaction. "The expression on your face is priceless, but be assured this little display is the full extent of today's theatrics. Now, let's discuss why you're here."

Master Marloh clasped his paws together beneath his chin. "I'll get straight to the point. I'm offering you a chance to become one of the most powerful shapers in Symoca. What do you think about that?"

Orville was stunned. "You want to teach me to be a shaper?"

"I wouldn't be the one teaching you at first. Someone else would tutor you on the basics, and later on I would assist with the more advanced training. You'll need a great deal of training if you're going to become a member of the Metaphysical Adventurers."

Orville stared blankly at Master Marloh. "What are the Metaphysical Adventurers?"

"I thought you might ask that. Shaping is an ancient mystical art with a long and sometimes checkered history. The first shapers we know of were the Thaumatarians, creators of the World Doors. I won't turn this into a history lesson, but it's an art that has been practiced for many thousands of years. In the past, shaping was performed in secret, usually behind locked doors, but the world is changing and so is its acceptance of shaping. Mice and rabbits are beginning to understand that shaping is not some dark magical power to be afraid of, but is simply a matter of science and deep physics."

"You mean compressing energy into physical objects using the power of the mind?"

Master Marloh smiled. "Excellent. I'm guessing you learned that from the same mysterious friend who told you about Mandora?"

"Umm... it may have been her."

"Indeed. To continue, over the centuries shapers gradually joined forces, forming small regional guilds. Those guilds eventually combined to form one large guild known today as the Shapers Guild. In many countries, such as Lapinor and Grymmore, the Shapers Guild practices openly and the citizens are more or less accepting of it. It's a little different here in Muridaan Falls, of course, which is why our Shapers Guild is still a closely guarded secret. I'm well aware you've noticed our mysterious guests who frequent the Book Emporium. They are members of the Shapers Guild visiting from neighboring towns and villages.

"Now, more to the point, I will tell you about a small elite group of shapers most Guild members are not aware of, a group known as the Metaphysical Adventurers. If you don't already know, metaphysics is the study of the profoundly deep mysteries held by our universe. The group's name is a rather antiquated nomenclature to be sure, but there is a great deal of history and proud tradition standing behind it."

Orville's mind was spinning. "I don't understand why you're asking me to join the Shapers Guild or this Metaphysical Adventurers group. I can't do anything. I don't know anything at all about shaping. I couldn't shape an orange if I tried for a month."

A light of understanding blinked on in Master Marloh's eyes. "Ahhh, of course you don't know why. I do apologize for my inexcusable lack of clarity. When a shaper is deeply connected to their inner self they gain an intuitive understanding of the mice around them. When I look at you with my intuitive mind, it is blindingly clear that you possess the innate potential necessary to become a truly legendary shaper. Let me ask you this, have objects ever appeared out of nowhere around you?"

"You mean like oranges?"

"Like oranges."

"And feathers, and leaves. How did you know about the orange?"

Master Marloh continued without answering Orville's question.

"You did not bring those objects back from your dreams as you suspected. You shaped them in your sleep. Your inner self was sending your outer self a message which would be impossible to ignore. Now, do you sometimes know what other mice are thinking? Do you know things about them that you have no reason to know? Perhaps on occasion you have found yourself suddenly standing in a different location with no idea how you got there?"

Orville's chest tightened, his heart pounding. "How did you... well... yes, that has happened. When I was a mouseling it happened twice. I was playing in the front yard and then I was in the back yard. It scared me badly and I never told anyone."

"No, I don't suppose you did. It's called spontaneous blinking. Very experienced shapers can blink themselves many miles away in a split second. You blinked when you were a mouseling. Are you starting to understand why I am asking you to join the Metaphysical Adventurers?"

"Kind of. I always thought there was something wrong with me."

"No, there is nothing wrong with you. To the contrary, you are the most gifted mouse I have ever met in all my years of shaping. There is one more thing I must ask of you. The Shapers Guild has some basic rules which must be adhered to by all members. Without going into great detail I will tell you there are two basic tenets. The first, you must never under any circumstances take the life of another living creature. If you are being attacked by a vicious beast or assailant you must defend yourself without harming your attacker. Second, you may not use your shaping skills for personal gain. No shaping crates of gold coins or bags of Nirriimian white crystals. Do you think you can live with those rules?"

Orville had no idea what Nirriimian white crystals were, but said, "I'm certain I can. Papa told me I shouldn't even kill a small bug. He said all life was precious, that it was a miracle."

"Very good. I thought as much." Master Marloh

pushed his chair back and stood up. "Well, my curious and eminently gifted friend, it's time you saw what's behind the mysterious blue door you've been eyeing for three long years."

Chapter 7

Orville's New Teacher

Orville's excitement mounted as they approached the blue door at the back of the shop. Master Marloh stopped in front of it and silently held up one paw, turning it slowly so Orville could see both sides. Using that paw he swung the door open and motioned for Orville to enter. Orville stepped into what appeared to be a large library, the walls lined with ornate wooden shelves holding thousands of dusty old tomes. A number of mice were sitting at tables reading. One of them looked up and nodded his hello to Master Marloh. Master Marloh gave him a quick wave.

"I'd like you all to meet Orville Wellington Mouse, the newest member of our Guild."

The mice at the tables greeted Orville cordially, then went back to their reading.

Master Marloh led Orville out of the library and closed the door.

"That's it? It's just a library?"

"That was the Symocan Shapers Guild library. It is the largest collection of shaping books in Symoca, covering nearly every conceivable aspect of the craft."

Master Marloh held up his other paw for Orville to see, slowly turning it. This paw was adorned with a large silver ring bearing the symbol of a single eye positioned between the letters 'M' and 'A'.

"This is the ring worn by all Metaphysical Adventurers. Watch what happens when I use this paw instead of my other paw to open the blue door."

When Master Marloh swung the door open this time, the library was gone. Instead, Orville stood facing an ancient spiral stone staircase worn smooth by the ages. He couldn't help but notice that the stairs were descending into inky blackness. Orville was unsure what he had been expecting, but this was not it. This was far scarier than anything he had imagined.

"Umm... what's down there?"

"There's only one way to find out, my friend."

Master Marloh flicked his wrist and a glowing sphere of light drifted out from his paw and floated down the stairway, gradually growing in brightness.

It took almost three full minutes to descend the great winding staircase, but Orville finally hopped off the last step, following Master Marloh through a long low archway.

When they emerged from the corridor Orville stood in stunned silence. He had never witnessed anything remotely like this.

Orville was looking out across a vast room, three hundred feet long and two hundred feet wide, with ceilings that towered fifty feet above the smooth stone floor. Running around the perimeter of the room were three enormous stacked walkways constructed of massive ornately carved wooden beams supported by a complex network of spiraling wrought iron rails. Each walkway was lined with wide iron mesh shelves holding thousands of gleaming, fantastical objects of every conceivable size and shape, their purpose a mystery to Orville.

He ran his eyes studiously across this monumental assortment of baffling contraptions, quickly realizing he could not identify even one of them. Many of the objects were fabricated from smooth gleaming synthetic materials, some holding strange sparkling glass spheroids or mysterious glowing cylinders with pulsing colored lights. A few of the larger objects looked as though they could be vehicles, but that was simply speculation on Orville's part. He felt as though he been dropped into another world, one of those imaginary worlds he had spent so much time dreaming about.

The main floor of the room was divided into six distinct sections, two of them were clear open areas, the other four were filled with long tables, shelves and workbenches piled high with curious instruments of unknown design and purpose. Orville counted over twenty mice in the room, many of them standing at workbenches in front of bubbling, gurgling glass cylinders and unidentifiable whirring mechanical devices. A few of the mice stood motionless in one of the open areas, eyes closed, paws extended out in front of them. Several of the mice were shooting brilliant streams of blue light from their paws at a ten foot wide black sphere which floated slowly across the room.

Orville noticed an area containing a roiling black cloud rimmed with miniature lightning bolts. Before his startled eyes a ragged looking mouse tumbled out of the dark cloud and rolled across the hard stone floor, quickly rising to his feet and brushing off his coat.

Orville turned to Master Marloh with a look of complete bewilderment. "What *is* this? Where are we?"

Master Marloh grinned, resting his paw on Orville's shoulder.

"I remember the first time I saw it. It's not something you soon forget. Only a few hundred living mice have ever seen this room. This is the main headquarters of the Metaphysical Adventurers, and it won't be long until this astonishing room feels like your second home."

"What are all those weird objects on the walkways?"

"What do you know about the universe?"

"What do you mean?"

"What do you know about the planets, stars, galaxies, dimensions, the concept that time is fluid and passes at different rates in different worlds, the true nature of our dreams, that sort of thing."

"Umm... not very much I guess. I know Earth is a round ball and there's millions of stars and planets and a lot have living creatures on them, some of them like us."

"That's a good start. Many mice aren't even aware of those things. As a Metaphysical Adventurer, you will be learning a great deal more than you currently know about the universe we live in. Metaphysical Adventurers often will travel to... shall we say, very unfamiliar and inhospitable environments. To survive in such worlds you must possess a broad range of skills, and a clear understanding of many different species and cultures.

"You'll learn it's possible for many worlds to simultaneously occupy the same space, as impossible as that may sound right now. These are called parallel dimensions, and there are many of them. But, to answer your question, all the objects you see on the walkways are highly advanced technological devices brought back from other worlds over the years by Metaphysical Adventurers. Such devices are often necessary on various missions, especially in the more hostile worlds.

Orville was overwhelmed. "Are you sure I should be here?"

"I have never been more certain of anything. How would you like to meet your new shaping instructor?"

Orville nodded, his eyes still scanning the massive room. "I guess so."

"Would you allow me just a little theatrical latitude?"

"Um, okay."

With a grin Master Marloh raised one paw above his head and announced dramatically, "Orville Wellington Mouse, I present to you a most proficient shaper, an honored member of the Metaphysical Adventurers, and now, your new shaping instructor."

There was a brilliant flash of blinding light followed by a deafening crash of thunder. A second blast of blue light followed and a mouse blinked into existence directly in front of Orville. Orville's jaw dropped. His new shaping instructor was Sophia.

"Hi, Orville! Surprised to see me?"

Chapter 8

Pavorak Gorge

The next morning when Orville arrived at the Book Emporium, Sophia was waiting for him on the front steps.

"Hi, Orville!" She glanced around to make certain no one was listening, then said in a low voice, "I'm sorry I couldn't tell you I was a member of the Metaphysical Adventurers, but I had to wait until Master Marloh told you about the group. Those are the rules. I was a member of the Shapers Guild on Quintari and was recruited there by a member of the Metaphysical Adventurers. They brought me here for two years of advanced training and even found me a boarding house to stay in. I still have a lot to learn but Master Marloh says I'm one of the best students he's ever had."

"That doesn't surprise me at all. You know a million times more about all this stuff than I do. How did you get here from Quintari anyway? Weren't your parents afraid to let you go to another planet?"

"I came here through a spectral door that Master Marloh opened."

"A what door?"

"A spectral door. It's a kind of pathway that lets you travel between two worlds without having to go through the space between them. I don't understand all the deep physics behind it, but I do know that only the most advanced shapers can open spectral doors. The Anarkkians used to have machines that could open spectral doors, and the more advanced civilizations had devices like that on their interstellar ships."

"Creekers, that sounds a little scary. Weren't your parents worried? My Mum would never let me do something like that."

"It's kind of hard to talk about it, but both my parents are gone. Mum died when I was a mouseling, and Papa died a little over a year ago. I was living with my mum's sister when they recruited me."

Orville desperately wished he hadn't asked Sophia about her parents. "Oh. I'm sorry, Sophia. I didn't know." Orville stared awkwardly at the ground.

"That's okay, there's no way you could have known."

Orville quickly changed the topic. "So, have you thought any more about the glowbirds?"

"I talked to Master Marloh and he feels the clockwork glowbirds are important, a link in a chain of events we need to follow. This is exactly the kind of mission Metaphysical Adventurers go on, and it will make a perfect first mission for you. It won't be too dangerous or too scary. Master Marloh wants us to find out where the glowbirds are going and how they are connected to a possible future war. He said you could take a few days off work so we can follow the glowbirds. We'll leave early tomorrow morning. I can start your shaping lessons during the mission, if you'd like."

Orville was thrilled. He rubbed his paws together. "I can't wait. My first big adventure *and* I'll be learning about shaping."

"I'm not sure how much of a big adventure it will be, but you never know what might happen. That's what makes them fun. And sometimes scary."

As the sun peeked up over the mountains the following morning it found Sophia and Orville heading due west through a dense forest, the falls several miles behind them.

"I brought my compass. Do we just keep heading west? How will we know if the birds change direction?"

Sophia swung her backpack off her shoulder.

"I have something that will work a little better than a compass." She flipped open her pack, rummaged around and pulled out a pair of brass goggles with fluorescent green lenses. There were two small dials and four silver tabs on the side panel. She tapped one of the tabs and a small light blinked on.

"What are those? What do they do?"

"Trackers use them on Quintari. Master Marloh had a box of them at the MΛ headquarters. It makes tracking a lot easier. Here, I'll show you. Put them on."

Orville took the heavy goggles from Sophia and strapped them on over his eyes. "I can't see anything. Everything looks dark green."

"How about now?" Sophia tapped several of the tabs and small blue light in the center of the goggles began blinking.

"Oh, that's good. Whatever you did worked. Now I can see really clearly. How do I track something with

43

them?"

"A glowbird's electrical field affects both the atmosphere and the space it flies through. Its effect on the atmosphere dissipates quickly, but it can take a week for its effect on space to fade away. These goggles track the effect of their electrical field on space, relative to the position of Earth. I'm going to slowly turn this dial and when it matches the residual electronic signature of the birds, you'll see something."

Orville watched the sky closely as Sophia turned the small brass dial. Moments later he cried out, "I see it! I see their trail! There are seven orange lines going through the sky and heading west. This is amazing – it's like magic!"

Sophia quickly corrected Orville. "You mean it's like science. Magic is science that mice don't understand."

"I know, but it still seems like magic."

Orville and Sophia continued heading west, following the orange trail lines of the seven glowbirds.

Six hours later they were trudging through the forest, both of them exhausted. Sophia came to a halt in a wide clearing at the top of a small hill.

"It will be getting dark soon. Let's set up camp here and have dinner. We can get up with the sun and continue tracking the glowbirds."

Orville set his pack down. "Whew, that was getting heavy. I can build the fire. I used to go camping a lot and I'm pretty good at making campfires."

"No need for that." There was a bright flash of light and a circle of stones appeared in the center of the clearing. Another flick of Sophia's wrist and there was a roaring campfire inside the ring of stones.

"Creekers! That's incredible!"

"Thanks. It won't be long till you'll be doing that. Are you ready for your first shaping lesson?"

"Sure. What do I have to do?"

"Let's sit by the fire and I'll tell you a little bit about how it works. It's probably a lot simpler than you think."

Orville unrolled his sleeping bag and plopped down on the ground next to Sophia.

"Okay, if you remember, Master Marloh told you it was your *inner self* who shaped the orange you found on your bedside table. It's important to remember that, because shaping is always done by your inner self, not your outer self. Your inner self exists outside of space and time but is fully capable of manifesting physical objects into this world. In order to be a shaper, you must first be deeply aware of your inner self. You have to be able to hear your inner voice, the deeper self who knows so much more than you do. You understand this so far?"

"I think so. It was my inner voice who told me you were my true friend and it was safe to tell you about the orange in my room."

Sophia smiled. "Yes, that's the one, and I really *am* your true friend, just in case you were wondering. Now, back to shaping. I want you to think of a simple object, something you own which holds great sentimental value. It could be something that belonged to your papa."

"Umm... let me think. I know, Papa gave me a big blue marble he found and told me it was magic. I still have it even though I never really did believe it was magic. It was the last thing he gave me before he went away."

"I'm sorry. I knew your papa was gone but I was afraid to ask you about it. What happened to him?"

"He was a fishermouse. He only took me out once because Mum said the Vesarak Sea was too dangerous. Almost two years ago he went out and there was a terrible storm. He never came back."

Sophia put her paw on Orville's shoulder.

"I'm sorry."

"What happened to your Papa, Sophia?"

Sophia hesitated, Orville instantly sensing she did not want to talk about it. An icy chill had shot through him, something he had never sensed from Sophia before.

"You don't have to tell me, it's okay. I know how hard it is to talk about stuff like that."

Sophia gave a weak smile and the chill faded away.

"Thanks. One day I'll tell you everything, but I can't talk about it now, not even to my best friend in the world."

There was a long silence, the pair of adventurers gazing into the flickering flames, lost in their own thoughts.

Finally Sophia said, "All right, back to business. I want you to close your eyes and imagine that magic blue marble your Papa gave you. See it as clearly as you can in your mind, move it around, turn it, examine it closely. What you're really doing is creating a good dense thought cloud. I'll be able to see it and in time so will you. When you clearly see the marble I want you to ask your inner self to bring the marble into this world. Then just let go and relax. Don't try to help. Let your inner self take over completely."

"Okay, here goes." Orville closed his eyes and began to visualize the marble. After several minutes it felt as though he could almost touch it. He smiled to himself. All those years of clearly imagining other worlds had not been a waste of time after all. When he was satisfied with what he saw he said, "Inner self, I would like you to bring this marble into the world. Please convert my thought cloud into physical matter."

He opened his eyes but saw nothing. "No marble."

"Shhhh. Just wait, I'm watching your thought cloud now. It's a good one, nice and solid. It's bright red which means there's a lot of love in it. That should help. Okay, it's swirling around like a little tornado, getting denser."

There was a sudden flash of light and a sparkling blue marble appeared on the ground in front of Orville. He turned to Sophia with a look of astonishment. "Did I do that?"

Sophia had a wide grin on her face. "Congratulations, you're officially a member of the Shapers Guild!"

The following day as they were making their way across a broad rocky pass, Sophia said, "I think I've figured out why you were able to shape that marble on your first try, a feat which takes most shapers many years to master. You've been unwittingly practicing the necessary skills for most of your life. All your years of imagining and visualizing complex worlds, plus listening to your inner voice since you were a mouseling."

"I was thinking the same thing. Maybe part of me knew what skills I should be practicing."

"That wouldn't surprise me at all. Hey, put these on and make sure we're still following the glowbirds."

Sophia handed Orville the tracking goggles. Orville slipped them on and tapped the tabs on the side panel and slowly turned the brass dial.

"Still there, heading west, but one of the glowbird trails has veered off from the others. It looks as though it may have landed. Maybe it was running low on power and stopped at one of those blue triangles."

"Maybe. Let's go see. We might get a good close look at one."

Orville and Sophia finally reached the end of the boulder strewn terrain, arriving at a small forest of tall spruce trees. Orville eyed the forest floor. "The orange trail ended right around here, but I don't see a glowbird anywhere."

It was Sophia who solved the puzzle. "Look up, not down."

Orville turned his gaze to the towering trees above him, immediately spotting the iridescent blue glowbird wedged between two branches. "It's not moving. It must have just stopped working."

Orville clambered up the tree, gingerly retrieving the fallen glowbird. He hopped down and held it out for Sophia to examine. "What do you think? It's really light."

"Look at the feathers, they're made of a synthetic material. This bird was fabricated, that's why it's so light. A real glowbird would weigh four or five times as much as this one. I've seen bio-form creations like this before, automatons made to resemble all manner of creatures. The Anarkkians used them extensively during the war. Papa showed me images of huge metallic spiders they created. They would drop thousands of the deadly silver spiders onto the surface of whatever planet they were invading. The Anarkkians weren't alone in this tactic either. The Elders had huge autonomous A6 Warrior Rabbitons which were virtually indestructible and armed with powerful vaporizing particle beam systems. It was a very dangerous time to be alive." Sophia gave a long sigh. "Enough about that dreadful war. These glowbirds were not meant for warfare, they have another purpose entirely. We just have to discover what it is, or what it was. Let's keep moving west and see where it takes us."

The two best friends hiked through the dense forest for most of the day, reaching the end of it late that afternoon when they stepped out only a few hundred feet from the edge of an enormous gorge.

"Creekers. There's no way we can cross that." Orville stared at the mammoth chasm, three or four miles across and well over a mile deep. He pulled a wrinkled map from his backpack and unfolded it. "This old map doesn't help too much, but it does show a gray area marked *Pavorak Gorge*."

"Can you see where the glowbirds went?"

Orville slipped on the brass goggles and twisted the small dial. "There are only six orange trails now. They veer down to the bottom of the gorge, head north for about a mile, then turn into a narrow ravine on the far wall."

Sophia stood motionless for several moments, her eyes closed. Orville did not interrupt her. Finally she turned to him and said, "We should head back to Muridaan Falls. We'll have to find another way to reach that ravine. Any attempt we make to climb down into the gorge would be far too risky. I might be able to blink myself to the bottom of the gorge, but that would be even more of a risk. Master Marloh says I need a lot more blinking practice before I can safely use it on a mission."

Sophia eyed the iridescent glowbird lying on the ground next to her pack. "Orville, I think it's time I paid a visit to the Mad Mouse of Muridaan."

Chapter 9

The Mad Mouse of Muridaan

The next month was a hectic one for Orville. During the day he worked at the Book Emporium and in the evenings he was tutored by Sophia, an unrelenting taskmaster who pushed Orville harder than his teachers at school ever had. She told him over and over that one day his life would depend on the skills he was now learning.

Master Marloh had cleared out a small practice room for Orville at the rear of the store. It was in the confines of this room that Sophia had him shape the blue marble again and again until he could shape it in a split second. Once he had mastered the marble, he began shaping larger, more complex objects. After three weeks of exhausting practice, Orville was able to shape almost any object Sophia requested.

"This is excellent. Master Marloh was right about you. I've never seen anyone advance so rapidly."

"How large an object can I shape? Could I shape a house?"

"No, there's not a shaper alive who could do that.

There is a limit to the size and the mass of an object a single mouse can shape, just as there is a limit to how much weight one mouse can lift. The greater your skill, the larger the object you can shape. There are some esoteric shaping techniques which involve two or more mice linking minds to magnify their shaping power, but that's well beyond my skill level. I'm not even sure if Master Marloh can do that."

Sophia reached into a basket filled with blue marbles shaped by Orville. She plucked one of them out and placed it on the floor in front of her.

"You have learned to create a thought cloud and compress it into a physical object, also known as a thought form. Now you will learn to convert a thought form back into a thought cloud. Watch, please."

Sophia flicked her wrist and with a small flash of light the blue marble vanished. "I have converted the marble from its physical form back to a thought cloud. The process involved is simply the reverse of shaping the marble. Now you try."

"Umm, so I look at the marble and imagine it as a thought cloud and then ask my inner self to convert it back to an energy field?"

"Precisely." Sophia set a blue marble down on the floor in front of Orville.

Orville focused on the glassy sphere and imagined all the compressed energy used to create the marble being released back into a field of energy. Once he had an image of the vaporous thought cloud clear in his mind he asked his inner self to convert the marble back to an energy field.

Five seconds later there was a flash of light and the marble vanished.

"Excellent, but far, far too slow. You have to be able to convert objects back and forth so quickly it looks as though they're blinking on and off."

Sophia pointed to the basket of marbles. "I want you to convert all these marbles back to thought clouds, and keep doing it until you can do it with barely a thought. I know this seems tedious, but at some point I guarantee this skill will save your life."

Three days later Sophia watched as Orville set out a row of fifty marbles and converted them one at a time to thought clouds, all in less than five seconds.

"Well done. You're ready for the next lesson, which combines everything you have learned so far. I'm going to teach you a skill which is commonly referred to as 'blinking'.

"There are three steps to blinking a marble. You have mastered each of the steps individually, but now you must combine them into one fluid motion. First, convert the marble to a thought cloud. Second, move the thought cloud across the room with your mind. Third, convert the thought cloud back to the physical form of the marble at its new location. You are essentially moving, or 'blinking' an object across the room.

"Once you are proficient at blinking an object around the room, you will learn how to blink your own physical form around the room. This is the skill which allows advanced shapers to blink themselves across great distances, something you must not attempt at this time under any circumstances. For now, I want you to practice with this marble. You must be able to blink it instantly from one point to another."

It took some time for Orville to grasp the rhythm of

blinking an object across the room, but once he was comfortable with it he progressed quickly. He practiced relentlessly for many days, often late into the night, until at last he could make the marble fairly hop around the room, blinking from place to place.

It was in the middle of one of these marathon practice sessions that Sophia burst into the room with a wide grin on her face. "It's time, Orville Wellington Mouse."

Orville looked exhausted, barely able to keep his eyes open. "Time for what? More lessons?"

"We're done with lessons for now. It's time for some fun. I have a surprise for you. Follow me!"

Sophia hurried to the rear of the bookstore and unlatched the back door. Orville was wide awake now, his curiosity piqued. "Where are we going? What kind of surprise?"

Sophia pointed to the old ramshackle barn behind the Book Emporium. "There. We're going in there." She hurried over to the barn's rickety wooden doors and put her paw on the heavy wrought iron latch. "Stand next to me and close your eyes."

"This isn't going to hurt is it?"

Sophia laughed. Orville squeezed his eyes shut and heard the rusty hinges squeal as Sophia swung the doors open. "You can open your eyes now."

Orville peaked cautiously through his eyelids then burst out laughing. "What *is* that thing?"

Orville stood facing what appeared to be a gigantic glowbird, eight feet tall and thirty feet long, its legs replaced with two metal spoked wheels. Behind the glowbird stood a rather disheveled elderly mouse wearing a long white coat and enormous round glasses, the grin on his face even wider than the one on Sophia's.

The mouse in the white coat waved his paw and called out to Orville. "What do you think of her? We named her *The Glowbird*. I guarantee there's not another one like her in this world or any other." He slapped his leg and gave very peculiar high pitched staccato laugh that reminded Orville of the Kukululu bird, a feathered denizen of the east Symocan jungles.

Even with this information Orville was still baffled. "So... what is it exactly that this very large glowbird on wheels does?"

Sophia gestured toward the eccentric looking elderly mouse. "Orville, I'd like you to meet the greatest inventor in all of Symoca. The Metaphysical Adventurers fondly refer to him as The Mad Mouse of Muridaan, but I can assure you he is far from mad and is in fact exceedingly brilliant. Say hello to Mirus Mouse. I brought Mirus the glowbird we found in the tree near Pavorak Gorge and asked if he could build a large scale version, one capable of flight, and one capable of carrying two mice. This magnificent craft is the product of his genius and of his tireless efforts, and it is also how you and I are going to get to the bottom of Pavorak Gorge."

Orville did four things in the space of five seconds. He looked at Sophia, then at *The Glowbird*, then at Mirus Mouse, and then back to Sophia. "We're going to do *what*??"

Half an hour later Sophia and Orville were seated comfortably in the cockpit of *The Glowbird*. Mirus Mouse was leaning in through the open door, pointing out the various controls of the ship.

"If you're going to ask me how she flies I'll tell you she's powered by duplonium. If you didn't know what duplonium was I'd tell you it's a rare element that reacts in a very particular way with water. Drop a piece of duplonium in a glass of water and the water will boil away in five minutes and you'd still have your duplonium. Put that duplonium in a closed system and it will produce all the steam you need to power *The Glowbird* for a hundred years. She'll fly until her wings fall off!"

"What?? Her wings might fall off?"

Mirus let out a great squawk. "No chance of that happening, my furry young friend. Now, how do you fly this contraption, you ask? I would answer by pointing to those two silver sticks on either side of your seat. It's easier than walking, I would tell you. The stick on your left, push it forward and the wings start flapping. The further you push it, the faster they flap. Stick on the right, pull back and she goes up, push forward and she goes down. To the left for a left turn, to the right for a right turn. Ready to take her up, my fine young friend?"

"What? No! Not so soon. I have to study all this first."

Mirus let out another raucous jungle bird laugh and slapped Orville on the shoulder. "Come with me back to the shop and I'll teach you a thing or two about flying this bird. It's a lot easier than it sounds, that's what I would tell you."

Chapter 10

Flight of *The Glowbird*

"Orville! You're going to be late for work!"

"Okay, Mum, I'm getting dressed. Master Marloh doesn't mind if I'm a bit late sometimes." Orville slipped on his favorite red plaid woolen shirt, a pair of sturdy canvas hiking shorts and his heavy leather boots, then dashed downstairs to breakfast.

"Good heavens, are you going to work dressed like that? You look like you're off to explore the deepest jungles of East Symoca."

Orville laughed. "Master Marloh is sending us out on a book hunting expedition and some of the mice we'll be talking to live a good distance from town. I'll be gone for several days."

"You be careful. Are you taking the train?"

"Umm... I thought instead maybe I'd fly there inside a giant mechanical glowbird."

Orville's Mum rolled her eyes. "Oh, you and that wild imagination of yours. You should write stories and sell them."

"Good idea. I have to go, I don't want to be late."

"All right, you be careful flying in that giant glow-bird of yours."

Orville hugged his mum and darted out the door. An hour later he stood at the front gate of the sprawling complex owned by Mirus Mouse.

"Let's see, Sophia said to meet her in the big red building." Orville swung the tall metal gate open and eyed the maze of buildings. He spotted the long, low red structure peeking out from behind a towering yellow barn.

He hurried past the barn and made his way over to the red building. Swinging a side door open he spotted Sophia and Mirus next to *The Glowbird*. Sophia looked up when she heard the door creak open.

"Hi, Orville! Mirus took *The Glowbird* up for some test flights and it flies like a dream, nice and smooth, even with the wings flapping up and down. This morning he took me up and let me fly it! It's so much fun and really easy to fly! It's not even a little bit scary. He added a set of controls on my side of the ship so you and I can take turns flying if we want to."

"That sounds perfect. You can take over when I get paralyzed with fear."

Mirus gave a great squawking laugh and slapped Orville on the shoulder. "You'll do fine. Hop in! I'll open the main doors and we'll roll her out. Don't forget, slow flapping until she hits twenty miles an hour, full speed till she hits forty, then take her up till you're soaring with the birds. Anything funny happens to the duplonium engine, just glide down and land somewhere smooth."

Mirus called out to Orville, "Help me roll her out onto the grass." Orville and Mirus lifted the tail and pushed the great bird forward while Sophia sat in the cockpit and steered the ship through the open doors.

Mirus stepped away from the craft and waved his arm at Orville. "What are you waiting for? Get in and get flying!"

Orville hopped into the cockpit. Sophia was almost bouncing with excitement. "Ready to take this bird up, Captain Orville?"

"Wait, I'm the captain? Shouldn't you be the captain?"

"I'll be captain of this side, you be captain of that side."

"That sounds fair. Okay, here we go!" Orville gave the paws up sign to Mirus and flipped on the duplonium motor, then pushed the left control stick gently forward. He watched as the craft's long feathered wings unfurled and began smoothly flapping.

"So far so good! The wings are working just as they should."

The Glowbird gradually picked up speed as it rolled down the grassy field. Sophia called out, "We just hit twenty miles an hour!"

Orville nodded and pushed the left stick forward as far as it would go. The wings became a blur, the wind whistling past Orville's ears as they sped down the runway. "Forty miles an hour! Take her up!"

Orville pulled back on the right stick and *The Glowbird* took to the air. They heard Mirus Mouse give a great squawking cheer. "Hoorah!! There she goes!"

Ten minutes later they were circling a thousand feet above Muridaan Falls.

Orville could barely contain himself. "This is incredible! We're flying! We're really flying! Look, you can see the falls. You can see the whole town! Everything looks so small from up here!"

Sophia gestured to the large compass sitting between the seats and hollered to Orville, "Head west! It shouldn't take us too long to get there. The dial says we're at fifty miles an hour. You can slow down if you want, now that we're up here. It won't be so windy then."

Orville made a slow banking turn and headed due west toward Pavorak Gorge. Sophia opened her pack and pulled out the brass tracking goggles. She slipped them on and pressed the tabs. "I see the six orange trails from the glowbirds. Just keep heading directly west."

Orville slowed *The Glowbird* down to thirty miles an hour and held it steady at a thousand feet. The sweeping vista of snowcapped mountains and lush green forests stretching out to the horizon was a sight Orville would never forget. He watched as the great forests passing below them gradually turned to green flowering pastures, and then to desolate and barren rocky terrain.

"Orville! Eyes on the sky! I don't want to smash into the side of a mountain while you're gawking at the scenery."

"Aye aye, Captain Sophia!"

Sophia rolled her eyes. She was about to give Orville some rather rude advice when she stopped and cried out, "I see the gorge! The glowbird trails veer down into it and turn directly north, continuing on for about a mile. Take us down into the gorge and head north. Nice and slow."

Orville pushed the right stick forward and *The Glowbird* began its gradual descent. Once they were in the gorge he banked gently to the north at an altitude of three hundred feet.

"Orville, there's the ravine up ahead on the left. The

glowbird trails go directly into it. The bottom of the gorge is smooth, so you can land here and we'll hike up into the ravine."

With barely a thump *The Glowbird* touched down onto the flat sandy floor of the gorge. Orville kept the wings flapping until they had taxied over to the ravine.

"Here we are!"

Sophia was grinning like a mouseling. "That was so much fun! We should go flying every day!"

Orville switched off the duplonium motor and hopped out. "This gorge is spectacular. Look at all the brightly colored layers of rock running through it."

Sophia nodded. "It's magnificent. Let's head up into the ravine."

Orville and Sophia scrambled up the steep mounds of rocky debris that led into the narrow crevasse.

"Look, it widens the farther in it goes."

After nearly a mile of walking over the jagged rocks Sophia stopped in her tracks, pointing to a mammoth stone cube almost a mile away.

"What do you think that is?"

Orville shook his head. "Please don't tell me that's where the glowbirds go."

Sophia peered through the tracking goggles. "That's where they go, so that's where we have to go. Don't forget your shaping skills. Don't forget to blink up a sphere of defense around you. We have no idea what might be waiting for us inside that building."

As they approached the stone cube Orville realized its truly mammoth proportions. The structure stood close to two hundred feet tall and was made of what appeared to be polished granite. Sophia pointed to three rows of round holes running around the upper perimeter of the cube. "The bird trails lead into those holes, each orange trail going into a separate hole. I see at least twenty other trails coming in from all directions. There are a lot more glowbirds besides the ones we're tracking."

Orville felt a growing sense of dread. "I don't like the feeling of this place. What do you think it is?"

"Well, it must have been built by the Anarkkians, but as for why they built it, I don't have the slightest idea. More than likely it's empty, abandoned a thousand years ago."

"I hope so, but somehow it doesn't feel empty to me. I suppose I could just be sensing the glowbirds inside it."

Sophia and Orville trekked on toward the stone cube, finally arriving at a mammoth set of gleaming metallic doors standing over twenty feet high. In the center of each door was embedded a large golden square, a silver spiral within it.

Orville pointed to the gold squares. "You were right, the Anarkkians built this. That's the same symbol we found on the blue triangle. How do we get in? These doors are massive and there's no handle or latch on them." Orville made a half hearted attempt to push the doors open. "They won't budge."

Sophia was studying the door's surface, running her paw gently across it. "Here, look at this grid of slightly raised circles. They're hard to see, barely visible. Five across and five deep, twenty-five in total. Maybe they're tabs you have to push."

"Could be. More than likely you have to touch them in a certain order for the door to open, if they even still work. There are so many possible combinations it would take us a thousand years to figure out which circles to tap and in which order."

Sophia rubbed her furry chin, deep in thought. "Try the goggles on them."

"Why?"

"Just try it. There could be some kind of electrical field that might help us."

Orville shrugged and slipped on the goggles, slowly twisting the brass dial.

"Creekers! You were right! Five of the circles are glowing. Those must be the ones. They're not all the same brightness, each one is different. I'll tap them in order of dimmest to brightest."

Orville reached out and touched his paw to each of the five raised circles. "Nothing."

"Hmmm... try brightest to dimmest."

Orville tapped the circles again and was rewarded with a deep rumbling noise. He skittered back, watching as the monstrous silver doors groaned open. Orville peered into the inky blackness of the cube's interior.

"This is scary. Are all your missions always this scary?"

"Sorry to tell you this, but this is nothing compared to most of them. Don't worry, we'll be fine. All right, let's practice your shaping skills. I want you to create a glowing sphere that will enter the cube, float up to the ceiling and then get brighter and brighter until it's like daylight in there. After that, pop up a sphere of defense around you."

Orville nodded. With a quick flick of his wrist a glowing orb appeared and shot in through the open doors. Moments later it flared brightly, illuminating the interior of the cube. A powerful sphere of defense then popped up around him.

"Excellent. Here we go. Eyes open, stay alert."

Orville gulped. He was now certain there was something other than glowbirds living inside the huge stone cube.

Chapter 11

Inside the Cube

Orville's eyes traveled across the brightly illuminated room, scanning for movement, but he found only stillness, echoing silence, and the musty smell of time.

"What *is* this place?"

Sophia studied the colossal rectangular room.

"The walls are covered with rows of those wide black rectangles. They resemble the old display panels we used to have on Quintari before holo screens were invented. Each panel has a long curved desk under it, and each desk has three or four high backed chairs in front of it. I'm not certain what was going on here. This technology looks too advanced for Earth, but the chairs are too large for Anarkkians. They were a scary looking bunch, with long green tusks and scales, but they weren't especially tall. If it wasn't Anarkkians sitting in those chairs, then who was it, and why is the Anarkkian symbol on the door? And then there's the puzzle of the glowbirds. What in the world were the Anarkkians doing with all those mechanical glowbirds?"

Orville shook his head. "It's beyond me. We should

search the upper levels of the cube. We might find something there. There must be stairs around here somewhere."

Sophia pointed across the room. "There's an entry-way. Let's try that."

The pair of adventurers hurried across the room and stepped through a stone archway.

"There's the stairs. Stay alert. If there's something else here besides glowbirds, more than likely it's at the top level of the cube."

They crept silently up the stairs, soon reaching the second level. Orville peered into a pitch black room, listening intently for any sound, any movement. There was neither, so he sent in a sphere of light.

"Nothing new here, it's the same as the first level. Desks, chairs, and display panels running along the walls. Let's keep going up."

Sophia tiptoed up the ancient stone stairs to the top level of the building. She held up her paw for Orville to stop, then sent him a thought cloud.

"The stairs end at this level. This is where we'll find the glowbirds. I can see light coming from the main room. It could be sunlight or it could be artificial light. I'm going in. Stay here."

Sophia hunched down and crept cautiously into the vast room. She heard no sounds, saw no movement. Finally she stood up straight and waved Orville in.

"This is the glowbirds' room. The walls are lined with hundreds of roosting compartments and some have glowbirds in them."

Orville eyes were locked on the motionless glow-birds. "They're not moving. It's as if they've been shut off somehow. This building is old, really old. Look at the dust covering everything. I count roughly four hundred roosting boxes but only see about thirty birds. If the birds are autonomous bio-forms it might be that they've just kept doing whatever it was they were built to do, long after the Anarkkians went home. Most of the birds seem to be in that one section over there."

Orville and Sophia strolled over to the area where the glowbirds were roosting. Sophia examined one of the glowbird boxes.

"This is interesting. Each box has an electrical panel on the left side. It looks as though when the birds return they connect themselves to–"

That was as far as Sophia ever got with her thought. She stopped in mid sentence because she was busy blinking up a powerful sphere of defense around her and Orville. One of the most commonly used shaping skills, the sphere of defense produces a virtually impenetrable wall of pure energy around the shaper. It's a skill that shapers practice over and over until it becomes a reflex. Any unexpected motion or sound and the sphere of defense seems to pop up of its own accord. In this case, the impetus behind Sophia's sphere of defense was the startling voice which had come out of nowhere behind her and Orville.

"Would anyone care for a light snack? Perhaps a warm beverage?"

The unexpected voice had taken Sophia and Orville completely by surprise, and they both whirled around in a panic. Orville froze, too stunned to even faint. He was staring into the eyes of a ten foot tall silver metallic rabbit with a look of grave concern on its face.

Orville could barely get the words out. "Uhh...uhh... what is it?"

Sophia answered in a hushed and raspy voice. "It's a Rabbiton. Do *not* make any sudden movements. They're autonomous bio-mechanical creations of the Elders, indestructible and heavily armed with deadly particle beam vaporizing weapons. It could obliterate us in a split second."

The tall Rabbiton laughed politely.

"Oh my, I do hate to be a Little Master Know-it-all and correct you, but I'm really nothing like that at all. How scary that would be! I think you may be slightly confused, perhaps mistaking me for an Autonomous A6 Warrior Rabbiton. They were quite fearsome creatures indeed. Just the thought of having an A6 Rabbiton in my lovely home gives me a rather severe case of the willies. Brrrrr! Now, who would like something to drink and a tasty snack? I'll fetch some comfy chairs so you can both sit down, relax, and rest for a while. You must be simply exhausted after climbing all those dreadfully steep stairs."

Sophia's initial fear had vanished like fog in the afternoon sun, replaced with an intense curiosity.

"If you're not an A6 Warrior Rabbiton, what are you? What are you doing here?"

"My, my, so many questions, my poor head is simply spinning! Let me dash off and get those comfy chairs and I'll be right back. I wouldn't be a proper host if I didn't offer you both a comfy seat. My goodness, I just had the most wonderful thought. I realized there's something about you two I like ever so much. I feel as though we're already old friends. Such a lovely feeling, wouldn't you agree? Now, you two stay right here and I'll be back in a jiffy!"

The silver Rabbiton strode over to an open doorway

and disappeared into a long alcove. Sophia and Orville turned to each other, Sophia raising her eyebrows. Orville snickered. They heard the Rabbiton rummaging about moving heavy objects around in the other room. "Would you prefer a blue chair or a green one? I have both, so each of you may choose whichever color you like."

"I'd like a green chair, please." Orville looked at Sophia and shrugged. "Green is my favorite color."

Sophia rolled her eyes.

"Green is fine for me also. Thank you!"

Moments later the Rabbiton returned carrying two large stuffed green chairs.

"Here you go, my friends, two comfy green chairs. Now, do have a seat and tell me exactly what kind of snack you would like, and if you would like a warm beverage or a chilled beverage. Or perhaps you would like a fizzy drink? I'm told fizzy drinks are quite popular among the younger crowd."

Sophia smiled politely at the Rabbiton. "Honestly, we're both fine. We just ate and had something to drink right before we arrived. I was wondering if you might possibly answer a few questions for me. It would be ever so gracious of you, but I certainly don't wish to inconvenience you in any way."

Orville gave Sophia a sideways glance. Why was she talking like that?

The Rabbiton beamed happily. "Most certainly, indeed, of course I would love to answer your questions. Would anyone care for some tasty chocolates? They're quite delicious and I have a wide variety to choose from. I'm told the lemon creams are especially delightful."

"Thank you so much for your kind offer, but we're really not very hungry just at this moment. I wonder if you might tell us something about your lovely home? It's so spacious and beautifully decorated, I must say."

The Rabbiton smiled brightly. "Of course, of course. Goodness me, where to begin? I suppose I should begin at the beginning. How does that sound to you? Would that be a good place to start?"

"That's sounds perfect *and* perfectly delightful!" Sophia beamed as brightly as she could. Orville grimaced. All this politeness was making him queasy.

The Rabbiton gave a cheery laugh. "Oh my, how clever you are with words! I'm so lucky to have such a clever new friend! Well, let me see now, it was the Anarkkians who built my lovely home, which I simply call the Cube. This was before the great war of course, and before the Anarkkians invaded all those poor unfortunate worlds. The Cube was originally created to house a highly secret and technologically advanced surveillance center. The Anarkkians wanted to keep a wary eye on all their enemies, and I believe they built surveillance centers such as this one on a great number of planets. It took the Elders five long years to discover the Anarkkians' secret surveillance network, but when they did, I assure you they acted without a moment's delay. In marched the Autonomous A6 Warrior Rabbitons and they sent those Anarkkians packing double time.

"The Elders' first impulse was to destroy the Cube and everything in it, but after some thoughtful consideration they decided to use it as their own surveillance center, keeping a sharp lookout for Anarkkian spies or any other such skullduggery. The Elders kept things humming along at the Cube until the day they packed up their bags and headed off to Mandora, a peaceful new world they created. Oh dear, you must be famished after a long story like that. Who would care for a tasty snack or a chilled beverage?"

"Not quite yet, but thank you so much for asking. If you wouldn't mind one more question, what in the world are all the lovely glowbirds for?"

"Oh dear, how embarrassing, I completely forgot to mention the glowbirds. They were the ones doing all the spying, you see. Once a day, groups of glowbirds would depart from the Cube and fly great distances to any number of towns and cities where they did their spying. These are not normal glowbirds, mind you, they are very special ones created by those crafty Anarkkians. Each bird has the most marvelous optical and auditory sensory input system you could ever imagine. My goodness, those glowbirds can spot things miles away *and* hear every word. Not only that, but they remember everything they see and hear.

"At the end of the day the glowbirds would return to the Cube, each one to its own little roosting box, where they would transfer all their secret information to crystalline storage cubes. Once the information was safely stored on the crystals, the Anarkkians would carefully review it for any suspicious activity. I imagine you must have seen all those display panels down on the first two levels. That's where they viewed the glowbird records.

"After the Anarkkians left, there were over a hundred Elders working here day and night, watching those panels and keeping a wary eye out for Anarkkian spies. I'm sad to say the number of active glowbirds has declined drastically since I first arrived at the Cube. There used to be almost four hundred glowbirds to take care of, but now there are just thirty-nine remaining. I'm afraid we lost another one only a few weeks ago. Quite sad indeed."

"If I might ask, when did you arrive here?"

"You're going to think I'm dreadfully old, but I arrived here well over fourteen hundred years ago. That's a rather a humorous story all on its own. I was one of the last Rabbitons ever to be created by the Elders, you know. In my day I was quite well known, some rabbits even saying I was famous. The Elders in charge of manufacturing Rabbitons had received many requests over the years to make Rabbitons behave more like rabbits. Customers said over and over they wanted Rabbitons to be friendly and caring, full of compassion and concern. I was the very first friendly Rabbiton ever built. I was what they called a Prototype, the first of its kind, and I was *very* successful, if you'll forgive a little boasting by an old Rabbiton. My official title was Prototype Model 10E Deluxe Rabbiton with the Expanded L7 Sincere Friendship Simulation Package.

"I spent the first six months of my life living with an extraordinarily delightful family of Elders. There were two of the most charming adult rabbits you could ever hope to meet, and they were blessed with three rambunctious, but ever so lovable young bunnies. It was a glorious time, simply glorious. I spent every moment of every day being their dearest friend and confidant, listening to every word they said and offering them an endless array of snacks, warm beverages, and all manner of other kindnesses. It brings tears to my eyes just to think of those days so very long ago."

"How lovely that must have been for you. How did you ever end up at the Cube?"

"Oh, dear, it was the war, that dreadful war. It changed everything. The family I lived with said I was ever so wonderful, their dearest and most cherished friend forever, but they felt quite deeply that I would be more useful somewhere else, perhaps helping with the war effort out on the front lines of battle. Such patriotic rabbits they were, giving up so very much for their country. I was deeply moved when I heard them tell the Rabbiton representative they should drop me from an Interstellar Battle Cruiser into the middle of a raging Anarkkian vape gun battle. I'm afraid the poor dears quite mistakenly thought I was an Autonomous A6 Warrior Rabbiton. I am quite tall, and I do have a rather commanding presence, so it's not surprising in the least they would assume that.

"The Rabbiton manufacturers knew better, of course, and since I was clearly not designed for warfare they sent me here. They were very concerned that the glowbirds were not receiving all the necessary care and attention they needed, and emphasized quite strongly that keeping the glowbirds happy was an absolutely vital part of the war effort. And, here I am, so many years later, still minding after my lovely glowbirds. Now, surely you must be ready for a snack. A warm beverage perhaps? Does it seem a little chilly to you? I could bring you a toasty warm blanket if you'd care for one. I also have some freshly baked oatmeal cookies, right out of the oven. Or, if you'd prefer, there are some tasty little frosted cakes."

Orville glanced over at Sophia. "You know, those

oatmeal cookies sound delicious. I think I'd like six oatmeal cookies, four tasty little cakes, a warm cocoa, a chilled glass of lemonade, a dozen lemon cream chocolates and six orange cream chocolates."

The Rabbiton let out a great gasp. "Oh, my! What a hungry mouse you are! How delightful! Yes, of course, of course, I would be more than happy to bring you everything you asked for. Sit right here and I'll be back in a blink!"

Sophia was gaping at Orville. "What is wrong with you?"

"What? I'm hungry. Besides, it will give us a little time to talk."

"A dozen lemon cream chocolates?"

"Um, the Rabbiton said they're delightful? Anyway, we know this Rabbiton is definitely not the one who's going to start a war, but we still have no idea why your inner voice wanted us to find out what the glowbirds were doing."

Sophia shook her head. "I don't know. Maybe if we keep talking to the Rabbiton something it says will make sense. All I know is I'll go nummers in the head if he offers me another snack."

Chapter 12

Proto

"Mmmmm... these little cakes are delicious! I don't think I've ever had anything so tasty. Thank you... umm... hey, we don't even know your name. What *is* your name anyway?"

"This is quite embarrassing, but I'm afraid I don't have a clever little name like you and Sophia do. I've always been Prototype Model 10E Deluxe Rabbiton with the Expanded L7 Sincere Friendship Simulation Package. One of the Elders who worked here used to call me the Silver Snackosaurus, but he never explained why."

"I bet it was because your snacks were so delicious. I think you need a new name, and we can't call you Prototype Model 10E Deluxe Rabbiton. How about if we just call you Proto? That's short for Prototype. It suits you well because there's not another Rabbiton in the world like you, and there's not another Rabbiton in the world who can make snacks as tasty as yours."

The Rabbiton stood quite still, its eyes blinking rapidly. "Oh, dear, I think I might just have to cry. I dearly love my new name, Orville. It's the most wonderful gift anyone has ever given me."

"You're welcome, Proto. Your snacks were the best treats anyone has ever given me."

Sophia looked at Orville with surprise, seeing him in a new light. This was a side of him she had never seen before, but she liked it.

Orville finished the last little cake and said, "Mmmm. So delicious. Say, Proto, what do you do here all day long? The glowbirds are gone during the day, so what do you do to keep busy?"

"I'm so pleased you asked me that, Orville, and I would love to answer your question. You would probably never guess it to look at me, but I'm quite a history buff. All the information the glowbirds ever gathered is still here on the crystalline storage cubes. Every day after the glowbirds leave, I watch exactly ten hours of the historical glowbird records. I've learned a great deal about the Anarkkians and the Elders, not to mention their marvelous technology. They had some of the most fantastical flying vehicles you can possibly imagine. It's all quite fascinating."

"Creekers, that's something. I wish you could meet the Mad Mouse of Muridaan. He's a mouse we know who loves to invent things. He built the flying ship we used to get here. You should take a look at it before we go. It looks just like an oversized glowbird except it has wheels instead of legs."

"Well, perhaps I could take a quick peek out the front door if you were both with me. I'm afraid my programming parameters are not very well developed in the area of bold adventuring. It takes me a good while to work up enough courage just to open the front door. It's been so long since I've spent any time in the wild and wooly outdoors that I'm quite fearful of what might be lurking out there now. You didn't happen to notice any silver Anarkkian Attack spiders skulking about the building did you? They're quite dangerous, as you might well imagine. Dreadfully powerful force beams. Simply awful creatures they are."

Sophia perked up. "I've read about them in history books. You're quite right, they were frightening creatures capable of devastating entire cities in only a few hours."

"Oh, yes, that's very true. My goodness, a marvelous idea just popped into my head out of nowhere! How would you two like to see some of those dreadful spiders in action? The glowbirds were watching when the Anarkkians released hundreds of them over the city of Cathne in Opar. I know exactly where those records are if you'd like to see them."

Orville sat up. "That would be amazing! I'd love to see that, Proto."

"Well, then, so you shall. Follow me down to the second level, but please be ever so careful on the stairs, they're quite steep and you wouldn't want to fall. Just thinking about a terrible fall on those stairs gives me a dreadful case of the willies."

Fifteen minutes later Orville and Sophia were seated comfortably in two cushioned lounge chairs, watching as Proto selected the correct storage crystal. "Ah, this is the one. I'm quite certain of it, Crystal 11091949. Who could forget a lovely number like that? Now, let me see.... I think it's right about... here."

A huge display panel in front of Orville and Sophia blinked on, a sharp colorful moving image appearing. Orville leaned forward, his eyes focused on the screen.

"What *is* that thing?"

"Ah, that is a Class 9 Anarkkian Interstellar Battle Support Cruiser. They're quite large, aren't they? If I remember correctly they're nine hundred and seventeen feet long and two hundred and twelve feet tall. Now, keep your eyes on the stern of the ship."

Orville watched in amazement as a huge door on the back of the cruiser yawned open. The ship was hovering silently several hundred feet above the city, flames sprouting from the nearby buildings, rabbits and mice running for their lives through the streets in a desperate attempt to escape the approaching Anarkkian ships. Massive thundering explosions rumbled across the city, brilliant flashes of green light from the blasts illuminating the night sky.

"Here it comes now, watch for the spiders!"

Orville let out a gasp as hundreds of monstrous eight legged gleaming metallic spiders spilled out of the battle cruiser in a silver cascade, tumbling down to the ground below. The hideous creatures hit the ground running, their fearsome red eyes a terrible sight to behold. Seconds later brilliant vermillion beams of light shot out from their eyes, blasting to pieces anything that stood in their path.

"Those are the force beams I mentioned! Quite dreadful, just as I told you. They're quite different from the A6 Warrior Rabbitons' particle vaporizing beams, but equally as destructive. Would you like to see a cloud bomb? They're far worse than those fearsome spiders. The Anarkkians released cloud bombs all over Opar, and I am told it takes over a thousand years for the vegetation to grow back after a cloud bomb attack."

Almost two hours later Sophia and Orville were still

watching scenes from the dreadful Anarkkian War, but Sophia had seen enough. "I'm afraid that's all the violence I can watch for one day, Proto. Do you have any recent records which might not be so frightening?"

"Indeed I do. Let me see, you said you're both from Muridaan Falls? Did I remember that correctly?"

"Yes, you're quite right. Orville was born there and I moved there from Quintari a year ago."

"Well, then, I have just the perfect records for you. If you look here at the map, you'll see we still have two active glowbirds in Muridaan Falls keeping an eye on things. Let me see, would you like to see yesterday's records? You might even see someone you know. Wouldn't that be lovely to see a dear friend?"

"That sounds perfect. Let's watch."

Proto popped in the storage crystal and pushed a blue tab. A brightly colored moving image of Muridaan Falls appeared on the display screen.

Orville laughed out loud, pointing at the screen. "Look, there's the bakery! And that's Madam Shearan! I always see her there. I think she has a crush on Master Fernelld, the owner. I can tell because she laughs way too loud at all his jokes. Look, the glowbird is flying... he's landing again... he's right near the Book Emporium! That's where I work, Proto. This is amazing! He's looking across the street now. There's two mice standing behind that building. I can't see who they are though."

Proto paused the record. "If you would like, I can enlarge the image to show much greater detail, and I can also focus the sound so we can hear every word they're saying. It's all quite marvelous, and the technology is fascinating to study. Watch what happens to those two mice now." Proto turned a small dial and the faces of the mice in the alley suddenly filled the screen.

"It's Master Marloh! This is amazing, I can't believe we're seeing this. What's he saying? He's probably trying to sell a book to the mouse in the red cloak. Or maybe he's telling him about the huge raise he's going to give me."

"I'll focus the sound so you can hear what they're saying."

Sophia and Orville grinned as Proto adjusted the sound. The cold raspy voice they heard was not that of Master Marloh, but came from the mouse whose face was hidden by the red hood.

"I won't tell you again. We can't afford to wait. He's getting too powerful. You know what might happen. Do it, Marloh. Kill Orville Mouse and his little friend Sophia. Kill them both or you will forfeit your own life."

Sophia gasped, slapping her paw over her mouth. She turned in horror to Orville. His eyes were enormous. "Did that mouse just say what I thought he said??"

Sophia grabbed Orville's arm tightly. "This is it! This is why my inner voice sent us here. Master Marloh is planning to kill us both."

Chapter 13

The Rising Storm

"Now, Orville, I've packed two large boxes of tasty snacks and some yummy beverages for your trip back to Muridaan Falls. I've also tucked away a very special surprise in your backpack. No peeking until you get home, though! That would ruin the lovely surprise."

"Thanks, Proto! You're sure you don't want to come down to the gorge and take a look at *The Glowbird*?"

"Perhaps on your next visit. I'm not quite ready to travel such a great distance from my lovely home. First I'll take a few short walks just outside the front door to get used to the great outdoors again. You're quite certain you didn't spot any of those dreadful silver spiders?"

"Not a single one. Besides, Rabbitons are completely indestructible. Nothing can hurt you."

"You're quite right of course, but strangely enough those dreadful spiders still give me a terrible fright."

Sophia stepped over to Proto and gave him a hug. "Thanks for everything, Proto. If it wasn't for you and your lovely glowbirds we never would have discovered what Master Marloh and the Red Mouse were up to. You very well may have saved our lives."

"How thrilling! I'm so glad I could help you both. Do be careful now, and have a very safe trip home. Keep a wary eye out for those awful silver spiders."

With a wave goodbye Sophia and Orville stepped through the front door of the Cube and headed back down the ravine toward Pavorak Gorge.

Sophia was anxious to get back to Muridaan Falls, but as she was hurrying across the gorge she stopped in her tracks. "Orville, why is it so dark this early in the day?"

"It is dark, isn't it? Maybe the clouds–" Orville turned to look at the sky behind them and gave a low gasp. He pointed to the monstrous pitch black rolling storm filling the entire northern sky.

"Creekers, it's heading this way! We can't fly through that. We'll have to go back and stay with Proto until the storm blows over."

Sophia's ears perked up. "Do you hear that? That roaring noise?"

Orville froze, his eyes focused on the ground. "Oh no! I just realized something! The floor of the gorge is smooth because when there's a storm it floods and washes everything away. That roaring noise is water coming down the gorge! We have to get to *The Glowbird* before it's destroyed! Run!"

Orville and Sophia sprinted madly to *The Glowbird*.

"Jump in! Hurry up!"

The roar of the water pounding through the gorge toward them was growing louder by the second. Brilliant bolts of lightning flashed in the ominous swirling black sky. Orville flipped on the duplonium motor and pushed the left control stick forward. *The Glowbird's* wings unfurled and began gently flapping.

82

"The wind from the storm will help us take off." Orville pushed the left stick forward. *The Glowbird* rolled across the sandy floor, powerful gusts of wind from the storm pushing them, helping to gain the speed they needed to take off.

Sophia cried out, "Twenty miles an hour!" The wind was buffeting the ship and Orville could barely hold it steady.

"Grab your control stick help me keep us going in a straight line!"

"Got it! Thirty miles an hour!"

Orville jammed the stick forward and the duplonium engine roared, the wings now a blur.

Sophia glanced behind them and let out a shriek. There was a massive thirty foot tall wall of water screaming through the gorge only a few hundred feet behind them. "The water is right behind us! Faster!!"

Orville pushed the left stick forward as far as it would go. The ship shot ahead, the gigantic torrent of water now a scant twenty feet behind them.

"Forty miles an hour! Take us up! The water's going to hit us!"

Orville yanked back on the right control stick and *The Glowbird* darted up into the sky. Sophia looked down and saw the massive wall of crashing water thunder through the gorge beneath them.

"We made it! We made it!"

"Head east, and keep it at top speed! We still have to outrun the storm. If we get caught in it we'll crash, and I'm not even going to mention what happens if we get hit by lightning!"

Orville held the control stick forward as far as it would go. "Okay! We passed sixty miles an hour. We should be able to outrun it."

Twenty minutes later *The Glowbird* had left the terrifying storm behind.

"Whew, that was close. Thank goodness you heard the water coming. I can't wait to get back to Muridaan Falls."

Sophia's face was grim. "Neither can I, Orville, neither can I."

"You're thinking about Master Marloh and the Red Mouse. Who do you think the other mouse was? He was scary. Even Master Marloh seemed afraid of him."

Sophia watched Orville thoughtfully as he gently corrected the course of *The Glowbird*. "You're my best friend, right?"

"Of course I am, you know that."

"So you would trust me no matter what?"

"There's not a mouse in the world I trust more than you."

"I'm glad, but I need to warn you. There's going to be serious trouble when we get back to Muridaan Falls."

"I already know that. We'll just have to keep our eye on Master Marloh and find out who that other mouse is."

"It's much more complicated than that, but I can't tell you everything right now. You'll just have to trust me."

"What do you mean, much more complicated? Wait, I just thought of something! If Proto had come down to look at *The Glowbird* he would have been washed away by that giant wall of water."

"Thank goodness he wasn't there. I really do like him very much. He's one of the nicest fellows I've ever met."

"Not to mention the most polite Rabbiton I've ever met. Well, he's actually the only Rabbiton I've ever met. Wouldn't it be fun if he moved to Muridaan Falls and was our friend there?"

Two things happened within a split second. First, Sophia let out a piercing shriek, and second, Orville gave a wild screech, briefly losing control of *The Glowbird*, swerving it wildly through the sky until he managed to grab the control stick again. A squawky voice had come from the storage compartment behind their seats.

"Oh my, that's the nicest thing I've ever heard. You two are the very best friends I've ever had. I knew we would be dear friends from the first moment I saw you."

"Proto?? What? Where are you?"

Sophia's eyes searched the small storage area behind them. "I don't see anything. Where is he? Proto, where are you?"

"Ha ha ha ha! This is my surprise! Sophia, open Orville's backpack. It's dark in here."

"What are you talking about, Proto?" Sophia grabbed Orville's backpack and flipped it open. She gave another shriek. There was a large glowbird sitting in the backpack, staring at her with big yellow blinking eyes. Proto's voice was coming out of the glowbird's mouth.

"It's me, your old friend Proto! I'm talking to you from the Cube through this glowbird. Isn't this marvelous? I'm safe and comfy in my lovely home, but I can see and hear everything through the glowbird. It's quite thrilling, although I'm glad I wasn't looking when you were dodging that deadly storm. Dreadfully frightening, even when I was hiding in your backpack. Sophia, would you mind holding me up so I could have a quick peek over the edge of the *The Glowbird*?"

Sophia lifted the plump glowbird out of Orville's pack and held it over the edge of *The Glowbird*.

"Aggghhhh!! Too high, too high! Put me back, please!"

Sophia quickly set the glowbird back in Orville's backpack. "Sorry. Wait, I just had an idea! Can you spy with this glowbird?"

"Most certainly, that's what glowbirds were created for, although I did think it also might help me to overcome my fear of the outside world. If I could safely experience the wild outdoors through the eyes of a glowbird, I might not be so afraid to venture out of the Cube."

"That's a wonderful idea, and very clever. How would you like your first adventure to be a secret spy mission? I was hoping you would be able to locate the mysterious Red Mouse who told Master Marloh to kill us."

"Oh, my, that does sound thrilling. A dark and sinister Red Mouse who is deadly intent on killing you. How frightening!"

"You don't have to get very close to him. Just close enough so you can hear what he's saying."

"I would be more than happy to spy on that dastardly Red Mouse. You know, it just struck me how lovely it is that I can talk to my two dear friends whenever I wish. It does get a little lonely in the Cube sometimes with just the glowbirds for company. Orville, have you tried any of the snacks I packed for you? There are several dozen very tasty chocolate cookies and some of those little cakes you like so much. Twenty-four of them, in fact. And two small boxes of assorted chocolate creams. Also some chilled lemonade. You should probably drink the lemonade before it gets warm. Oh, and there's also some of that warm cocoa you like so much. You might want to drink that before it gets cold. Goodness, how high up are we? That quick peek I had at the ground below was quite terrifying. How long do you think it will be until we arrive at Muridaan Falls? Did I ever tell you about the time I was almost attacked by one of those dreadful Anarkkian silver spiders?"

Sophia looked over at Orville and raised both eyebrows as high as she could. Orville snickered. "You never told us that story, Proto, but I'll let you in on a little secret. Sophia *loves* stories like that. Tell us everything that happened, and don't leave out a thing, not even the tiniest detail."

Sophia leaned back in her seat and covered her face with her paws, but not before she had punched Orville's arm.

"Oww! What was that for??"

Chapter 14

Proto's Discovery

I'm home, Mum!"

"Hi, sweetie! I hope you had a pleasant trip. Did you find everything you were looking for?"

"Yes, I found everything and had a marvelous time. I brought you back a box of tasty snacks. You should try the little cakes, they're delicious."

"Thank you so much. I do have a fondness for little cakes."

"How lovely!" A squawky voice popped out of Orville's backpack.

"What's wrong with your voice? Are you sick?"

Orville cleared his throat loudly.

"Oh, umm... I think I might be getting a cold or something. Anyway, I'm really tired from my long trip, so I think I'll run up and take a quick nap." Orville grabbed his backpack and dashed upstairs to his room.

"Shhh... quiet, Proto! No one can know about you. If you're going to be a spy you can't go around talking to everyone about tasty snacks. Besides, how would I ever explain a talking bird to my Mum? I don't know about other planets, but on Earth birds don't talk."

"Oh, I completely understand. I was just so excited

to hear how much your Mum likes little cakes that I forgot about my secret spy mission. I do wish there was a way I could send you more of those little cakes."

"Well, maybe one day you can come visit us in Muridaan Falls. It might take a while for the mice to get used to seeing a Rabbiton strolling around town, but I'm sure it wouldn't take long until you had ever so many new friends."

"You make it sound quite lovely, not the least bit scary."

"It's not scary at all in Muridaan Falls. Now, I think it's time to send you out to track down the Red Mouse who– wait, I just thought of something. What happens if you need charging?"

"Oh dear, I almost forgot about that myself. Hmm... is there any chance you might be able to shape a battery?"

"Good idea. That's one thing I do remember from science class, especially the part about never touching both terminals of a battery at the same time. Ouch."

Orville flicked his wrist and a large rectangular battery blinked into existence. "How's that?"

"Marvelous work. Now, we'll need two cables, one connected to each battery terminal. To charge myself I'll just grab one cable with each foot."

"Creekers, isn't that dangerous?"

"It would most assuredly be quite dangerous for you, but not for me. My feet are wired directly to my internal power supply core."

"Oh, that sounds all right then." Two copper battery cables appeared and Orville carefully connected each one to a battery terminal. "There you go. Would you like to try it?

"Most certainly, I would." Proto waddled over to the battery cables, sat down and grabbed one cable with each foot. Orville jumped back when a few sparks shot out, but Proto seemed quite comfortable.

"Ahhh... quite lovely, nice and toasty warm and my power core is charging right up. This really hits the spot."

Two minutes later Proto released the cables and stood up.

"I'm ready to hunt down your dastardly Red Mouse. I'll be on my way if you would be kind enough to flip that window open."

Orville swung the heavy sash open and Proto scrambled up onto the sill, spread his wings, and soared out over the trees.

Orville sighed. It was time to face Master Marloh and feign ignorance of his murderous scheme.

"How could I have been so wrong about him?"

He closed the window just enough so Proto could squeeze back in, then headed downstairs, calling out out a hurried goodbye to his Mum as he stepped out the front door. He didn't want to be late and risk any unnecessary conversation with Master Marloh. Orville was definitely not an accomplished liar and was afraid his face would instantly betray him.

Orville groaned to himself when he entered the Book Emporium. Master Marloh was standing behind the long wooden counter adding up the previous day's receipts.

Before Orville could say anything, Sophia darted out from behind a tall bookshelf and scurried over to him, saying in a voice loud enough for Master Marloh to hear, "Hi, Orville! I already told Master Marloh about our trip and how we discovered the Anarkkians used the glowbirds to send each other secret messages during the war, but we still don't know how they are connected to a future war in Symoca."

Orville played right along with Sophia's story. "Oh, right. Kind of a wasted trip, but it was fun flying in *The Glowbird*. Maybe we can go flying again sometime. Well, I guess I should get to work."

Orville attempted a friendly wave to Master Marloh, then hurried back to the loading area. He wanted to spend as much time as he could away from Master Marloh.

Sophia joined him a few minutes later and said in a hushed voice, "Did you send Proto out to look for the Red Mouse?"

"I sent him about an hour ago. I also shaped a battery so he can charge himself. You should come over for dinner tonight in case Proto finds something."

"Good idea. I'll come by around six o'clock. It's okay with your mum?"

"Oh, sure, Mum likes you a lot."

Orville spent a good portion of his day doing his best to dodge Master Marloh. He only had to talk to him once, about a crate of scientific journals being shipped to one of their best customers. Orville thought the conversation was going well until Master Marloh stopped and said, "Are you all right, Orville? You seem nervous."

"Umm...sure, everything's fine. I'm... uhh... still a little jittery from flying in *The Glowbird*. It's the first time I've been up that high. It was a lot of fun but also sort of scary."

"Ahh, of course, I completely understand. I'm not

especially fond of heights either. Feel free to take a few hours off if you need to recuperate from your trip."

"Thanks, Master Marloh, I'm sure I'll be fine soon."

Orville wasn't sure how convincing he had been, but Master Marloh seemed to accept his explanation.

The day ended with no further confrontations, and a much relieved Orville hurried home to check on the success of Proto's first spy mission. Flinging open the front door, he hollered a greeting to his mum and ran up to his room. Proto was resting comfortably on Orville's bed, curled up in a mound of blankets.

"How did it go? Did you see anything? Did you find the Red Mouse?"

Proto's eyes blinked open. "I hope you don't mind, but I took the liberty of making a comfy little nest out of your blankets. You have quite a marvelous bed."

Orville heard his Mum call out, "Orville! Sophia is here to see you!"

"I'll be right back, Proto. Sophia wants to hear what you found."

Orville dashed downstairs and waved hello to Sophia.

"I'm glad you could make it. Mum, can Sophia stay for dinner?"

"Of course she can. You're always welcome here, Sophia."

Sophia thanked her, then turned to Orville. "Do you have that history book you found at the Book Emporium? The one about the Elders? I'd love to see it."

"Oh, sure... it's up in my room. Come on, I'll show you."

Sophia followed Orville upstairs and they found Proto snuggled in the blankets.

"Did you find the Red Mouse?"

Proto's eyes popped open and he stood up.

"Ha ha ha ha, that is quite an amusing story. I haven't forgotten how much you love long engaging tales, so I won't leave out a single detail."

Sophia gave Orville a secret glare.

"Well, as preposterous as it may sound, I found a total of *nine* mice all wearing red cloaks, and I had to follow each one to determine if they were the dastardly Red Mouse I was searching for. Quite a merry mix-up, I must say. The first mouse I trailed was acting *very* suspiciously. After a time, however, it became quite evident to me that he was engaged in nothing more nefarious than planning a surprise birthday party for his wife. He picked out such a lovely card for her, covered with delicate lacy hearts and flowers, and filled with such heartwarming sentiment that it brought tears to my eyes. Without hesitation, I can affirm that his choice of cards was thoughtful and sensitive, but I have a difficult time believing the gift he finally purchased for her was entirely–"

Sophia gritted her teeth and interrupted Proto's story. "That's a marvelous tale, and quite engaging, but do you think we could save all those luscious details for another day? Perhaps you could just tell us about the dastardly Red Mouse, since we don't have much time just now."

"Ahh, yes, of course, of course. Well, after following eight mice in red cloaks, I finally spotted a red cloaked mouse who was glancing about furtively, as though to make certain he was not being followed. Very suspicious indeed, and quite clearly he was up to some sort of skullduggery. I trailed him all the way across town to a ramshackle barn behind your very own Book Emporium, where he had a secret meeting with the mouse you call Master Marloh. They're up to no good, I can tell you that. Devious characters they are, both of them."

"What did they say? Can you show us the record?"

"Oh dear, let me think. I don't have a display panel here, but perhaps if I reroute the storage crystal data through the glowbird's optical system and reverse the grid sensor polarity... and the auditory input... yes, that should work. Hold on while I position myself next to that wall." Proto scuttled down from the bed and stood several feet away from the wall.

"Now, if I have made all the correct adjustments, I should be able to project the glowbird's record through its eyes onto the wall."

The glowbird's eyes blazed brightly and a colorful moving image appeared on Orville's bedroom wall.

"Even better than I had expected. I'll reroute the sound so you can hear what those two underhanded scalawags are saying."

The moving image on the wall clearly showed the Red Mouse standing face to face with Master Marloh. Orville recognized the interior of the old barn immediately.

The Red Mouse had a horrid sneer on his face, his raspy voice dark and threatening.

"This is your last warning. I want them both dead and I want it done now. You have three days. Here's the map. Hide it in the secret compartment behind the front counter. If those mice get their paws on it, two things will happen – our invasion plans will be worthless and carnivorous centipedes will be feasting on your bones." The mouse's eyes glowed with a terrifying red light.

"Creekers, that is one scary mouse." Orville looked up at Sophia. Her face was grim, her eyes filled with a fierce light. Orville felt the dreadful chill pass through him. He did not like seeing this side of Sophia.

"Umm... are you all right?"

The chill faded. "I'm fine. I'm sorry, I was just thinking. We have to get that map. It shouldn't be hard to find the secret hidden compartment. We'll go tonight. Whatever these invasion plans are we have to put a stop to them."

During dinner Sophia chatted pleasantly with Orville's Mum about the Symocan Institute of Mechanistic Studies, mentioning that she had decided to return to Muridaan Falls after graduation to work with Mirus Mouse.

"Mirus is a brilliant and revolutionary inventor. It would be such a thrill to work with a mouse like him."

Orville was extremely happy to hear her new plans. The last thing he wanted was for her to move back to Quintari, but he couldn't mention anything about Quintari in front of his mum.

They had a wonderful evening except for the part when Mum told Sophia the snow bear story, a tale which Orville would have been happy to forget.

The incident occurred three years ago in the middle of a brutally cold winter. Orville had just finished breakfast and was late for school. He hollered goodbye to Mum and flung open the front door, greeted by a gigantic growling snow bear who had made its way down from the upper slopes of the mountain. He let out a piercing shriek of terror, barely managing to slam the door shut. His Mum raced out of the kitchen when she heard his scream. Before she could reach him an intense wave of heat rolled up through his body and he fainted away, sliding down to the floor like a sack of walnuts.

Sophia did her best, but could not stop laughing. Orville was dreadfully embarrassed for a minute or two, but in the end Sophia was his best friend, and he did like to see her laugh.

When the evening wound down, Sophia bid her farewells, heading for the front door. She whispered to Orville, "Midnight tonight. The Book Emporium. Bring Proto. I don't know when we'll be coming back."

Orville gulped. What in the world did she mean by that? She didn't know when they'd be coming back? Coming back from where?

Chapter 15

Welcome to Periculum

Because Orville did not have the slightest idea where he and Sophia were going or when they were coming back, he decided he'd better write a letter to his Mum disclosing the truth about Sophia, Quintari, the Shapers Guild and the Metaphysical Adventurers. He promised her he would be safe, but did not know precisely when he would be returning. He neglected to mention the Red Mouse and his murderous plans.

With Proto tucked safely in his backpack, Orville tiptoed downstairs, set the letter to his Mum on the kitchen table and slipped silently out of the house.

His paws were cold, his anxiety steadily increasing. He had no idea what Sophia was planning. He trusted her, but he also knew she was a mouse who took far greater risks than he ever would. As he hurried along through the gloomy night his whirling thoughts were abruptly interrupted by his inner voice.

"You are entering a period of great chaos and confusion, a time where you will face nearly insurmountable obstacles. These are called the fires of life, and they bring with them great change. Your actions during these times will determine the kind of mouse you shall become. If you remain true to your heart in the midst of such fires, you shall return to this world in possession of great wisdom and power beyond imagination."

"Return to this world? What do you mean?"

There was no reply from his inner voice.

Orville tried to calm himself, taking a deep breath and looking up at the starry night sky that blanketed Muridaan Falls. The moon was rising above the mountain range, its soft light casting purple shadows across the rugged landscape. He would do what his inner voice asked, he would follow the truth he found in his heart. Orville swung his backpack up onto his shoulder and hurried forward into the darkness.

As he approached the Book Emporium a figure darted out of the shadows. It was Sophia. She whispered sharply, "You brought Proto?"

"Yes, I have him and the key to the shop. Have you seen anyone?"

"No, it's all quiet. Let's go."

"I don't understand where we're going. My inner voice said something about the fires of life and another world. What does that mean?"

"I can't tell you. Trust me."

"I do trust you, but I just–"

"Follow me. No talking. Send thought clouds to communicate."

Sophia crept over to the front door, motioning for Orville to unlock it. He silently swung the door open and they entered the store. Sophia shaped a small glowing light in her paw and padded quietly over to the front counter.

She sent a blue thought cloud to Orville. "The map is in here somewhere. Look for a hidden panel."

Sophia and Orville froze when the room was suddenly flooded with light, neither one of them able to move a muscle. They weren't frozen with fear, it was something quite different, a strange paralyzing force which Orville had never encountered before. He could move his eyes, and would have gasped if he could when he saw the two dark figures standing at the far end of the room. One was Master Marloh and the other was the Red Mouse. The Red Mouse's face had a vicious smirk plastered across it.

His mocking voice echoed through the room.

"Well, well, if it isn't Orville Mouse and Sophia Mouse in search of a mysterious map which doesn't even exist. Did you really think I wouldn't notice your comical little snooping glowbird trailing behind me? It's going to be a new world when I am Supreme Counselor of the Metaphysical Adventurers, and it's going to be a new world without two nosy little mice who never learned to mind their own business. Marloh! Open the spectral door. Sending them to Periculum is the only good idea you've ever had. This will be more fun than killing them myself. Have a wonderful trip, my precious little mouselings. I do hope you remembered to pack plenty of insect repellent."

The Red Mouse let loose a horrific high pitched laugh that sent chills through Orville.

Master Marloh looked haggard, his face grim as death. He stumbled as he made his way across the room toward Sophia and Orville, stopping ten feet away from them. Without a word he cupped his paws together. A small diaphanous wavering sphere formed above them and began to grow in density, its color changing to a translucent blue green, pale clouds swirling about within the undulating sphere. As the sphere grew in size, tiny blue sparks appeared around its periphery, quickly transforming to brilliant flashes of lightning. The frightening sphere was expanding rapidly, now a maelstrom of dark gray roiling clouds and deafening claps of thunder. Master Marloh released the sphere and stood back, watching without expression as it moved toward Sophia and Orville. They could hear the swirling black storm shrieking and moaning, the horrific deadly tempest inching inexorably toward them. It was all over in a split second. The sphere exploded with incomprehensible fury, blasting Orville and Sophia into unfathomable darkness.

Orville was past fear, beyond feeling. He was hurtling through a narrow black tunnel, small lights flickering past him at impossible speeds. His body was a blur of flowing liquid light. He managed to glance behind him and saw the brilliant elongated fluid figure of Sophia flashing through the tunnel. Before he could even begin to comprehend what was happening they were both tumbling wildly across a hard rocky surface. Sophia smashed up against him and lay motionless. Every bone and every muscle in Orville's body cried out in exquisite agony.

"Unnnhhhh. What... what... how did we..."

Sophia's eyes blinked open. "That was so much worse than I thought it would be. Nothing at all like my trip from Quintari."

"You knew this was going to happen? Why didn't you tell me? Wait, what *did* just happen?"

"We're on Periculum. Master Marloh created a spectral door and sent us through it to the world of Periculum."

"Huh? How do you know where we are?"

"Because I asked Master Marloh to send us here."

"You asked him to send us here? I'm so confused. I also think I'm either going to throw up or faint."

"That will pass in a few minutes. The spectral door I came through from Quintari was fun, not at all like this one. Let's figure out where we are, and then I'll tell you the whole story. Master Marloh is on our side. You weren't wrong about him, Orville. He's a good mouse and a dear friend."

"That's a relief. I couldn't imagine him trying to kill us."

Orville peered out into the inky blackness, the only illumination coming from the flickering stars in the night sky. He crawled forward across the gritty stone floor, feeling his way with his paws, stopping when he felt the rocky surface abruptly drop off.

"I reached the end of it. I think we're on a cliff or something."

Orville's eyes were gradually adjusting to the dim light.

"It looks like we're on the top of a column of rock about twenty or thirty feet across. It's hard to see, but I think there's water way down there. I can see the waves glinting. We might be on a tiny island in the ocean."

Sophia peered over the edge, studied the waves for a moment, then stood up. "Come over here, Orville."

Orville rose to his feet and stepped over to Sophia.

"What is it?"

"I want you to put your arms around me and hold me tight."

"Huh? Why? Ooooh, wait, is there something you want to tell me, Sophia? Or do you just need a hug?"

"Stop talking and put your arms around me."

Orville put his arms around Sophia and held her close.

"This is nice. I like hugging you. This was a good idea, I feel a lot better now. Not so worried."

"Orville, there *is* something I want to tell you. I know when you get scared you get a little wobbly and you have been known to faint. Like that time you opened the front door and the snow bear was standing on your porch. I wanted to make sure you didn't fall and bump your head."

"Why would I do that?"

"Because that's not water down there, it's hundreds of enormous millipedes."

Orville gave a small whimper and collapsed in Sophia's arms. She grinned, gently lowering him to the ground.

"My hero." She ran her paw across Orville's furry head. She was truly lucky to have him for her best friend.

Orville woke up with a groan a moment later. "Did you say giant millipedes?"

"I'm so sorry, I checked again and I was mistaken."

"Whew! I *hate* millipedes. They're so creepy. So I was right, it's water down there?"

"No, it's not water and it's not millipedes. In case you didn't know it, millipedes are actually quite harmless. I'm afraid what we have down there are giant carnivorous centipedes." Sophia burst out laughing.

"That's not funny! I feel sick. What are we going to do? How do we get off this rock?"

Sophia heard a muffled croaky voice coming from Orville's backpack. "Where are we?"

Orville flipped open his pack and let Proto out. "We're on the planet Periculum surrounded by giant carnivorous centipedes. Nothing to worry about, Proto. Things couldn't be better. It's going to be a lovely sunny day with a good chance of being devoured by centipedes."

"Did you say Periculum? I believe at some point I read a rather detailed report written by the Elders regarding the world of Periculum. If I remember correctly Periculum is one of the twelve worlds accessible through the Thaumatarian World Doors, through the fifth World Door to be quite precise. Parts of it are lovely this time of year, especially near the seaside. It goes without saying I'm not referring to the areas where the dreaded carnivorous centipedes live. Awful creatures, simply awful. Quite frightening with their hideous razor sharp prehensors, quite commonly referred to as fangs. Perhaps I could have just a quick peek at them?" Proto seemed oddly delighted to learn they were surrounded by carnivorous centipedes.

"Why does everyone think this is so much fun? What are we going to do?"

Sophia rubbed Orville's arm. "We're shapers and we're Metaphysical Adventurers. We can shape whatever we need to get off this rock. Don't let your fear control you. We can create impenetrable defense spheres and as scary as they look, those centipedes down there can't hurt us. Although I suppose they could swallow us whole."

"That's not helping! I guess you do have a point about my sphere of defense though." Orville blinked up a protective field of energy around him. "All right, let me think, how to get off this rock... I know, how about a long rope? It's about thirty feet to the outer wall of the centipede pit and there are all those big trees there. We could shape a heavy metal ring to the rock floor, tie a rope to it and tie the other end of the rope around one of those trees."

"How exactly are we going to tie the rope to a tree on the other side of the pit?"

"Oh, good point. Hmmm... I know, Proto could do it! He could grab the end of the rope and fly it across the pit. Proto, could you fly circles around the tree with the rope? About five times should work."

"Yes, I believe I could do that. Oh my, this is quite a thrilling adventure. Did you remember to pack plenty of snacks? Some of those little cakes you like so well?"

"Sorry, they were so delicious that Mum and I finished them all. She did say they were the tastiest cakes she's ever had."

"Oh my, that's quite lovely to hear. Now, where's that rope? It's time I rescued you from these dreadful centipedes."

Sophia looked at Orville with a bright smile. "Thank goodness Proto is here. I don't know what we'd do without him."

Proto let out a delighted laugh. "Oh my, thank you so much! It's my pleasure to assist you."

Orville shaped a light but strong rope while Sophia shaped a heavy iron ring securely bolted to the pedestal's rock floor. "This will hold a hundred mice. We're all set."

Orville held the rope out for Proto, who grabbed it with his feet.

"I'll fly it around that tall tree five times, then you pull it tight and secure it to the iron ring."

Orville lay the coil of rope down and Proto took off, flying across the centipede pit, the rope trailing behind him. He soared around the tall spiky tree again and again until Orville called out, "That good, Proto! I'm going to pull in the slack now!"

Together Sophia and Orville hauled the rope in as tightly as they could and tied it to the iron ring.

Sophia grinned. "We're all set. Did you want to give the giant centipedes a hug and a kiss goodbye before we go?"

"How did I ever wind up with such a cruel friend?"

Sophia snorted. "You go first. Here, put these on." A pair of sturdy gloves blinked into Orville's paw. He nodded his thanks and slipped them on. Grabbing the rope with both paws he stepped off the edge of the rocky pedestal, swinging out above the wriggling mass of centipedes far below. Traveling paw over paw he made his way across the deadly creatures, soon arriving safely on the other side.

Two minutes later Sophia was standing next to him.

"I told you we could do it,. Now you're officially a shaper *and* a Metaphysical Adventurer."

Orville laughed. "Any day you don't get eaten by a giant carnivorous centipede is a good day indeed."

Chapter 16

Cry of the Gnorli

Sophia eyed the dense tangled foliage surrounding them. "It's probably best if we get out of this jungle as soon as possible. We escaped the centipede nest but there's bound to be more of them slithering around in the undergrowth."

Orville grimaced, but took out his compass and studied it. "Let's head east and see where that takes us."

He tucked Proto into his backpack and they began their trek through the nearly impenetrable Periculum jungle. "This is awful, I wish I had something to cut through all these vines. Hey, what am I thinking?" With a flash of light a long silver brush hacker knife appeared in his paw.

Sophia grinned. "Now you're thinking like a Metaphysical Adventurer."

Even with the brush hacker it was slow going and several times they were forced to climb up into the jungle canopy to avoid swarms of the giant centipedes. Despite all the obstacles, they were making some headway through the sweltering rainforest.

Orville was hacking away at a particularly thick vine when an idea popped into his head.

"Hey, Proto, what was that you said about World Doors and the Thaumatarians? Who are they again?"

"The Thaumatarians were an ancient civilization quite unknown to most mice today. They were the first beings to colonize this universe, and they were the creators of the World Doors. If you've read anything about deep physics you'll remember that it's possible for many worlds to simultaneously occupy the same space. These are called parallel worlds, or parallel universes. There is a kind of space lying in between those parallel worlds known as the Void, an infinite black emptiness possessing some rather peculiar properties, but it also acts as a gateway to the parallel worlds. The Thaumatarians built a set of twelve World Doors within the Void. In reality there is only one set of World Doors, but it exists simultaneously in all twelve worlds."

"I'm confused. How do the doors work?"

"It's far simpler than you might think. On each world there is a single door which appears to be floating by itself several inches above the ground. If you open the door you will find a hallway lined with six doors on each side. Each door leads to one of the twelve worlds. I believe the Third World Door opens to Earth in a rather dismal area known as The Swamp of Lost Things."

Sophia added, "One of my physics teachers on Quintari mentioned the World Doors, but he didn't know as much about them as you do, Proto. Are you saying if we find the World Doors here on Periculum we can walk through Door Three and be back on Earth again?"

"Precisely. There is one small but very vital detail,

however. You need a key to open the door to Earth. Each of the twelve doors has its own key, and they are by no means ordinary keys, I assure you."

"How do we find a key?"

"I'm afraid it would be quite impossible for you to find one on Periculum. I may have a solution, however. I believe there is a set of twelve World Door keys tucked away down on the third sub level of the Cube, left there by the Elders. I could take the Third Key to the Swamp of Lost Things, enter the hallway and wait for you. When you entered the hallway on Periculum I would be right there with the key to open the Third Door."

"But... you'd have to leave your lovely home and travel to the Swamp of Lost Things."

"Yes, yes, that is quite true, I would have to do that. You are quite correct about that."

"Proto, are you all right?"

"Yes, perfectly fine indeed, just as right as rain. I do, however, have a sudden overpowering urge to bake great numbers of tasty snacks and both of my hands seem to be trembling rather severely."

"It's all right, you don't need to worry about leaving your home right now. We don't even know where the World Doors are on Periculum."

"Yes, quite correct, no need to worry just now. One moment while I pop up a holomap of Periculum and have a look. Let me see.... here it is, the symbol for World Doors. Drat, it would appear you are quite a distance from the World Doors. You'll need to travel directly east for three hundred and twenty-nine miles to the Senyph Ocean, cross the ocean, then travel another forty-nine miles inland to a rather bleak looking desert.

That's where you'll find the World Doors."

Sophia frowned. "Exactly how wide is that ocean?"

"The distance across the Senyph Ocean is precisely one thousand, nine hundred and forty-nine miles."

Sophia looked at Orville in dismay. "I don't think that's possible."

Orville did his best to sound optimistic.

"Getting down into Pavorak Gorge seemed impossible too. Besides, we don't have a choice. We have to get back home. We have to."

"You're right. We'll take it one step at a time. Who knows what tomorrow will bring? We could find towns and villages along the coast with boats that cross the ocean every day."

Proto gave a great squawk. "Centipedes! I hear them coming! A huge swarm of them!" Orville heard it too, a dreadful slithery rustling sound coming from all around them.

"Hurry! Up into that tree!"

Orville and Sophia scrambled madly up the vines into the dense forest canopy. "We'll be safe here until they leave."

Orville groaned as he watched several dozen of the ferocious creatures darting and slithering through the jungle below, gathering in a great tangled wriggling mass beneath their tree. The centipedes were huge, at least thirty feet long, with many dozens of spiky yellow legs capable of propelling them through the thick jungle vegetation. Orville tried not to look at their monstrous razor sharp fangs, and their jaws... opening and closing. A sudden rush of heat roll up through him, and he closed his eyes so he wouldn't have to look at the dreadful creatures. The last thing he wanted to do was faint and tumble down into a mass of writhing carnivorous centipedes.

Sophia cried out, "They're trying to cut down the tree!"

Orville opened his eyes and looked down. Sophia was right. The centipedes were using their huge mandibles, making a unified effort to hack through the tree trunk. Orville popped up an impenetrable sphere of defense around himself and Sophia.

Proto wriggled out of Orville's backpack.

"I just had a marvelous idea. I was doing a little research on the infamous centipedes of Periculum and I believe I may have a solution to your current dilemma. Hold on, I just realized this very moment how much I enjoy rescuing you two. Quite invigorating to dash in and save my two dear friends from their imminent doom. Perhaps I should become a Metaphysical Adventurer."

With a flurry of feathers Proto swooped down from the tree and landed on the back of a gigantic centipede. He spread his wings and opened his beak wide, letting out a raucous, discordant shrieking cry unlike anything Orville had ever heard.

"Oww, that hurts my ears! Proto! What are you doing? Get back up here before something happens to you!" Proto ignored Orville's cries and let loose another jarring shriek that echoed and vibrated through the rainforest.

The centipedes became wildly agitated, racing frenetically around the tree and making dreadful hissing noises. One of them bolted off into the jungle and seconds later the others followed suit. In less than twenty seconds every centipede had vanished.

Proto flew back up into the tree and landed next to Sophia.

"What in the world did you do, Proto? How did you get them to leave?"

"It's a simple fact of life that every living creature is afraid of something. I simply had to discover what the centipedes were afraid of. A quick search through the Elder's crystalline database told me they are afraid of a very large bird indigenous to this area known as the Gnorli bird. I was able to mimic quite accurately the Gnorli's piercing cry as it swoops down from the sky to snatch up a tasty centipede."

"Ummm... a bird that eats thirty foot long centipedes? Exactly how big *is* this bird?"

"An excellent question, Orville, and the answer is quite straightforward. The Gnorli bird is a very, very, very large bird indeed."

Orville gulped. "Oh, wonderful. Now we have to worry about giant Gnorli birds screaming down from the sky and gobbling us up in a single bite." His eyes nervously scanned the brilliant blue jungle sky.

Orville and Sophia continued moving eastward toward the distant shores of the Senyph Ocean. Proto was soaring high overhead, keeping a watchful eye out for centipedes. When he spotted one he would swoop down, shrieking out the raucous cry of the Gnorli bird and watch with glee as the centipede slithered away in terror.

After nearly two weeks of the punishing overgrown jungle, the two adventurers finally broke through, finding themselves facing a broad vista of rolling emerald green hills extending out as far as they could see.

Sophia gasped. "Oh, this is beautiful! I've never seen such a sight, not even on Quintari. Look at the wildflowers! There are millions of them, and so many different colors. And those magnificent shade trees standing alone in the midst of such beauty. They remind me of the big tree in your dream except they have green leaves, not blue. This is simply glorious." Sophia set off through the long lush green grass and the great swaths of brilliant wildflowers. An hour later she flopped down beneath one the towering shade trees, calling out to Orville, "Let's camp here! This is lovely and I need a rest after that dreadful jungle."

"I couldn't agree with you more." Orville dropped his backpack on the ground and took a seat next to her.

"We did it. We survived the pit of giant carnivorous centipedes and we found our way out of that dismally creepy jungle."

Sophia smiled, knowing full well there were innumerable obstacles still standing between them and their safe return to Muridaan Falls. She leaned back against the tree with a long sigh, gazing out at the endless fields of sunlit wildflowers.

Chapter 17

Sophia's Revelation

Sophia had shaped a tent, sleeping bags, and a picnic table. Orville had shaped all the necessary ingredients for the delicious dinner now simmering over their blazing campfire.

"Mmmm... that smells delicious, Orville."

Thanks. Hey, I think Proto needs your help. He's looking a little wobbly."

Sophia watched Proto shuffling around in a small circle, rocking precariously back and forth, finally toppling over with a loud squawk.

"I do hate to bother you, but would you mind giving me just a smidgeon of a charge?"

"Sure." Sophia picked up Proto and set him down in front of her on the table. "I'll charge you right up. Shaping is manipulating energy, so it's easy enough for me to convert it to electrical energy."

With a small flash of light two copper wires appeared next to Proto. Sophia picked up one with each paw. "Okay, I'll be your battery. Take a seat and grab one wire with each foot. This should take about twenty minutes."

Orville sat down across the table from Sophia. "You

never did tell me why you asked Master Marloh to send us here." A sudden thought popped into his head. "It's about your papa, isn't it?"

"Yes, it's about Papa and how he died. I couldn't tell you this until now, but my his name was Rowland Mouse and he was a highly regarded Metaphysical Adventurer. I was always told that I inherited his natural shaping ability, and my teachers told me I was a shaping prodigy. That may be true, but I also worked harder than most mice did at my craft. I loved Papa and I wanted to be just like him. He used to go out on missions to the most amazing worlds, always returning with gifts for me – gadgets and books and technological relics from long before the Anarkkian war. I was always so happy to see him come through that front door and couldn't wait to hear his stories.

"A little over a year ago he left on a mission to Periculum. It wasn't supposed to be dangerous, they were only searching for an old monastery. He couldn't tell me why they were trying to find it, but he told me not to worry because there weren't any scary creatures where they were going. Besides, Papa was a powerful shaper. He could blink himself fifty miles away if he needed to, and his sphere of defense was one of the most powerful ever recorded by the Metaphysical Adventurers.

"He was accompanied on the mission by a Metaphysical Adventurer named Draken Mouse. Papa was his superior and also his mentor. He told me in confidence that Draken was a gifted shaper and quite ambitious, but was not a very likable fellow. Papa thought he was too ambitious, that he hadn't joined the Metaphysical Adventurers for the right reasons, that he was more interested in personal power than making the world a better place. He had moved quickly up through the ranks of the Metaphysical Adventurers, but was never satisfied with his current position. His desire for power seemed insatiable.

"Draken volunteered to help Papa look for the ancient monastery and even though Papa wasn't especially happy about it he thought some good might come of it. Papa hoped Draken might gain some insight into the true and noble purpose of the Metaphysical Adventurers. Papa always said the only thing in the world that mattered was love. That's what he told me almost every day."

Orville was getting a very bad feeling about what was coming next.

"Are you all right?"

"I'm fine. I've wanted to tell you about this since I first met you, but Master Marloh said I should wait. You've probably guessed it, but Papa never came back from that mission. He died somewhere on Periculum. Draken Mouse said their scout ship suffered a catastrophic CDETS failure and crashed, killing Papa. When Draken returned he had severe injuries, though none of them were life threatening. He said Papa had tried to bring the ship down safely but they lost power and..."

Sophia looked up at Orville, her eyes welling up with tears. "I miss him. I miss him every day."

"I'm so sorry." Orville reached across the table and gently took her paw.

"AAGGGGHH!!!"

Sophia shrieked, letting go of the copper wire she was holding.

"Owww! I forgot you were charging Proto."

Sophia burst out laughing, quickly putting her paw over her mouth. "Sorry, I didn't mean to laugh."

Orville grinned. "Well, at least I made you laugh. That's something. I still don't understand why you asked Master Marloh to send us here."

"Everyone in the Metaphysical Adventurers knows the risks we face, and as painful as it was, they accepted Papa's death as a tragic mishap. I never thought about it when Draken took Papa's position in the Metaphysical Adventurers. I never thought about it until I was going through Papa's desk and found a letter he had written to me. Orville, Papa had been warned by his inner voice about Draken and his overpowering ambition. Papa knew Draken wanted his position and he was afraid the day might come when Draken would resort to violence. In the letter he said if anything happened to him I should go to Muridaan Falls and show his letter to Master Marloh. They were very old friends and he trusted Master Marloh.

"I contacted Master Marloh and he arranged for me to come to Muridaan Falls through a spectral door. When I showed him the letter he said he would look into it, but told me to go no further with my own investigation.

"The Red Mouse is Draken Mouse. When I saw the glowbird's record of Master Marloh talking to Draken, at first I thought Master Marloh had been lying to me, that he was collaborating with Draken and maybe even had something to do with Papa's death. When we returned to Muridaan Falls I accused him of betraying Papa.

"I've never seen Master Marloh so upset. He told me

he had been cultivating a friendship with Draken in order to find proof that he had killed Papa. He had many conversations with Draken and discovered that Draken Mouse thinks Metaphysical Adventurers should have the option of using lethal force if necessary. Draken eventually took Master Marloh into his confidence, revealing that his ultimate goal was to be Supreme Counselor of the Metaphysical Adventurers. He said he would change everything. Lethal force would not only be allowed, it would be encouraged and used against any mice who disagreed with his new order. Draken wanted the Metaphysical Adventurers to become a military force. He said with the combined shaping power they possessed they would be unstoppable. Master Marloh had not told me any of this because he feared for my life. He was afraid if I knew too much Draken Mouse would try to kill me.

"You were a surprise to everyone, especially Master Marloh. He knew right away you were special, a gifted mouse with the potential to become a far more powerful shaper than Draken could ever be. Draken sensed this also and it frightened him. That's why he ordered Master Marloh to kill us both. Draken wasn't aware of my connection to Papa. He thought I was simply a friend of yours who could cause trouble if you disappeared."

"So you and Master Marloh hatched this plan together?"

"We did. The plan had two parts. First, Draken must believe that Master Marloh had killed us both, and second, I needed to find solid, tangible proof that Draken killed Papa. Master Marloh came up with the ingenious solution, telling Draken he was going to send us through a spectral doorway into a nest of huge carnivorous centipedes on Periculum. Draken couldn't stop laughing when Master Marloh told him, assuming we would meet our end inside the belly of a hungry centipede. Master Marloh didn't tell him about the pillar of rock in the center of the pit. Now that we're here and we've survived the centipedes, I need to find proof of Draken's guilt."

"Do you know where... where your papa was when he died?"

"That's what we have to find out. How hard could it be to search an entire planet for something which may or may not even exist?"

Orville said nothing.

"I do have two possible leads. First, when Papa and Draken came to Periculum they arrived in a small Quintarian scout ship. It's a silver egg-shaped craft used by the Elders during the Anarkkian Wars. The Metaphysical Adventurers found an ancient storage depot on Nirriim with half a dozen scout ships still in working order and brought them back to Earth. We know for certain that Draken returned from Periculum without the scout ship. If we can locate the ship then we've probably found where Papa died."

"What's the second lead?"

"The second lead is what Papa and Draken were searching for, but did not find – the ancient monastery."

"You have no idea where it might be?"

"Papa thought it was near the ocean, that's all I know. He also said the Anarkkians had been looking for it during the war but never found it."

"It's not much to go on, but it's something. We have to cross the Senyph Ocean to get to the World Doors, so we may as well just keep heading east. We can rest here for a few more days and then move on. At least we don't have to fight our way through that jungle."

Sophia let go of the two copper wires she was holding. "Okay, Proto, you're fully charged, and it's time for me to get some sleep."

Proto gave a squawk. "Have a lovely rest, and don't worry about a thing. I shall be soaring through the night sky keeping a sharp lookout for monstrous nocturnal creatures gnashing their teeth, slithering and slinking about, hunting for tasty snacks."

Orville frowned. "Thanks, I'll sleep like a little mouseling now."

Chapter 18

The Blue Mouse

A gentle breeze carried the delicate fragrance of ten thousand newly bloomed orange blossoms across the balmy summer air. It was far too early in the season for the trees to be bearing fruit, but the intoxicating scent of the blossoms floating through the grove was more than enough to satisfy Orville Wellington Mouse.

"Isn't this an amazing place, Sophia? I could sit under one of these orange trees for a hundred years."

"Orville, you're having the dream again. The one about the orange grove and the big blue tree."

"Mmm hmmm... lovely summer day, I must agree."

"It's a dream. You're having a dream."

"I'm sorry, did you say something? Aren't the orange blossoms lovely this time of year?"

"Orville, I want you do something for me, all right?"

"Sure. Did you want me to pick a few of those orange blossoms for you?"

"Please pay attention, Orville. I want you to look very, very carefully at your paws. This is something

Master Marloh taught me. Look very carefully at your paws and focus on them until they become sharp and real."

"Okay." Orville held out his paws in front of him. There was a soft, hazy cloud-like look about them and it was difficult to hold them still, hard to focus on them.

"Hmm... this is not as easy as I thought it would be. Wait, I think I've got it–" Orville stopped in stunned surprise. A very strange thing happened when he finally brought his paws clearly into focus. Not only did his paws became real, but so did the dream world around him. A powerful sense of awareness flooded through him and he was fully present in the moment. He was wide awake. He was wide awake inside his dream of the orange grove. He gazed dumbstruck at the world around him, then looked at Sophia. "What is this place? Is this real?"

"It's real for now."

"Wait, are you saying every time I dream I'm creating a real world?"

"It's real enough while you're here, that's what I'm saying. Think of a bubble floating up from the bottom of the ocean, a lovely silvery round bubble. As you watch it floating up through the water it looks solid, with a very defined form. But what happens when the bubble reaches the surface of the water? Where does that bubble go? Where does the roundness go? Has anything been lost, or are you just looking at the bubble from a new perspective?"

"I'd never thought of that before. So when I wake up from a dream it's still there but I'm just seeing it differently?"

"Exactly. The dream is still inside your head, but

your center of awareness is no longer inside the dream, it's now outside the dream. Everything changes when you're outside the dream."

"Why does everything seem so real now? The orange trees look just like they would if I was awake and in Muridaan Falls."

"You are awake, you're just not awake in Muridaan Falls. You're awake in this orange grove dream."

"Well, whatever the reason, I like this place. Now that I'm awake, I'm going to go take a good close look at that big blue tree."

Orville set off through the orange grove toward the enormous blue tree.

"What an amazing tree. I wonder how old it is? Wait, maybe it's not old at all. Maybe I just created it. Maybe it's brand new but it only looks a thousand years old."

He stepped closer to the huge tree and ran his paw over the smooth white bark. Out of the corner of his eye he caught a sudden movement. "Sophia?"

Orville looked up, but instead of Sophia he saw a plump elderly mouse wearing a bright blue robe peering out from behind the tree trunk. Orville popped up a sphere of defense. "Who are you? What are you doing in my dream?"

The blue mouse's gaze was unwavering, but he did not answer.

"Why are you staring at me like that?" Orville dropped his sphere of defense. He sensed the blue mouse was not here to harm him. When he focused his awareness directly on the blue mouse he felt something quite unexpected. He felt great love and deep compassion.

"Do I know you?"

Orville heard a quiet voice echo through his mind. "Is he true?"

Orville approached the blue mouse.

"Is that you talking? Is who true?"

Orville heard a second voice in his head.

"Perhaps I am not in your dream, perhaps it is you who are in my dream."

With a flash of light the blue mouse vanished and Orville found himself back in his sleeping bag, gazing up at a starry Periculum night sky.

"Creekers, what was that all about?"

Chapter 19

A Sticky Wicket

"Sophia, did you dream about the orange grove last night? I dreamed about it again and you were there and there was an old mouse wearing a blue robe. He said he wasn't in my dream, but I was in his dream."

"That's strange. Now that you mention it, I do seem to remember dreaming about the orange grove, and I think you were there."

"You taught me how to wake up inside the dream by focusing on my paws."

"I do that all the time! It's something Master Marloh taught me."

"Creekers, that's what you told me in my dream. Well, in someone's dream. Why am I dreaming about this loopy orange grove anyway?"

Sophia shook her head. "I don't know. These kind of dreams take time to understand. Master Marloh says our inner voice can't tell us too much, that we have to experience life without knowing what's going to happen next. That's how we learn. You'll find out one day what it all means. In the meantime, we have to get to the Senyph Ocean."

Proto swooped down from the tree and landed on the

picnic table.

"Good morning, fellow adventurers. I trust you had a delightful sleep? I kept a watchful eye out for dreadful predatorial beasts with razor sharp teeth but there were none to be found." Proto sounded disappointed.

"When do you sleep, Proto?"

"Rabbitons have no need for sleep. We are at the ready twenty-four hours a day. While everyone else is sleeping, I am usually in the kitchen preparing tasty snacks and beverages. Being on this adventure is quite a change for me. I must say it's making me feel quite bold. Only yesterday I stepped out of the Cube and made the long and treacherous trek down the rocky ravine. I even peeked out into Pavorak Gorge and was quite taken by how lovely it was. I have seen it many times on the glowbird records, but it's different to be right there standing next to it. Quite different indeed. I am also pleased to report there was not a single Anarkkian Attack Spider in sight."

"That's wonderful, Proto! Good for you! I have high hopes that one day you'll visit us in Muridaan Falls."

"Oh my, that would truly be an adventure, but first I'll need to get you two safely home to Muridaan Falls. We must press on and discover the truth about Sophia's papa, although I'm quite certain that dastardly Draken Mouse was behind it all. What a vile creature he is. I'd like to send a few A6 Warrior Rabbitons his way to give him a taste of his own villainous medicine."

Sophia laughed. "I'm glad you're on our side and not his."

She converted their supplies back to thought clouds and the three adventurers headed east, Proto soaring high above them, scouting the area for carnivorous creatures with a hunger for tasty mice.

The lush grassy plain with its patchwork of brilliant wildflowers continued on for mile after mile, the air permeated with the most delectable fragrances. After five days of trekking over the picturesque landscape Orville noticed an irregular dark line running across the horizon. "How many miles did Proto say it was to the ocean?"

Sophia halted, setting her pack down. "Three hundred and twenty-nine. I think we've come almost a hundred miles, maybe a little more. We're making good time."

"That dark line on the horizon must be a forest. It could be slow going depending on the kind of trees. Hard to tell from here how dense the growth is. Hopefully it's not another jungle." Orville scanned the sky, quickly spotting Proto high overhead and waving him down.

"Proto!!"

Proto banked sharply, performing two quick barrel rolls and a spectacular loop de loop maneuver as he shot down from the sky and skidded to a halt on the grass.

"I'm impressed, Proto! I think you might be just the Rabbiton to pilot *The Glowbird* on our next adventure. You're quite a gifted flyer."

"Thank you, Orville. I must admit, I am beginning to feel a certain confidence which I have never felt before. I believe adventuring suits me quite well. Now, how may I be of assistance?"

Orville pointed to the dark line of trees in the distance. "I thought you might fly down to that forest and scout around so we don't get surprised by some hideous beast slithering out from behind a tree, gnashing its razor sharp teeth."

"Oh my, an excellent idea. I'll be right back!" Proto shot up into the air, swooping and soaring his way across the open plains until he was only a black speck in the brilliant blue sky.

Two hours later he had not returned.

Sophia frowned. "I'm worried about Proto. He really should have been back by now. Something may have happened to him."

"Do you think he ran out of power?"

"No, I charged him this morning and it should keep him powered up for several days."

Orville slung his pack onto his shoulder. "We'd better go look for him."

Even walking at a brisk pace, it took Orville and Sophia four hours to reach the edge of the forest. It was farther away than it appeared, the trees being much taller than Orville had initially thought they were.

"I don't like the way this forest feels. Something's not right. It's too dark, for one thing."

Sophia nodded. "I feel it too. It's as though there is something here that doesn't belong here. It's hard to describe the feeling."

"What do you think happened to Proto?"

"I don't know. The good news is the real Proto is sitting back in the Cube watching a big bright display panel, and probably frosting little cakes while he's doing it."

"Mmmm... those little cakes were good."

"Focus. We need to find Proto. He has to be in here somewhere. Better pop up a defense sphere. I really do not like what I'm feeling."

"Done. Let's go." Orville and Sophia stepped into the unnaturally dark forest. A bright light shot out from Orville's paw, illuminating the path in front of them.

Sophia studied the forest floor carefully, then raised an eyebrow. "Orville, look at the path. What do you see?"

"Umm... well, nothing on the path itself. That's... strange. There are leaves and fallen branches and those seed cones all over, but nothing on the path. It looks as if someone went through with a wide broom an hour ago and swept it clean."

"Let's go." Sophia moved further into the darkened forest, Orville's orb of light leading the way. "Look, there's another path, and it's been cleared the same as this one. It's getting darker."

An orb of light shot out from Sophia's paw and joined Orville's. "That's better."

"Sophia! Look!" Orville pointed to the edge of the path.

"Oh, dear." Sophia leaned over and picked up a feather, examining it closely. "It's synthetic, one of Proto's."

"We're on the right trail at least."

"But on the trail to where? To what? What happened to him? He was flying. How could something... catch him?"

The two adventurers pushed deeper into the forest, their eyes scanning the ground for fallen feathers. Sophia found two more.

"It's getting darker. I have a feeling whatever has Proto is causing this darkness. We should probably move toward the darkness, not away from it." Orville sounded less than enthralled with his own suggestion.

Sophia looked around her.

"Over that way. It's almost pitch black over there." Another brilliant sphere of light flashed out from Sophia's paw and sped through the forest to the darkest area.

"Orville, do you see what I'm seeing?"

"What is that? It's not a rock, it's too round. It's shaped like a giant ball."

"Keep your sphere of defense as strong as you can. I don't like this at all. It's too strange, and it's much too dark here."

Sophia and Orville crept silently through the trees, carefully avoiding any dry twigs or sticks that would give them away. Sophia sent out a soft green thought cloud to Orville. When the cloud touched him he heard Sophia's voice in his mind.

"Just use thought clouds from now on. I think something might be listening to us."

Orville sent back a pale blue thought cloud. "Good idea. That big ball looks like it's all covered with moss. Or something that looks like moss."

Orville was now only fifteen feet away from the huge mossy ball. "It's at least ten feet tall. I think it might be... moving." That was the moment he spotted Proto lying motionless on top of the mossy sphere. "It's Proto! I found him!" Orville let go of caution and dashed toward the sphere.

Sophia hollered, "NO! Don't touch it! Don't touch it!"

It was too late. Orville had made a tremendous leap up onto the ball in an attempt to grab Proto. Unfortunately, that was as far as he got. When he tried to climb down, he could not. He couldn't move his arms or his legs. The surface of the ball was coated with a horrible sticky green substance which had first trapped Proto and now Orville.

"It's okay! My defense sphere is– aagghh! Wait! Something is oozing right through my defense sphere! It burns! I think this thing is trying to dissolve me! Help, Sophia!"

Sophia's heart was pounding. She knew if she tried to pull Orville off the sphere she would become its third captive. The creature was trying to eat Orville, trying to dissolve him with acid and then absorb his body. The creature's stomach was on the outside, not on the inside.

"I have to try something, but I don't know if I can do it. If it doesn't work, it might kill you!"

Orville shrieked out, "Do it, Sophia! Whatever it is, do it now! It's burning me!"

Sophia held out both paws and a brilliant blue light blasted out. The instant the light hit Orville he vanished. A split second later he appeared on the ground next to Sophia. A hundred small lights flashed from her paws and water spilled out of the air onto Orville, washing away the deadly acid that covered him.

"You did it! You did it!" Orville stood up and threw his arms around Sophia. A moment later he pulled away. "What did you do, exactly?"

"I blinked you away from the creature. I've never done it to anyone except Master Marloh. I was so scared I wouldn't be able to convert you back to your physical self. I was afraid I'd do it all wrong and you'd be... not the same."

"Can you blink Proto away from that thing?"

"I think so. He's a machine so it's not so tricky."

The blue light shot out from her paw and Proto disappeared, reappearing almost instantly on the ground in front of Sophia. Proto staggered to his feet, his feathers covered in the thick goopy acid.

Sophia shaped a shower of warm water, quickly rinsing him off.

"Oh my, what a dreadful experience, but also rather thrilling! Thank goodness my synthetic feathers were resistant to that creature's digestive acids."

Sophia gave a shout. "It's moving!" The huge ball was rolling away from them down the forest trail.

"Look! It's picking up everything on the path as it rolls. That's why the paths are so clean. Proto, what happened? How did it catch you?"

"It was all my own doing. I flew down to investigate the peculiar darkness, saw the big green ball and decided to land on it and have a look around. Of course I became stuck immediately, and when it started rolling again I was pressed flat against it."

"Do you know what it is, Proto?"

"I'm not completely certain, but if I were to guess I would say it's more than likely a creation of the Anarkkians. It has all the hallmarks of one of their dreadful bio-form creatures. I have no idea how it's able to absorb the light around it, creating that most peculiar darkness."

A voice popped into Orville's head. "Follow the green orb. You must follow it."

"Sophia, we're supposed to follow that green ball creature."

"Are you sure?"

"I'm sure. It came from my inner voice."

"Let's go, then.

"Proto, why don't you hop into my backpack? There might be more of those creatures rolling around the forest."

Proto jumped up onto Orville's shoulder and scrambled into the his pack, pulling the flap shut behind him.

"Good idea. When I think about it, there might other Anarkkian creations out there, too. Creatures far, far worse than the monstrous sticky green ball that devours tasty little mice."

Orville looked at Sophia, raising his eyebrows. "Thanks, Proto, I feel much better now."

Sophia grinned as they headed down the forest path after the green ball creature.

Chapter 20

Tasty Little Cakes

"You're sure that's it, Proto?"

"Quite so, then I bake them for twenty-eight minutes, let them cool and slather on the frosting."

"Here we go, I'm going to try it."

Orville was looking quite doubtful. "I don't see how you can do it. They won't be the same."

"You wait and see. This isn't the first time I've shaped tasty snacks you know." Sophia's face became a mask of concentration as she held both paws out. An orange light flowed out of them and onto the forest floor. There was a bright yellow flash and a large metal tray appeared, filled with tasty little cakes identical to the ones made by Proto. "All right, Orville Wellington Mouse, you're the snack expert. Go ahead and try one."

Orville looked at the cakes, then at Sophia, then back at the tasty little cakes. "They look about the same as Proto's." He plucked one from the tray and waved it back and forth under his nose. "Hmmm. It smells good." He took a tiny bite. "Mmm." He took a large bite. "Mmmmmm! You did it, these are excellent." He whispered loudly to Proto, "Not quite as tasty as yours, but still delicious."

Orville shaped a carton for the tasty little cakes and placed them carefully in his backpack. "Don't crush these, Proto."

"Most certainly not. In fact, I have decided to fly ahead and scout the area for that hideous green ball creature. This time I will most definitely not land on it, however." Proto flashed off through the trees, his wings a blur.

"Proto's getting a lot braver, isn't he?"

"He is. It's nice to see him having fun. I think it's helped that you've been so nice to him and never laughed at him for being afraid of things."

"Oh, I know what it feels like to be afraid. Like with those centipedes. I've always been afraid of bugs like that, even the little ones. That's one reason why I was surprised that Master Marloh wanted me to join the Metaphysical Adventurers."

"It's good to be afraid. You wouldn't last very long in the Metaphysical Adventurers if you didn't have a healthy fear of strange looking creatures. You'd wind up being a tasty snack on your first mission."

Orville gave a snort. "I'm not lacking in the fear department."

Moments later Proto came streaking back through the trees and swooped down in front of Sophia. "I found the lair of that dastardly green menace!"

"That's wonderful, Proto! Lead the way."

Sophia and Orville followed Proto through the forest for over a mile. Finally he stopped, pointing with one wing. "There, in that cave. That's where he went."

Orville gave a loud groan. "Caves! Why do they

always live in dark caves?"

Proto gave a great squawk. "That's it! I think I know why your inner voice sent us here!"

"What do you mean?"

"When you mentioned dark caves I remembered something I read back at the Cube. In the book I am thinking of, a very distinguished Elder wrote, *'The darkest cave holds the brightest light.'* That's our answer right there. This is a very dark cave indeed, so it should contain the brightest light, which I believe refers to an object or an idea which we desperately need."

Orville looked dubious, glancing over to Sophia. "Well, I guess you could be right, Proto. I just meant it seems like creepy creatures always live in dark caves, and I don't really like them. I'm not scared of caves, I just don't like them or going into them. Or thinking about them."

Sophia smiled to herself and flicked her wrist. A brilliant orb of glowing light shot out. "It won't be a dark cave for long." The adventurers followed the orb into the cave's interior.

"Creekers, this is not what I was expecting." Orville looked around in surprise. "It's not even a cave. It's a metallic structure of some kind, and it's big. This room must be fifty feet long and twenty feet tall. It looks like a section of long curving corridor. Maybe we're in an old building."

Sophia shook her head. "No, it's something else entirely." Her eyes swept the walls, which were composed of a gleaming pale blue metallic substance. She rapped the smooth surface with her paw. "It's not metal, it's an artificial substance called Morsennium. I learned about it in science class on Quintari. The

Anarkkians built their ships with it, even their interstellar ships. It's the strongest substance known to mice and is completely unaffected by the elements. We're inside an Anarkkian ship, Orville. It's been here since the war ended fifteen hundred years ago and it will sit here just like this for another hundred thousand years at least."

"Creekers, this is amazing. Look at all those panels covered with dials and levers running along the walls. Some have display panels like the ones in the Cube. They could be for communication or something, or maybe for seeing what was outside the ship. Look, there's a door over there."

Orville stepped over to a tall recessed section of wall with two glowing discs next it, one yellow and one violet. "What you think? Should I touch it? The green ball creature could be on the other side."

"Pop up a sphere of defense, tap the violet disc, and back away from the door."

"Okay. Here goes." Orville tapped the violet disc and stepped back. The tall rectangular panel slid open, revealing a large circular room. A dozen soft lights inside the room blinked on.

"The lights still work. How is that possible after so long?"

"These ships didn't run on electrical power the way glowbirds do."

Proto scrambled out of Orville's pack and jumped onto a counter covered with small lights, colored tabs, switches and silver control sticks.

"Sophia's quite correct. The Anarkkian ships were powered by CDETS. All Rabbitons are powered by a single CDETS, but ships like this had huge banks of them. CDETS is short for Cross Dimensional Energy Transfer Sphere. Very simply, what they do is siphon energy from the tenth dimension, a dimension of pure energy. It's quite possible there might be living creatures there, but so far no one has been able to detect any."

"That's incredible. I think this must be the central control room, Sophia. It looks as though the ship has a round room in the center that's surrounded by a wide circular corridor partitioned into separate rooms."

Sophia looked puzzled. "Where did the green ball creature go? Proto saw it enter the ship, so where is it?"

"I don't know. How could it open the doors?"

"Maybe it can change it's shape. You know, sort of ooze under the doors?"

"Eeww. I don't like the sound of that. Let's go back to the first room. We can make our way around the outer rooms."

Orville stepped out of the central control room back into the curved corridor. "Over there, there's the door leading to the next partition."

Orville hurried over to the door on the far end of the curved room and tapped the violet disc. The door slid open but the overhead lights did not blink on. He tried to contain his fear.

"It's really dark in there. Really, really, dark." He sent out a glowing orb and a moment later gave a terrified shriek, slamming his paw against the yellow disc. The door hissed shut.

"What is it? What did you see?"

"Unnh... dizzy... so hot..."

Sophia jumped over and grabbed Orville in case he fainted.

"Thanks. I'm okay now, I think. At least this time I didn't actually faint. I found Proto's dastardly green menace. I also found about five hundred other dastardly green menaces in all different sizes. There's a huge colony of those things in there."

Sophia grimaced. "This is not good. I have a feeling Proto was right about the darkest cave holding the brightest light. I'm afraid your inner voice may have sent us to find something inside that room. That's how the universe usually works."

Orville groaned. "This is just like a scary bad dream."

Sophia leaned back against a wall. "All right, what do we know about these things?"

Proto squawked out, "They like to eat tasty mice and glowbirds."

Orville perked up. "That's a good start, Proto. We know they like to eat. There are hundreds of them in there and they all like to eat mice and glowbirds. Maybe that's not such a good start after all."

Sophia laughed. "Mice and glowbirds can't be the only thing they eat. We could be the only two mice on Periculum, Orville. They have to eat other things or they wouldn't have survived."

"Maybe they eat those giant centipedes. Proto, could you go grab a few and bring them back here?"

"Ha ha ha ha!"

"Let's think of something else, then. I know, we could shape something for them to eat, something that might distract them while we sneak past. Maybe your tasty little cakes."

Proto gave a great squawk. "Excellent idea. There's not a creature alive who can resist my tasty little cakes.

Toss a few into the room and see what they do."

"Hmmm.... I don't know, tasty snacks from another planet?"

"It won't hurt to try."

Orville flipped open his pack and took out a pawful of tasty little cakes.

"Mmmm... they do smell good, don't they?" He stepped over to the door, blinking up a sphere of defense. "Here we go." He tapped the violet disc and as the door was opening he tossed the tasty little cakes into the room, quickly slapping the yellow disc. The door hissed shut. Orville put his ear to the door, jumping back an instant later. "What is that??"

Loud thudding and thumping noises were coming from the next room. There was a wild cacophony of crashes, shattering glass, and the sound of heavy objects slamming into the walls and floor.

Sophia cried out, "The tasty little cakes are driving the creatures mad! Proto, you were right!"

The entire ship was rattling and shaking from the frenetic activity in the next room. Finally the noises died down and the ship was still again.

Orville stood next to the door, his paw next to the violet button. "I'm scared to look."

"Just take a quick peek."

Orville tapped the button and the door slid open. He sent in an orb of light and jumped back. There were hundreds of the green balls clustered around the doorway. If he didn't know better he'd swear they were all looking at him, waiting for something.

"Uhh... I think... I think maybe they want more tasty cakes." He reached into his pack and took out the rest of them, tossing them all into the room. The chaos was instantaneous, the room filled with five hundred manic bouncing green balls trying to grab a tasty cake. It was the strangest sight Orville had ever seen. He slapped the yellow button and the door slid shut.

"Okay, Proto, your tasty cakes are a hit with those sticky green fellows in there. We need to make more of them. This might take a while, there's a big crowd of hungry creatures in there."

Sophia shaped tray after tray of the tasty little cakes, and Orville tossed tray after tray of them into the room with the green ball creatures. Each time he threw in the cakes the creatures went wild, bouncing across the floor and walls, rattling the ship. Finally the creatures slowed down. Orville tossed a tray of little cakes into the room and watched. A few of the green ball creatures twitched slightly then sat still. "I think that's it. I think they're full!"

"It could be the sugar. That might be why they went wild and why they're not moving now. They're acting just like mouselings do. Let's go in while they're still sleeping."

Orville nodded, stepping cautiously through door-way. "Don't touch them, they'll stick to you!" A small green ball creature had stuck to Orville's foot. He shook it wildly and the creature flew across the room, sticking to the far wall.

Step by careful step Sophia and Orville gingerly made their way into the room. They were halfway across when Sophia gasped.

"Over there! That's what we need. That's why we're here." Sophia was pointing to a gleaming brass box sitting on the counter. Unfortunately, the box was surrounded by immense green sticky ball creatures.

Orville shook his head at Sophia. "I don't think I can get to it. There's too many of them, and they're too big. I'd have to squeeze in between those two huge ones. I'd never make it. What's in the box? How do you know it's what we need?"

Sophia slapped her paw to her forehead. "What am I thinking??" She shot a blast of blue light across the room and the brass box vanished. A split second later it blinked into her paws. She flipped the lid open and looked inside. "Yes! This is it! I found it!"

"What is it? Wait, the creatures are starting to move. We'd better get out of here." Sophia nodded and they hurried back through the green creatures and into the other room. Orville grabbed a tray of tasty little cakes and hurled them through the doorway, slapping the yellow disc. He put the rest of the tasty cakes in his backpack. "That should keep them busy for a while. Let's get out of here."

Five minutes later the party of adventurers was heading east through the dense forest toward the Senyph Ocean. Sophia had the mysterious brass box clutched tightly in her paws. She grinned at Orville.

Chapter 21

The Gnorli Bird

"Well, don't keep us in suspense. What's in the brass box?"

Sophia gently set the gleaming box in Orville's paws. "Find out for yourself."

Orville hesitated. "Wait, this isn't a trick is it? One of those boxes full of paper snakes that spring out and scare you?"

"I guess you'll find out soon enough, Orville Wellington Mouse."

Orville held the box away from him and gingerly raised the lid. He blinked several times, looking puzzled.

"Goggles and a red hat?"

Sophia gave Orville her very best know-it-all smirk, carefully removing the brass goggles and a bright red stretchy cap covered with dozens of small gleaming gold spheres.

"It's not just any pair of brass goggles and any old winter cap. It's far more than that. Papa spent years searching for these. He discovered a reference to them in an old Anarkkian manuscript when he was young. A few years ago he showed me an ancient image of the goggles sitting in a brass box just like this one. I recognized it the instant I saw it. The more Papa studied the old Anarkkian technology, the more he came to believe that goggles such as these really did exist."

"What do they do?"

"Hold on to your adventuring hat. These are four dimensional goggles. They allow you to look back in time."

Orville burst out laughing. "That's not possible. When something is over, it's over. That's the end of it."

Sophia glared at him. "Orville Wellington Mouse, you should know by now I am never wrong. My science teachers on Quintari taught us that time passes at different rates in different environments depending on a number of factors. Time is affected by gravity and also by how fast you are traveling, although those two factors are closely related. My teachers also said given the right circumstances, it was possible for time to flow in reverse. That's what these goggles do. When you look through them you see time flowing backwards. You can also adjust the speed and direction of the flow."

"You're saying I could look through those and see something happening a million years ago?"

"No, that's not what I'm saying. They have limited power and can only look back a finite amount of time. I don't know how far, though. Papa didn't know either. I'm certain the ship with the green ball creatures was an Anarkkian Command Control Scout Vessel. There were not many of them and the technology they utilized was shrouded in secrecy. Maybe to some advanced civilizations this would be antiquated technology, but during the war there was nothing better."

"I don't know. I know how much you loved your papa, but if you really think about it – goggles that let you see into the past? That's kind of silly."

Sophia gave groan of exasperation. She held out the goggles and the cap for Orville. "Put them on. No talking, just put them on."

Orville slipped the stretchy red cap on over his head and strapped the goggles on tightly.

"Do you think this is a good look for me?"

"Quiet, I said no talking." Sophia pulled two thin cables out from the side of the brass goggles and plugged them into the red cap. She grabbed Orville's shoulders and turned him so he was facing the path they had been walking on. Sophia tapped three silver tabs on the top of the goggles and slowly turned the brass knob sitting between the two bright red lenses. "Tell me when you see something."

"The only thing I see is your paw turning the–" Orville let out a shriek. "No! That's not possible. I can't be seeing this!" He tore the goggles off his head.

"I saw us! I saw you and me walking backwards down the path! That's not possible. It can't be real."

"And yet you saw it with your big brown eyes."

Orville frowned. "You're right. I did see it. I can't deny that. I suppose I should know better after all the things I've seen in the last month – Rabbitons, mechanical glowbirds, shaping, all those strange devices in the Metaphysical Adventurers headquarters, gigantic centipedes, and those green ball creatures. It's almost too much."

"I know this is all new to you. I grew up with shaping and advanced technology. You'll get used to it. It won't take long, I promise."

144

"Maybe you're right. Wait, why do we need those four dimensional goggles anyway? What are you going to do with them?"

"I'm going to do something I dread with all my heart, but it's something I have to do. I'm going to watch my papa being murdered by Draken Mouse."

Orville had no idea how to respond.

They walked silently through the great forest for several more miles until Orville spoke again.

"Sophia, if it would help at all, I could watch it instead of you. We'd have the proof you needed and you wouldn't... you know, have to see it happen."

Sophia squeezed Orville's arm.

"I couldn't ask for a better friend than you, but I need to see it for myself. It's something I have to do. I guess it's one of those things you called the fires of life. Things that change us forever."

"Well, if you change your mind, just– hey, look at that weird tree. I've never seen a bright yellow trunk like that before."

"That is strange. Usually trees grow in clusters. It's odd that there's only one of them."

"There's another right over there. They're kind of pretty, aren't they?"

One of yellow trees abruptly slid several feet across the forest floor. Sophia skittered backwards with a shriek, grabbing Orville's arm. "Look up! Look up!"

The first thing Orville noticed was that the two bright yellow tree trunks were not tree trunks at all, but were in fact a pair of legs, a pair of legs connected to the body of a gigantic black bird. A gigantic black bird who was staring at Orville with intense curiosity.

Orville was feeling dizzy but managed to snap a

sphere of defense around Sophia and himself. He stammered, "G-g-giant bird. Giant bird looking at me."

"I don't think he wants to eat us. He's just watching us."

Orville gave a tentative wave at the bird and whispered, "Hello, very, very large bird."

The bird's enormous black eyes blinked rapidly. "Gnorli. I'm a Gnorli bird. I was looking for something, and now you've made me forget what it was. Drat. Double drat."

Orville gaped at the Gnorli bird. "Good heavens, you can talk?"

"Of course I can talk. Why shouldn't I talk? You can talk. Plenty of creatures can talk. What are you doing in my forest anyway? Wait – don't tell me. You're a couple of rough and tumble adventurers looking for treasure and you're going to plead with me to fly you somewhere. You know, ride on my back and that sort of thing. You're thinking, oh, my, what a lovely adventure that would be, soaring through the sky on the back of a great Gnorli bird. Am I right? You know I am. You'd be surprised how often I run into adventurers like you in this forest."

Sophia gave the Gnorli bird her brightest smile. "I'm Sophia, and it's a great pleasure to meet you. I've never met a Gnorli bird before. Do you have a name?"

"Gnorli."

"You're a Gnorli bird and your name is also Gnorli?"

"You're a clever one, figuring that out so quick like that."

"Well, it just seems a bit odd that you don't have a different name than the kind of bird you are. You know, like Blacky or... Feathers..."

"Feathers? Who has a name like that? All Gnorli birds have the same name. We're all called Gnorli. That way when I see another Gnorli bird, I just say, 'Salutations, Gnorli. Seen any yummy centipedes?'"

"Well... suppose you're talking to one Gnorli bird about another Gnorli bird? How would he know which Gnorli bird you were referring to?"

"Are you dim? He'd know I was talking about Gnorli. You're giving me a terrible headache. What did you want again? Why am I talking to you?"

"You said you might be able to fly us somewhere on your back. We're adventurers."

"Adventurers? Why didn't you say so? I've flown plenty of adventurers on my back. My name is Gnorli, by the way. What's yours?"

"Sophia, my name is Sophia. This is my best friend, Orville." Sophia pointed to Orville, who had a very puzzled expression on his face.

"Are you hunting for treasure? I like treasure, especially when it's sparkly and shiny. Where are you headed?"

"We're trying to get to the Senyph Ocean."

"Oooohh... scary. You're not going to go swimming are you? Not a good idea to go swimming in the Senyph Ocean." Gnorli threw his head back and let out a great cackling laugh that shook the forest.

"Well, we hadn't planned on going swimming. We're going to spend some time along the coast and then cross the Senyph Ocean."

Gnorli pulled his head back and stared blankly at Orville and Sophia, his eyes blinking rapidly. "Say what?"

"We need to cross the ocean. It's the only way we can get home."

Gnorli threw back his head again gave the great cackling laugh but stopped abruptly. "Hold on, what was I laughing about? Drat. It was something funny... something about... oh, I don't know. Okay, so what are we doing again?"

Orville studied the Gnorli bird carefully. "Gnorli, you were going to fly us to the Senyph Ocean, remember?"

"If you say so. Here, I'll stoop down and you can scamper up onto my back. Just sit on my neck and hold on to my feathers. I've flown a lot of adventurers around, you know. You're not my first adventurers."

Gnorli squatted down on the forest floor while Sophia and Orville grasped his feathers and clambered up his side, then scooted across his back to his neck. Orville sat down, his legs straddling Gnorli's wide neck. He grabbed a pawful of feathers and held on tightly. Sophia sat down behind him and put her arms around Orville's waist. "Gnorli, I think we're ready to go!"

"Okay, my adventuring friends! We're off to fight the deadly giant carnivorous centipedes!"

"No! No, Gnorli, we're going to the Senyph Ocean."

Gnorli let out a great cackling laugh. "Just kidding. Hold on tight. Next stop is the Senyph Ocean."

Gnorli flapped his gigantic wings and took to the air.

"Yikes! We're flying on the back of a gigantic bird! Tell me again why we're doing this?"

Sophia could not stop grinning. "This is amazing! It's more fun than flying in *The Glowbird*!

Orville gripped the feathers tightly as the Gnorli bird

148

rose into the sky. The ride was surprisingly smooth and after a while he began to relax. "It is kind of comfortable sitting on all these feathers. Hey, Proto, do want to come out and take a look?"

"No, thank you. I'll just stay in your backpack if you don't mind."

"Why aren't you afraid of heights when you fly by yourself?"

"Oh, that's quite different, I assure you. Yes, quite different indeed."

The Gnorli bird abruptly let out a terrible shrill shriek, veering wildly across the sky. "What is that? What is that on my back?? What are you doing there?"

Sophia was quite aware by now that Gnorli had a dreadful memory, and in fact he couldn't remember much of anything for more than a few minutes.

"It's just us, Gnorli. Your two adventuring passengers, Sophia and Orville. You're taking us to the Senyph Ocean, remember? We're hoping to find some nice shiny treasures for you."

"Oh, that sounds nice. I do like shiny treasures. You're not the first adventurers I've carried on my back, you know. Say, would you like to see some of my shiny treasures? It'll be fun, hold on!"

Gnorli took a sharp banking turn and headed north.

Orville cried out, "Gnorli, we need to get to the Senyph Ocean – that's east, and you're heading north."

Gnorli laughed. "There it is up ahead! That's where I live."

Sophia peered across Gnorli's gigantic head. "You live on that mesa? Good heavens, Gnorli, that's gigantic! Can you fly that high?"

"Oh, I don't live on the top of the mesa. That would

be crazy, unless you don't mind a bunch of scary looking invisible creatures walking right through you. I have a glorious nest on a spacious ledge with a breathtaking view only a few hundred feet from the top. Here we go!" Gnorli began flapping his wings in earnest, rapidly gaining altitude. Orville was beginning to feel very warm, panic setting in.

"We're pretty high up, Gnorli. Are you sure this is safe?"

"I've flown plenty of adventurers on my back, you know. You're not the first. Look, we're almost home!"

Orville looked ahead at the rapidly approaching mesa. The mountain range surrounding Muridaan Falls was a little over twelve thousand feet tall and this mesa looked taller than that. His best guess was the massive formation towered almost three miles above the ground and was ten or twelve miles across.

Gnorli was now circling the mesa several hundred feet below the top. "Here we are! My marvelous nest!" Gnorli swooped in and landed in a gigantic nest built with thousands of tree branches, filled with enormous mounds of soft dried grass.

"Okay, everyone off. Time for the grand tour."

Orville and Sophia slid down from Gnorli's back into the mammoth grassy nest.

Orville was trying to conceal the overwhelming terror he was feeling sitting on a rocky ledge nearly three miles up in the air.

"A lovely nest indeed, Gnorli. Well, I suppose we should get going. You remember, you were taking us to the Senyph Ocean?"

"The Senyph Ocean? Scary place, that Senyph Ocean. Whatever you do, do *not* go swimming there.

Not a good place to go swimming." Gnorli let out another great cackling laugh, but stopped abruptly. "Oh, yummm! Are you seeing what I'm seeing?" Gnorli pointed with a wing to some distant invisible object.

"See what? We're three miles up, Gnorli. We can barely see the ground from here!"

"Centipedes! Yummmy! My favorite!" Gnorli leaped off the ledge and dove straight down for a thousand feet, then spread his wings and soared out across the great forest, disappearing into an enormous bank of puffy white clouds.

Orville quickly realized at that moment he and Sophia were trapped in a gigantic Gnorli bird nest three miles above the ground. His eyes were still on the cloud bank where Gnorli had disappeared. "Umm... do you think he'll remember he left us here?"

Sophia put her paw on Orville's shoulder. "I think we have two choices. We can climb up, or we can climb down."

Orville peered over the edge of the nest at the smooth vertical rock face dropping three miles down to the forest below.

"Up it is, then. One question. What do you think he meant by 'invisible scary looking creatures who walk right through you'?"

Orville was interrupted by the squawky voice coming from his backpack. "Oh, my, that does sound quite intriguing! Do you think these ghostly creatures will have poisonous fangs and great long claws?"

Chapter 22

The Looper

Orville was lying on his back in the Gnorli nest, his eyes on the smooth vertical granite wall leading to the top of the mesa. "This is kind of a comfy nest. I can see why Gnorli likes it. The dried grass is nice and soft. What do you think, Sophia? Some kind of rope ladder to the top? I don't see anything to tie it to though. It's just smooth rock for the whole two hundred feet up."

"I'm not sure. Hey, Proto, could you fly up there and take a look around?"

"No, thank you. Would you be a dear and make sure the flap is buckled tightly? I don't want to fall out of Orville's pack while he's climbing."

"I thought you didn't mind heights when you were the one flying?"

"My maximum altitude is two hundred and fifty feet. If you will note, we are currently well over fourteen thousand feet above the forest floor."

Orville nodded. "You make a good point. Sophia, back at the centipede pit you shaped that iron ring into the rock. Do you think you could do the same thing here? Could you shape a metal ladder and bolt it to the rock face?"

"That's a great idea. I could shape a section of ladder, climb it, and then shape another section above it."

"Wait, can't you just blink us up there?"

"I'm not ready for that. I blinked you off the sticky green ball but that was a life or death situation. I still need a lot more practice and instruction with Master Marloh."

"Okay, metal ladder it is. I'll shape some sturdy safety harnesses for us that hook securely to the ladder."

"Good idea. I don't think a sphere of defense will help much after a three mile fall."

"I wish you hadn't said that. Wait, we won't fall all the way to the ground, we'll just fall two hundred feet down into the Gnorli nest."

"Did you hear what you said? Just fall two hundred feet?" Sophia stood up and stepped cautiously across the mounds of spongy dry grass to the rock face. With a flick of her wrist two ten foot metal poles appeared, bolted securely into the rock wall. A series of solid metal rungs then blinked into place between the two poles. Orville handed Sophia her safety harness and hooked her to the ladder. Sophia scampered up to the top rung. Two more metal poles appeared and one by one the connecting rungs blinked into place. It was slow going and rather tedious, but an hour later they were halfway to the top of the mesa. Orville was being exceedingly careful not to look down. He only slipped once, but his safety harness functioned perfectly, averting a sudden and very dismal end to their adventure.

Almost two hours later Sophia clambered off the final rung up onto the surface of the mesa. She turned around and grabbed Orville's paws, hoisting him off the ladder up onto solid ground.

"Whew! We made it!" Orville's eyes were roaming across the mesa. He squinted, trying to focus on a very peculiar misty, wavering shape. "Do you see that? I can't tell what it is. It's kind of cloudy, sort of ghostly looking."

Sophia shaded her eyes with one paw. "That is strange. I see it too, but I'm not certain what I'm looking at."

She strode across the mesa for a hundred feet then stopped. She was looking at a barely visible silver wall that curved upward for several hundred feet. She squinted her eyes, trying to follow the path of the wall across the mesa. Finally she had her answer. "It's a ship. It's an Anarkkian Attack Cruiser." Sophia reached out cautiously to touch the barely visible craft. "My paw goes right through it. I don't understand what's happening here."

Orville stood at the far end of the ship. "Wait, re-member what Gnorli said about scary looking invisible creatures walking right through you? This must be what he was talking about. This ship is at least three hundred feet long. Why can't we touch it, though? Maybe it's some kind of advanced Anarkkian technology. You know, so the enemy can't see it?"

"Even if that were true, we'd still be able to touch it."

Orville let out a screech and dashed toward Sophia. "Defense spheres up! We're being attacked!" He pointed to a hoard of heavily armed ghostly creatures dashing wildly across the mesa toward them. A few of the them were holding up clear glass tubes and shooting barely visible beams of light at whatever was chasing them.

"I don't think they can see us. I think they're running for the ship. They're trying to get away from something."

"You're right, they're heading up that ramp that just opened and going into the ship. Let's go look."

Proto called out, "I'd like to get out of the backpack, if you wouldn't mind! This sounds quite thrilling. Transparent creatures being chased by some dreadful unknown monster with huge poisonous fangs?"

Orville unbuckled the flap and let Proto out. "I didn't say anything about huge poisonous fangs."

"Oh, I just assumed they would have them." Proto shot up into the air and soared past the Anarkkian Attack Cruiser. "I'm going to see what manner of beast is chasing them!"

Five minutes later Proto was back. He swooped down onto Orville's shoulders. "It's far worse than I thought. Far worse. There are at least a dozen Autonomous A6 Warrior Rabbitons heading this way, and they look very, very angry."

"A6 Warrior Rabbitons? How could that be? The war ended fifteen hundred years ago. I don't understand what we're watching. We can't touch the ship and the Rabbitons and warriors can't see or touch us. Sophia, could you tell what kind of creatures the warriors were?"

"Anarkkians. They have long green tusks and scales. They were definitely Anarkkian troopers and it appears they were running away from a group of A6 Warrior

Rabbitons. I wonder if they're really even here?"

"What do you mean?"

"Well, we can't touch the ship, we can barely even see it. I'm not sure it's in this world. I'm not sure the Rabbitons or the Anarkkians are here either." Sophia rubbed her chin. "I'm trying to remember... there was something in one of Papa's books about the Mintarians. What was that?"

"The Mintarians? Who are the Mintarians?"

"They were a nonviolent race of creatures who fought in the war against the Anarkkians."

"How could they fight if they were nonviolent?"

"The same way the Metaphysical Adventurers do. They used very effective non-lethal methods. Especially–" Sophia's eyes opened wide. "That's it! You're brilliant, Orville! I know exactly what is happening here!"

Sophia put her arms around Orville and gave him a great hug.

"Proto! I need your help. We have to search the surface of the mesa for a blue iridescent sphere. It will be small, no larger than four or five inches in diameter. We have to find it. It might be our ticket off this mesa."

Proto looked at Orville, then at Sophia. "You do realize the top of this mesa covers over a hundred square miles?"

"You're right. Let me think. Can you use the glow-bird's special vision? The advanced optical system it uses for spying?"

"I suppose so, but even with that it would take weeks to search such a large area for a tiny sphere."

"Sophia, would the blue sphere you're looking for produce an electrical field?"

"Brilliant! What would I do without you?" Sophia reached into her pack and pulled out the Quintarian tracking goggles. She slipped them on and waved Orville forward.

"Let's go! We have to find that sphere."

After walking for nearly an hour toward the center of the mesa Sophia spotted a small glowing light in the distance. "I see something. It's not moving. This could be it."

Fifteen minutes later Sophia was standing over a blue sphere the size of a small orange which was emitting a pale pink light. "Do not touch it! Nobody touch it!"

"What is it?"

"A Mintarian weapon, and it's still active."

"Do you think it might explode?" Proto was slowly backing away from the sphere.

"No, that's not how it works. It's called a Time Looper. Most of the weapons used by the Mintarians manipulated time. They never killed anyone, but sometimes I think what they did was worse. Mostly they used a weapon called a time throttle. They had big ones and little ones. If a world was causing them trouble, the Mintarians would drop a time throttle on it. The inhabitants of the planet wouldn't notice any change, but time on the planet slowed to a crawl. It's hard to cause any serious trouble when it takes you a thousand years to put your boots on. Life went on as usual on the planet, but they were no longer a threat to anyone."

"That's unbelievable. They really did that?"

"They did. They even had megalithic time throttles which could shut down entire galaxies. This is different, though. It's called a Time Looper. Time progresses normally for short while, but then it loops. It starts over again from the moment the looper was dropped. Those Anarkkians we're seeing have run to that ship countless millions of times over the last fifteen hundred years. I imagine a Mintarian scout ship saw them down there and dropped a looper on them."

Sophia gingerly picked up the Time Looper, placing it carefully in her backpack. "Let's go back to their ship. I want to see if I can stop the time loop."

Orville and Sophia made their way back to the ghostly Anarkkian cruiser. When they were almost there Orville gave a shriek as several dozen Anarkkian warriors ran right through them, heading up the ramp into their ghost ship.

"That was creepy. Now I understand what Gnorli was talking about."

Five minutes later Sophia was sitting on the ground holding the looper gingerly in her paws. She looked at Orville nervously. "If I do this wrong we could be caught in a time loop. We could be here forever."

"Sophia, you're the most brilliant mouse I know. I know you can do it. Besides, there's no one else I'd rather be trapped in a time loop with than you."

"Thanks. Just don't say anything dumb that I might have to listen to a hundred million times. All right, here goes. Keep your eyes on the ship."

Sophia gently twisted off the top half of the blue sphere. Inside the looper was a small panel containing six colored tabs. "Orville, put on the tracker goggles and tell me what you see here."

Orville slipped on the goggles and examined the looper. "Four of the tabs are glowing orange and two are not. The two blue tabs are not glowing."

"Good, that's what I thought. This is good. I think I have it. Watch the ship and tell me when all the Anarkkians are inside it."

Orville waited nervously, his eyes searching for the group of Anarkkian warriors. Finally he spotted them running toward the ship and shooting beams of light at the A6 Warriors behind them. He watched as the ramp dropped down and the warriors dashed up into the ship. "They're inside the ship!"

Sophia took a deep breath and simultaneously pushed down both blue tabs.

Orville was watching when the Anarkkian Attack Cruiser burst into this world, transforming from a ghostly spectre to a magnificent gleaming silver leviathan. The noise of the ship's propulsion unit was deafening, shaking the ground around them. The warriors were shouting, firing a fusillade of blinding vaporizer beams at the rapidly approaching A6 Warrior Rabbitons. The front row of the A6s held out their right arms, their fists glowing with a brilliant purple radiance. A split second later intensely concentrated beams of purple light sizzled through the air, smashing into the side of the attack ship, only to be repelled by its powerful energy shields. The ship glowed brightly and went silent as its gravitational disrupters came online. It rose into the air, slowly circling above the group of A6 Warrior Rabbitons. With a dreadful shrieking whine a dozen focused beams of dazzling orange light blasted out from the bow of the ship toward the A6 Warriors. There was a sudden and terrible silence. Without warning the Anarkkian Attack Cruiser and the group of A6 Warrior Rabbitons simply vanished.

Orville stared blankly at the silent, empty landscape. "What happened? Where did they go?"

Sophia stood up, carefully reuniting the two halves of the Time Looper. "They're back where they belong, Orville, fighting a battle that ended fifteen hundred years ago. They won't even realize what happened. They won't know they were caught in the Mintarian time loop for fifteen hundred years." Sophia placed the Time Looper gently in her pack and headed out across the mesa. "Let's go, we need to find where those A6 Warrior Rabbitons landed. If we're very, very lucky they may have left us a way off this mesa."

Chapter 23

The Door

Orville and Sophia trudged along the broad rocky plains that formed the upper surface of the mesa, their eyes scanning the area for any sign of the A6 Warriors' landing site.

"Hey, Sophia, the mountains surrounding Muridaan Falls aren't as tall as this mesa and they're almost always covered in snow. Why do you think this mesa isn't covered in snow? It's a little bit cooler than it is down in the forest, but not by much."

"You really are good at finding puzzles. I hadn't even thought about that. I'd say that Periculum more than likely has a much thicker atmosphere than Earth does. Think of the atmosphere that surrounds a planet as a big warm blanket. If the blanket is really thick and heavy, the planet stays toasty warm. If it's thin and light, the planet is freezing cold. That's also why the creatures here on Periculum are bigger than the ones on Earth. It's warmer and there's a lot more oxygen in the air."

"Oh, that makes sense. Did you learn that in your science classes on Quintari?"

"I learned a lot of it there, but I also read a lot, and

Papa taught me almost everything I know about the old technologies. He was an expert on them and studied the ancient tech his whole life. He even wrote four books about it. He always made it sound so interesting and would bring home old tech artifacts to show me. Once he even brought home a vape gun and let me shoot it."

"A vape gun? What's that?"

"That's short for vaporizing gun. It shoots out some kind of heavy particle beam that disrupts matter and turns it into energy fields. Kind of like when I convert a physical object into a thought cloud except you don't need to be a shaper to shoot a vape gun."

"Oh. Maybe we'll find one when we find the A6 Warrior Rabbitons' scout ship."

"Maybe. I'm not exactly sure how those A6 Warriors arrived on the mesa. I really hope they didn't just get dropped off by a troop transport vessel."

"We should try the tracker goggles. Maybe we'll spot something."

"Good idea." Sophia pulled the goggles out of her pack and slipped them on, adjusted the small brass dial, and swept her gaze across the mesa.

"That's it, Orville! I'm picking up a strong energy field almost straight ahead of us, behind those big slabs of jutting rock. Hey, Proto, fly down there and tell us what you see."

Proto gave an excited squawk. "Excellent idea, Sophia. Who knows what manner of fiendish creature might be lurking behind those rocks, just waiting to devour us."

Proto shot off across the barren landscape and disappeared behind the huge rocky outcropping. Moments later he was streaking back toward them. He made a quick barrel roll and skidded to a halt on the ground in front of Sophia.

"No deadly creatures, I'm afraid, but there is a rather mysterious and onerous looking trapdoor that appears to lead down inside the mesa. I suppose there could be dozens of horrible creatures skulking about down there, snarling and snapping."

"You forgot to mention their fangs, Proto."

"Oh, most certainly they would be equipped with dreadful poisonous fangs, not to mention long, razor sharp claws. Quite terrifying!"

Orville laughed. "I think you might be curing me of my fainting episodes, Proto. The creatures you describe are so frightening that when a real creature shows its face it will probably seem about as scary as a little mouseling."

"I'm so pleased I was able to help you. I only hope the creatures in the Senyph Ocean aren't as dreadful as the Gnorli bird suggested. He seemed to become rather distraught just at the mention of them. They sound quite hideous."

"Thanks, Proto. Sophia, what do you think, should we take a look at Proto's terrifying trapdoor?"

"Absolutely. We even might find a passageway that takes us down to the base of the mesa."

"That's a good thought."

Proto's mysterious trapdoor proved to be an eight foot square, heavily armored slab made of pure Morsennium with no obvious means of entry.

Sophia frowned. "How do we open it? There's no disc grid on it like there was on the front door of the Cube."

"Can you blast a hole in it with shaping energy?"

"It's made of Morsennium, and I think that absorbs shaping energy. I'll try though." Sophia stood back and shot out a blast of purple light from her paw. The trapdoor glowed brightly for a moment, but was ultimately unaffected by Sophia's powerful beam of light.

"Nothing. It glows when it absorbs the shaping energy, but it would take a particle fusion beam to blast through it. It's stronger than the rock that surrounds it."

"Wait, I know! How about we just knock on the door and one of Proto's scary friends will open it for us?" Orville gave a wide grin and rapped loudly on the door.

Sophia was rolling her eyes when they heard the soft mellifluous voice coming from the door.

"I'm sorry, this door is for emergency use only. I'm sorry, this door is for emergency use only. Please use the main entrance. Thank you for your cooperation."

The two adventurers gaped at each other.

Sophia rapped loudly on the door again.

"Hello, door. Where is the main entrance, please?"

"I'm sorry, the main entrance is currently undergoing routine maintenance. Please use the emergency entrance. I'm sorry, the main entrance is current undergoing routine maintenance. Please use the emergency entrance."

Orville rapped on the door again. "Since we can't use the main entrance, would you mind opening this emergency entrance?"

"I'm sorry, this door is for emergency use only. I'm sorry, this door is for emergency use only. Thank you for your cooperation."

Sophia stood up, took a deep breath, then shrieked as

loudly as she could, "Emergency! Emergency!! This is a dire emergency! We're being attacked by hundreds of Anarkkians! Open this door right now! Emergency! They're shooting deadly vape guns at us!!"

The huge Morsennium door made a slight whirring noise and slid smoothly open. Orville grinned at Sophia, then peered down into the square shaft. "There's a big metal ladder and lots of lights. It goes down about a hundred feet or so."

The soft sultry voice spoke again. "In the event of an emergency, please use the ladder to enter Norrich Bunker. In the event of an emergency, please use the ladder to enter Norrich Bunker. Thank you for your cooperation."

Orville snickered. "You should learn how to talk like that, Sophia."

Sophia curled her lip at Orville. "Eeww, you make me sick. Down the ladder, before I throw you down."

Orville snickered again, gingerly backing down onto the wide metal ladder. "Creekers, these rungs are really far apart. Whoever used this ladder must have been tall."

"I'm guessing this is one of the bunkers the Elders built during the war. Now that I think about it, it's also more than likely where the A6 Warriors came from."

"Do you think there might still be any of them down there? They looked kind of scary."

"I guess we'll find out soon enough. What I'm really hoping for is an elevator that goes to the bottom of the mesa."

Orville stepped off the final rung onto a dark green metallic floor, turning toward a twelve foot tall arched entryway. Sophia hopped down from the ladder and peered in through the archway. Orville heard the trapdoor above them slide shut.

"It looks like a cloakroom or something. There's a bunch of big coats hanging on hooks with boots sitting under them."

"Those coats are enormous. How tall were the Elders anyway?"

"They were the same size as Proto, about ten feet tall."

"Look, there's a door over there. I'll knock on it and see what happens." Orville stepped across the room to a tall, pale green rectangular panel. He rapped loudly on the door. "Hello, door! Open, please!"

"Please insert your Military Identification Card now. Failure to do so within one minute will result in your immediate vaporization. Thank you, and welcome to Norrich Bunker."

Orville skittered backwards. "What?? What did it say? It's going to vaporize us?"

Sophia's mind was racing. "The coats! Check all the pockets for an identification card!" Sophia darted over to the long row of hanging coats and began rifling through the large flapped pockets. "Hurry, help me look!"

Orville dashed over and jammed his paw into a coat. "I've got something! It feels like a card!" Orville yanked out a slender translucent rectangle. "I think it's made of glass, or something like that. I guess it could be–"

"Orville!! Hold the card up in front of the door!"

Orville raced over to the door and held up the pale yellow card. "Here's my card, door."

"Please insert your Military Identification Card into

the slot within fifteen seconds. You are now facing imminent vaporization. Thank you for your cooperation."

Orville gave a shriek. "Slot! Slot!" He spotted a narrow four inch opening next to the door with several incomprehensible symbols above it. He jammed the card into the slot.

"Thank you, Senior Mechanist Bletchley Rabbit. Welcome to Norrich Bunker. Please report immediately to the Order Room. You have one new message."

The green door slid open with a loud hiss, revealing a vast shadowy room extending fifty feet in either direction. Orville squinted into the gloomy depths, then sent in a brilliant orb of light. He eyes scanned across dozens of dark blue chairs scattered across the floor and came to rest on a long gray metallic counter at the far end of the room, an odd flickering light emanating from behind it. Bright overhead lights blinked on as Orville entered the room.

"Kind of stark and bare, isn't it?"

Sophia nodded. "It definitely has that military bunker look to it. Do you think this room is the Order Room the weird voice was talking about?"

"I have no idea. Let's see what that flickering light is." Orville and Sophia wove their way through the maze of blue chairs to the other side of the room.

"I can't see what it is, the counter is too high."

"Here, stand on this." Sophia slid one of the chairs next to the counter and Orville hopped up onto it. "Creekers! The flickering light looks like a rabbit, but it's kind of creepy and ghosty looking."

Sophia jumped up on the chair for a look. She saw the wavering image of a tall rabbit in a military uniform standing at attention, paws behind his back. "I think that's a holo image, Orville. It's not a real rabbit, but we might be able to talk to it. It probably has engineered intelligence. Sophia waved to the flickering figure. "Hello, there! Can you tell us if there is an elevator that goes down to the base of the mesa?"

The tall holo rabbit stepped briskly over to the counter.

"Name, please?"

"Ummm... Sophia Mouse."

"I'm sorry, I couldn't quite hear that, would you mind repeating it?"

"Sophia Mouse."

"I'm sorry, I couldn't quite hear that, would you mind repeating it?"

"MY NAME IS SOPHIA MOUSE!"

"I'm sorry, I couldn't quite hear that, would you mind repeating it?"

Orville grabbed Sophia's arm. "Wait, let me try something." Orville leaned over the counter and said loudly, "I am Senior Mechanist Bletchley Rabbit, here to check my messages."

The holo rabbit glowed brightly. "Senior Mechanist Bletchley Rabbit, you have one new message. Please use booth number 31. Please use booth number 31. To retrieve your message simply insert your Military Identification Card into the appropriate slot." The holo rabbit flickered, returning to its original position, standing at attention, paws behind its back.

Sophia pointed to a long hallway. "Down there. I can see a long row of doors."

Two minutes later the two adventurers were standing in front of a door adorned with the large red numeral

TOM HOFFMAN

'31'. Orville pressed the violet tab next to the door and
it slid silently open, revealing a room no bigger than a
small closet. He stepped in and an overhead light
blinked on. He heard the sultry, sensuous voice again.
"Please insert your Military Identification Card to
retrieve your messages."

"Hey, can you teach Sophia to talk like that?" Orville grinned at Sophia.

"Orville! Do what it says before I tell it to vaporize
you."

"Just joking." Orville located the narrow slot on the
wall in front of him and slipped in the Military
Identification Card.

"Good evening, Senior Mechanist Bletchley Rabbit.
You have one new message. To receive your message,
please say, 'This is Senior Mechanist Bletchley Rabbit,
and I am here to receive my new message.'"

Orville groaned, repeating, "This is Senior Mechanist Bletchley Rabbit, and I am here to receive my new
message."

The overhead light blinked off and a massive room
appeared in front of Orville, the very angry face of an
enormous rabbit wearing heavy blue coveralls glaring
at him.

"BLETCHLEY!! Get down to Level Six right now,
do you hear me?? Right now!! I don't know what your
game is, but we got four damaged blinkers that need to
be back in the air by tomorrow morning. Two with
major and two with minor damage but all no-flies. You
got it? Get on that lift and get down here now! I want to
see you walking the green line before I count to three!!"

The room went dark and the overhead light blinked
on.

Sophia turned to Orville. "We have to find Level Six. There might be blinker ships down there we could use to get off this mesa. Maybe we could even fly one across the Senyph Ocean."

"Good idea. We need to find the lift that angry rabbit was talking about."

Orville and Sophia hurried down to the end of the corridor, reaching a set of tall red doors. Orville inserted his card into the card slot next to the doors and they whirred open, revealing a small metal room. "Is this a lift? I don't really know what they look like."

"I think so. Look on the wall at those seven colored tabs. If you push one of them it probably takes you to a certain level."

"Which one should I push?"

"Good question. He said you should be walking the green line. Try pressing the green one."

Orville hit the green tab and the red doors slid shut. The lift shot down so quickly Orville felt as though he was in free fall. "Aggghhh!!"

Sophia grabbed the rail on the wall with both paws, her eyes wide. After rapidly descending for fifteen seconds the lift came to an abrupt stop, almost sending Orville to the floor. The red doors slid open.

"Please follow the yellow line. Please follow the yellow line. Mind the gap between the car and the platform."

Orville stepped out of the elevator into a long dark corridor.

"There's a line of little yellow lights here. Maybe they take us to the green line, whatever that is."

Sophia and Orville headed down the long corridor but found no sign of a green line. "This is a little troubling. I think we might be on the wrong floor."

"You're probably right, but let's just go a little bit farther and see. The hallway turns left here. Maybe the yellow line ends and the green line begins in the next hallway."

"Maybe." Sophia did not sound convinced.

They reached the end of the corridor with the yellow line of lights and turned left.

"Uh oh." Orville was looking down the length of the corridor. His eyes had followed the yellow line all the way down to an enormous Rabbiton standing at attention – an enormous Rabbiton who was now looking at them with a dreadfully severe frown.

"He's way bigger than Proto. I think he's one of those A6 Warrior Rabbitons, and he doesn't look very friendly."

"We should go."

"HALT!" The huge Rabbiton bellowed down the hallway at them. "NAME??"

"What?"

"NAME AND RANK, TROOPER!!"

Orville thought quickly. "I'm Senior Mechanist Bletchley Rabbit, at your service, sir!"

The huge Rabbiton was now striding quickly toward them, his glowing red eyes scanning Orville's form.

"What's your game? You're not Bletchley Rabbit! You're not even a rabbit, you're a mouse! Do you think I'm some kind of dimmer? Stand at attention so I can vaporize both of you!" The A6 Warrior stretched out his immense silver arm and it began to glow with a brilliant purple light.

"Run, Sophia, run!!" The pair of adventurers turned and ran just as a mammoth blast of purple light exploded behind them, vaporizing a six foot wide hole in the corridor wall. Orville shrieked as they sprinted at top speed down the echoing hallway.

Sophia hollered, "Back to the lift, back to the lift!" Orville reached the lift first and slapped the violet button. He heard the familiar sultry, mellifluous voice.

"The lift is currently undergoing daily maintenance. We apologize for any inconvenience. Please try again in ten minutes. Thank you for your cooperation."

Sophia cried out, "Here he comes again! Run!"

The two best friends dashed wildly down the wide corridor, the Rabbiton booming out, "WARNING! WARNING! ANARKKIAN SPIES HAVE INFILTRATED NORRICH BUNKER!!"

"Aggghh! Faster! Turn right!" They skittered and careened around the sharp corner, racing down the hallway.

"Orville, into that room! We have to hide, there's no way we can outrun an A6 Rabbiton."

Orville flung the door open and they dashed in, quickly closing the door behind them. "Lots of big desks. Let's hide under one near the back of the room."

The pair of adventurers scuttled across the room and slipped under one of the huge desks.

"We should be safe here."

Sophia heard the A6 Rabbiton thundering past the door and down the hall.

"We're safe for a while, but we can't hide here forever. The problem is that A6 Rabbiton can wait in the hallway forever. He's probably been here guarding the bunker for the last thousand years."

Proto poked his head out of Orville's backpack. "Great heavens, you two certainly do manage to get into some dreadfully awkward predicaments."

"Proto, this isn't funny, we're in real danger now. That A6 Warrior Rabbiton thinks we're Anarkkian spies and is trying to vaporize us. We don't have a chance against a creature like that."

"Yes, I completely understand, it's all quite clear to me. You want me to rescue you again, but you're too embarrassed or too proud to ask for my help. Orville and Sophia, my dear, dear friends, you should know better than that. Of course I'll rescue you."

"I know you mean well, but–"

Proto's beak opened up and Orville's voice came out of it. "I know you mean well, but–"

"Hey, how did you use my voice like that?"

"I am fully capable of perfectly mimicking any sound or any voice. Don't you remember how I used the cry of an attacking Gnorli Bird to scare away the carnivorous centipedes?"

"Of course I remember that, but how are you going to rescue us using my voice?"

"Trust your old friend Proto to come up with a fool-proof escape plan. If you wouldn't mind cracking the door open, I will fly through the corridors until I spot that dreadfully fearsome A6 Warrior Rabbiton and lead him on a wild Gnorli bird chase he won't soon forget. It will be quite exhilarating, I'm sure."

"That could work! If you can lead the A6 away from us, then we'll head back the other way to the lift."

"Precisely, you have grasped the essence of my ingenious plan. My weapons shall be misdirection, confusion, and a variety of extremely rude insults. I'll infuriate him, distract him, and then fly back to the lift and hit the violet tab, opening the lift doors. Be ready to dash back down the hallway and into the lift!"

"All right, Proto, I'm opening the door for you."

Proto waddled out of the room, flapped his wings and shot off down the hallway.

"COME AND GET ME IF YOU DARE, YOU GREAT ENORMOUS SILVER NINNY!"

Orville heard the A6 Rabbiton's deafening voice boom through the corridors. "ANARKKIAN SPY MOUSE! I'VE GOT YOU NOW!"

Sophia nodded and they crept out of the room, heading back the way they had come. They could hear Proto shouting dreadfully rude insults at the A6 Warrior Rabbiton. "Good heavens, where did Proto learn words like that?"

Orville snickered. "Let's run for the lift." Sophia and Orville darted down the long hallway. When they reached the end of the corridor Orville peered cautiously around the corner.

"All clear!" They raced madly toward the lift.

"There it is! Proto opened the doors!"

They could hear Proto still shrieking vulgar invectives at the Rabbiton.

"I think he really likes this. We may have created a monster."

Seconds later Proto flashed into the lift. "Hit the purple tab! I found a sign showing purple is for Level Six!"

Proto stuck his head out between the lift doors and shrieked, "TOO LATE, NINNY FACE! BIG SCARY A6 RABBITON COULDN'T EVEN CATCH A MOUSE!!"

Proto pulled his head in just as the doors to the lift slammed shut and the car rose up one level. When the doors opened again Sophia peered out, then smiled. There was a lovely line of green lights leading out from the lift and down the corridor.

"You did it Proto! You really did rescue us!"

Sophia picked up Proto and kissed him on the top of his head. "You're the best! I really do not know how we ever got along without you."

Chapter 24

Sophia's Plan

Sophia and Orville exited the lift, following the line of green lights down the wide hallway. Orville sent a bright glowing orb out from his paw.

Sophia slung her pack up onto her shoulder. "That's better, now we can see. This is the level where they repair the damaged ships, but I can't image how they get them down here."

"There must be a gargantuan lift that goes up to the surface of the mesa."

"You're right, and if it still works we can use it to take a blinker up to the surface."

The trail of green lights turned sharply to the right, stopping in front of a set of wide green metal doors. Orville slid his card into the slot and the doors whirred open.

"Creekers, this place is huge!"

"Over there! Those are the four blinker ships the angry rabbit was talking about, but two of them are almost crushed flat. The other two look okay though."

"That angry rabbit called them 'no-flies'. I guess that means they don't fly. Let's take a look around. They must have left this place in a hurry."

Sophia scanned the room. At the far end was a large silver scout ship with a great jagged hole in the port side, and sitting next to it was a large white boxy craft with an array of odd glowing cubes and antennae running around the top of it.

"What's that big box thing?"

"I think it's an interstellar ship. They don't work the same as scout ships and blinkers. They don't actually travel through space, they just... well, they're here and then they're somewhere else. I don't really understand how they work, but it has something to do with creating a fold in space."

"Oh, that doesn't sound like something we could use. The only ships I see here look badly damaged. Let's take a look at the two blinkers that aren't in such bad shape."

"I want to search this scout ship first. Maybe there's something in there we can salvage." Sophia climbed through the ragged tear in the side of the ship and studied the craft's interior. She spotted a rack on the wall holding six clear glass cylinders, each about three feet long with a pair of silver tubes running down one side. At the base of each cylinder was a round violet tab. She strode over to the wall and gingerly removed one of the cylinders. After searching the rest of the ship and finding nothing, she climbed out of the scout ship and held the glass cylinder up for Orville to see.

"What is it?

"It's what you hoped we might find. It's a vape gun. They're easy to use, but incredibly dangerous. Papa let me shoot one."

"I remember you said that. What do they actually do?

Sophia looked around her then pointed to the wall. "See that picture hanging on the wall?"

"Yes?" Orville was not certain he wanted Sophia to be firing ancient and incredibly dangerous weapons in a closed room. "Wait, is something going to explode? We probably shouldn't–"

Sophia aimed the vape gun at the wall and pressed the violet tab. There was a loud humming sound and the picture vanished, along with a twelve inch wide circular section of wall. "That's what it does. It vaporizes matter."

Orville stepped over and examined the hole in the wall. "Creekers, don't point that thing at me. Should we bring it with us?"

"Let's leave it here. We're shapers, we don't need weapons like this. Let's go check out the two blinkers." Sophia set the vape gun gently down on the floor and they made their way across the cavernous room to the damaged blinkers.

"We're in luck, they never took them off the lift. If by some chance they do fly, we can take them back up. That looks like the lift control panel on that brass pedestal."

"Well, the two crushed ships obviously won't fly, but how can you tell if the other ones will?"

"There should some sort of indicator lights in the cabin."

"Do you know how to fly these?"

"Not exactly, but it can't be too hard."

"Sophia..."

"Quit being a nervous ninny, Orville." Sophia stepped into the first blinker, studying the control panel. "Hmmm... it looks fairly simple. Two control sticks and that bank of colored tabs. Let's see, violet means on and yellow means off. So I'll just tap this violet tab."

Orville backed away from the ship. "Be careful, please!"

Sophia pressed the violet tab and a blaring alarm shrieked. All the tabs were blinking bright yellow. "That doesn't look promising. I'll try the other ship."

Orville covered his ears and a minute later a similar alarm blared from the second ship. Sophia peered out of the main hatch at Orville.

"Well, we won't be flying these anytime soon. Drat, I was hoping we'd find a ship that was still in working order. Help me look and we'll see if there's anything we can use."

Orville stepped into the blinker ship and looked around. "This is amazing. How did they fly without wings?"

Proto pushed his head out from under the flap. "They were powered by CDETS and utilized anti-microgravity units with force displacers. Some of the later ones had inertia deadeners which allowed them to stop almost instantly."

"What?"

"It's quite simple really. They warp the space around them to alter the gravitational pull. When they shoot forward they are actually falling, attracted by the enhanced artificial gravitational pull they create."

Sophia was eyeing the ceiling of the ship, her jaw slowly moving back and forth. "There is one option, but I don't think you're going to like it."

Orville's eyes narrowed. "Does it have anything to do with carnivorous centipedes or big green sticky ball creatures?"

Sophia snorted. "Nothing even remotely like that. Stand outside the ship and keep your eyes on the top of it. Tell me if anything happens." Orville exited the craft and stepped away from it.

"Okay, I'm watching. What are you going to do?"

"Here goes!" There was a sharp squealing of metal on metal, followed immediately by a small explosion on the top of the ship. A gigantic orange canopy burst into the air above the craft, then drifted slowly down, draping itself over the craft. Sophia dashed out of the blinker, poking her head out from under the orange canopy. "It worked!"

Orville stood silently, staring at the huge orange canopy. "I don't get it. What is that thing?"

"It's an emergency sailing canopy. If the ship loses power and begins to fall, the blinker pilot pulls the release lever and the sail canopy pops out, allowing them to glide safely to the ground."

"Ummm... are you saying we're going to jump off a three mile high mesa holding onto that big piece of orange fabric?"

"No, of course not, that's not what I'm saying at all. We'll be safely inside the last blinker. We just have to roll the ship to the edge of the mesa, climb inside, rock it back and forth until it rolls off the edge, and when we're falling I'll pull the emergency canopy release."

Orville's legs began shaking. "That really doesn't sound like a very well thought out plan. It's three miles straight down to the very hard ground below."

"Pay attention. It's just physics. The canopy will billow out, increasing our air resistance and drastically slowing the ship's rate of descent. We should glide at least five miles, probably much more. The Elders wouldn't have installed these in blinkers if they didn't work."

"You make a good point." Orville stared at the bright orange canopy covering the blinker Ship. "I'm guessing it's our only choice?"

"Perfect. We'll use that blinker ship there. The emergency canopy release looks in good condition."

"Wait, what? Suppose this one doesn't pop out like the first one did?"

"Then you'll probably be very angry at me, but not for long, if you know what I mean." Sophia slapped her paws together with a loud smack, raising one eyebrow.

Orville groaned. "If you're trying to make me faint, it's not going to work. All right, I trust your judgement more than I trust my own when it comes to ancient tech. What do we do now?"

"Well, first we have to see if the lift still works. If it does then we'll raise these ships up to the surface. If the lift doesn't work, then all this has been for nothing. Okay, hop on the lift and we'll see what the universe has in store for us."

Orville stepped onto the platform and stood next to Sophia. "The violet disc?"

"That's the one. I'm holding my breath."

Orville slapped his paw down on the violet disk. There was a loud groaning and clanking sound as the huge lift began moving upward.

Sophie held both paws up and cheered loudly. "It works, Orville! It won't be long now and we'll be off this mesa and back on the ground again."

Orville had a painfully forced smile on his face. Back on the ground again. He was imagining himself inside a metal ball screaming down through the air toward the forest floor three miles below.

Sophia looked up and saw a square of bright light high above them. "The upper lift doors have opened! I can see daylight."

Ten minutes later they were standing safely on the surface of the monolithic mesa.

Orville was feeling more dubious than ever, but did his best to maintain a positive attitude. "What next?"

"This is the perfect location. The lift is only a hundred feet from the edge of the mesa. We just have to roll the ship right up to the edge, but not too far. If it rolls over the edge then we're back to square one."

Orville and Sophia stood behind the blinker, rocking it back and forth. The outside of the craft was perfectly smooth and without a great deal of effort they rolled the ship off the lift. Fortunately for the two adventurers there was a gentle downgrade leading to the edge of the mesa. Orville set down a row of large rocks at the edge of the precipice to keep the blinker from accidentally rolling over the side.

Twenty minutes later the ship was perfectly balanced only a few feet from the three mile high drop off.

Sophia stepped back and studied the ship. "Excellent. The rocks you set down worked just as I'd hoped. I think we're ready. We'll remove the rocks, hop inside, lock the hatch, and rock the ship back and forth until it rolls over the side. Once it's falling I'll pull the emergency canopy release."

"Okay. I think. Is it getting hot or is it just me?"

They slid the heavy stones out of the way and the two intrepid adventurers climbed into the blinker ship, closing the main hatch behind them. Orville twisted the locking mechanism tightly. "We can use those harnesses to strap ourselves in."

"Perfect, they'll help during the landing, in case we roll." Sophia buckled herself in tightly, making certain she could reach the canopy release lever.

"Okay, I have a good grip on the emergency release. We're all set. Start rocking the ship!"

The ship was already teetering on the edge, and after only fifteen seconds of rocking it rolled over, tumbling over the side into the three mile deep abyss.

Orville would have shrieked like a mouseling if he hadn't been so disoriented. He was upside down and the ship was plummeting toward the ground so rapidly his insides felt like they were being pushed up into his boots. Sophia managed to cry out, "Here we go!"

She yanked the canopy release lever and was rewarded by the sound of a sharp explosion from outside the ship. Seconds later the craft flipped right side up with a wild jarring movement, violently pushing Orville downward until he felt as though he was being crushed by a giant hand, his stomach doing flip flops as the ship swung crazily about like wind chimes in a tornado.

Gradually the swinging diminished until it was only a gentle swaying motion. Sophia peered out of the small porthole. "We did it, and we're drifting away from the mesa, just as I hoped we would. It should take us about twenty minutes to reach the ground."

Orville was shaken, but thrilled to still be alive. "Creekers! I don't think I've ever been so scared in all my life! Hey, I didn't faint!"

Five minutes later Orville was still giddy with relief. He peered out the porthole behind his harness. "That canopy is huge! It won't be long now, I can see the trees!"

183

Sophia had been concerned about how jarring their landing would be, but as fortune would have it the blinker ship descended into a dense grouping of gigantic trees. They heard a series of splintering, snapping sounds from outside the ship as it careened through the thick branches, slowing the ship's descent and bringing them to a gentle halt. Sophia peered out the porthole and grinned. The ship was dangling six feet above the forest floor. She unhooked her harness and swung open the ship's hatch. "Everyone out! We've landed!"

Proto scrambled out of Orville's backpack. His eyes were wide. "It's gone. It's really gone."

Chapter 25

The Senyph Ocean

"Well, I can't say I'm sorry to leave that forest behind us. Especially our round sticky green friends, although I was getting quite *attached* to one of them." Orville looked at Sophia with a silly grin on his face.

"What?"

"I said I was getting *attached* to one of the green ball creatures. Get it? Attached?"

"I'm sorry, I guess I'm not in a very funny mood. I'm starting to worry."

"Did you see a centipede?"

"No, nothing like that. I asked Master Marloh to send us here so I could find proof that Draken Mouse was responsible for Papa's death, and I haven't discovered anything yet. It's taken all our efforts just to survive."

"What about those time goggles? The four dimensional goggles you found in the Anarkkian Command Control Vessel. Can't you use those somehow?"

"If I could find the exact location where Papa died I could use them to witness the murder and prove Draken's guilt. The monastery they were looking for is somewhere near the ocean, but the coast is hundreds of miles long. I don't know where to start looking. Even if we send Proto out to do an aerial search it would take weeks to find the monastery – if it's even there."

"All right, let's start from the very beginning. How did your Papa get to Periculum?"

"They came through a spectral doorway in a small Quintarian scout ship. That's all I know."

"Well, how about when we summit that ridge ahead of us we use the time goggles to look back in time for their ship?"

"The time goggles might work. It happened too long ago for the tracking goggles to work, but the time goggles should work. We should have a good panoramic view of the coastline from way up on the ridge and a silver scout ship flying through the sky shouldn't be too hard to spot."

"That's our plan, then. We'll camp here for the night and in the morning we can take on those hills. They're not as steep as the mountains around Muridaan Falls, but it's still a tough climb."

Orville shaped a blazing campfire and prepared dinner while Sophia shaped sleeping bags and a large waterproof canopy in case of rain.

Soon they were relaxing by the campfire eating a tasty meal prepared with a healthy portion of excellent culinary advice from Proto.

"Mmmm... your vegetable soup recipe is delicious, Proto. You should open an inn. I'll bet it would be a great success."

"Thank you, Sophia. Would you mind terribly if I discussed a rather personal matter with you? Something has happened which is quite confusing to me."

"Something has happened? Are you all right?"

"Yes, quite all right, thank you. I suppose I should begin at the beginning. Over the last several years I've spent a good deal of time thinking about the tasty snacks and warm beverages I make, and why I feel so compelled to make them. When the Elders created me, their intent was for my behavior to simulate that of a very friendly and likable rabbit, one who is kind, compassionate, and thoughtful. They selected what they felt were the most admirable qualities of rabbits, and altered my engineered synthetic neuronic intelligence to act according to this new set of parameters." Proto hesitated. "Is this too personal? Am I talking too much about myself?"

"Proto, we love hearing about you. You're our friend, and friends tell each other their deepest thoughts and feelings without fear."

"Thank you, Orville. Well, as I said, I was engineered to please rabbits and that is all I have ever known. For many hundreds of years, to the very best of my ability I remained true to my original design, and found this behavior quite gratifying. When a rabbit liked my tasty cakes or chocolate creams, I felt happy and fulfilled. But, as the centuries rolled by I began to fccl something odd, something... unfamiliar. It felt like the tiniest, gentlest tickle of emptiness inside me, as light as the brush of small glowbird feather. It came from far beneath my neuronic patterning and it felt as if an infinitesimal speck of me was missing. The years went by but the feeling did not go away. In fact it grew stronger until eventually, no matter how many tasty snacks I made, I felt as though a part of me was missing. That tiny tickle of a glowbird feather had grown to become a dreadful ache which was consuming me.

"Two days ago everything changed in a single moment. As we were tumbling off the mesa in the blinker ship and I lay curled up in your backpack, terrified that you and Sophia would not survive the fall, I realized my dreadful feeling of emptiness was gone. It was gone and I hadn't made a single tasty snack in weeks. I have thought about nothing else since that moment. I believe it is your friendship and Sophia's friendship which filled that empty space. I am certain now there is a deeper purpose for me than pleasing rabbits with tasty snacks, a purpose which I believe was quite unforeseen by my creators. A purpose that comes from another place, a place I am unable to describe or name."

For a moment Orville could not speak. He was absolutely stunned by Proto's revelation. "Proto... this is incredible. It's... miraculous."

Sophia ran her paw over Proto's feathered back. "It is well known among mice that all living creatures have a hidden destiny, a hidden purpose that comes from a far deeper place than this physical world. I am astonished that you have discovered this on your own. I agree with Orville, it is miraculous. Many mice and rabbits go through their whole lives without realizing this truth."

"You said all *living* creatures have a hidden purpose, Sophia. Are you saying you think I'm alive?"

Sophia thought for a moment. "I can't answer that question. I can't say for certain either way. All I can say is you are our dear friend and we would love to have you join us on our adventures, wherever they may take us."

Proto snuggled down between Orville and Sophia in

front of the roaring campfire. He was silent for a long time, but finally poked his head up and said, "Perhaps tomorrow we shall encounter some dreadfully terrifying creatures with great pointy scales and razor sharp teeth just itching to devour us, and I will rescue both of you."

Sophia rubbed Proto's back. "I would like that. Wouldn't that be fun, Orville? Maybe we'll even get attacked by a swarm of those dreadful carnivorous centipedes."

As the sun rose the next morning it found the three adventurers scaling the rugged ridge to the east. More precisely, Orville and Sophia were scrambling up the jagged slopes while Proto soared overhead in search of dreadful predatorial beasts.

"Look behind us, Sophia. You can see most of the dark forest. And look at that mesa! I can't believe we climbed into a big metal ball and rolled over the edge. If someone had told me a year ago I was going to do that I believe I would have fainted on the spot."

"I think you might be turning into an intrepid adventurer, Orville Wellington Mouse."

Proto sailed over them, calling out, "Not much farther to the peak! Just another mile or so. There's a wonderful view of the ocean from up there!"

Orville groaned. "Only another mile of climbing? Sometimes I wish I had wings like Proto." He grinned, "But then I'd have to eat those tasty little cakes with my feet. Eeww."

"Thank you so much for sharing that with me."

"If we find proof that Draken was behind your papa's death, what are you going to do? Who will you tell?"

"Master Marloh and I discussed that. We'll announce it at the Grand Assembly of Metaphysical Adventurers. If we do it during the assembly, everyone will witness it at the same time and I don't think Draken Mouse would dare to harm us in front of all the Metaphysical Adventurers. I hope not, anyway."

"That seems like a good plan. What kind of proof do you think we'll find?"

"That I don't know. I really have no idea."

It was late afternoon when Orville and Sophia crested the great ridge overlooking the coastal region. Orville gave a loud cheer and sat down on a flat boulder to catch his breath.

"Look at that view. The ocean is beautiful, isn't it? How high up do you think we are?"

Sophia glanced behind them. "Probably six or seven thousand feet above the ocean. It will be a lot easier going down the slopes than climbing them."

"That's good news. Are you ready to try the time goggles?"

"I am, although part of me is a little afraid of what I'll see. Maybe more than just a little afraid."

"I can look if you'd like."

Sophia gave long sigh. "Thank you, Orville, I think I would like that."

Sophia gave him the brass box and Orville slipped on the goggles and the red cap. Sophia connected the cap to the goggles and pushed the silver tabs. A small blue light blinked on between the bright red lenses of the goggles.

"You're all set. Just turn the little brass dial. That determines how far back in time the goggles take you. I really don't know their limit, but I hope it goes back far enough to spot the scout ship. It's an egg-shaped silver craft about fifty feet long. It should sparkle in the sun, and more than likely they arrived during the daytime. As you rotate the dial you'll see the days turn to night and back again. This little counter on the side displays how many Anarkkian days have passed. You should probably start looking about... maybe... umm... three hundred and ninety days ago. I'll keep an eye on the number of days while you turn the dial."

"Okay, here goes." Orville began twisting the small brass knob. "Creekers, you're right, it's flickering from day to night. It goes fast! Whoa – I just saw a huge Gnorli bird flash past! Hold on – I see something in the ocean." Orville turned the brass dial back until he had found the right place in time. "Creekers! Now I know why Gnorli told us not to go swimming in the Senyph Ocean. Something leaped up out of the water. It was enormous, bigger than anything I've ever seen. I can't even describe it except I'd rather be dropped into the centipede pit than be swimming in the water when that thing showed up. It was nothing at all like a fish. Scary."

Orville twisted the dial and left the terrifying creature behind.

Sophia watched the counter spin on the side of the goggles. "Okay, you just passed three hundred and ninety days. You can start looking for the scout ship."

"I'm turning it slowly now, scanning up and down the coastline. This is going to take a while. I don't want to miss anything. I've seen three more Gnorli birds fly past so I know it's working."

Sophia gazed out across the ocean while Orville searched through time for the scout ship. She never imagined that one day she would find herself on

Periculum trying to discover who had killed her father. In her heart she knew Papa was in a better world than this one, but she still wished he was here. Life was full of surprises, good ones and bad ones. She also knew that events which at first were impossibly painful and sad could change a mouse's life in the very best of ways. She glanced over at Orville and smiled. She would never have met Orville if her papa hadn't been killed by Draken. The universe closed some doors and opened others. Who would have thought her best friend in life would be a mouse who fainted at the sight of giant centipedes? Or a mouse whose kindness would transform the life of a lonely Rabbiton.

"Hold on! I think I have it! I see it, I see it! An egg-shaped silver vehicle just popped out of a black stormy cloud to the north of us, right over the ocean. I'm reversing the time flow now. It's heading inland... slowing down... descending. I see where it landed! Right near that big rocky area that pokes out into the ocean!"

"They landed safely? There wasn't a crash?"

"No, they were in control of the ship the whole time. It descended slowly and disappeared down behind the trees."

Sophia knew the time was approaching when she might have to watch her father being killed. She felt sick inside. "Orville, I can't do this. I thought I could, but I can't watch what happened to Papa."

"You don't need to. I'll do it for you. We'll find out the truth and then we'll tell Master Marloh and all the Metaphysical Adventurers."

Chapter 26

The Letter

The following morning after breakfast Sophia and Orville headed down the steep rocky slopes to the Senyph coastline. Orville watched as Proto swooped and soared through the sky ahead of them. "Sophia, what do you think about Proto, about him sensing a deeper purpose than making tasty snacks for rabbits? Do you think it's really possible for a Rabbiton to make the transition from a machine to a living creature?"

"Stranger things have happened. I suppose it just depends on what you mean by being alive. I have a physical body and so does Proto. I have a physical brain and so does Proto. I sense a deeper purpose to my life than scurrying around hunting for food and now so does Proto. I don't believe his transformation was part of the Elders' plan, but it does seem as though he's become self-aware. That sounds like life to me. And also, when you think about it, a little bug doesn't have deep self-awareness or a sense of purpose and we don't question for a moment whether they're living creatures."

"That's a good point about the bug. I think Proto's probably right that our friendship is what changed him. He told me yesterday he's taking walks almost every day down in Pavorak Gorge. When we first arrived he wouldn't even leave the Cube."

"That makes me wonder."

"Wonder what?"

"About the true purpose of our adventures. I've been so focused on finding the truth about Papa's death and I've been gauging my success by how that one task is progressing. But look at what happened along the way. Proto was transformed. Was that really just a coincidence, or was his transformation the grand plan, and my personal quest just a means to that end?"

"It could be both. You said everything is connected and everything affects everything else. My inner voice told me to always follow the truth I find in my heart. If we do that, then everything we do brings positive change to the world, like Proto's transformation."

"That does makes sense. You're a lot smarter than you look."

"Wait, what?" Orville gave a loud cackle and pretended to punch Sophia's arm. "Hey, we're almost at the ocean. Mmmm, smell that salt air. It reminds me of the Vesarak Sea. I only went out once with my Papa on his fishing boat. Mum didn't want me to go because she thought the seas were too rough." Orville trailed off, his thoughts drifting back to the Vesarak Sea and the day his Papa didn't come home.

"Hey, let's do something fun. Let's skip stones across the water. I don't want to boast, but I was a champion stone skipper back on Quintari."

Orville rolled his eyes. "The only thing you're the champion of is making up big phony stories. Grab a stone and we'll settle this here and now. My record is twelve skips with one stone."

Sophia snorted. "A mouseling could beat that. Watch and learn, little mouseling." Sophia picked up a smooth flat stone from the sandy beach and stepped closer to the water. With perfect form she flicked the stone smoothly just above the surface of the water, counting the number of skips. "One, two, three–" Unfortunately, before she could say 'four' a terrifying creature resembling an angry buzzing centipede with six wings and a jaw filled with razor sharp green teeth flashed out of the water and swallowed Sophia's stone.

Sophia and Orville stood gaping at the foaming white water, barely able to breathe. Finally Orville said, "Okay, that's three skips for you. Now it's my turn."

Sophia gave a shriek and pounded Orville on the arm. "This contest is over. I'm never setting foot near that water again. Now I know why Gnorli told us not to go swimming."

Orville laughed, but the creature who swallowed Sophia's stone had made him realize that crossing the nearly two thousand mile wide Senyph Ocean was quite clearly an impossible feat.

The two adventurers headed north along the sandy beach, both of them keeping a safe distance from the water's edge. They had no idea what kind of bizarre beasts might come shooting out of the water up onto the sand.

Other than the dreadful creatures in the ocean, the coastal area was quite idyllic and their walk along the shoreline to the scout ship's landing spot was leisurely and enjoyable. Three hours later they were approaching the small rocky peninsula that jutted out into the ocean. The silver scout ship had landed about one mile directly inland. Orville pointed past the tall beach grass swaying in the warm ocean breeze. "The ship landed about a mile in that direction. I saw it land, but I didn't see it leave." He glanced over at Sophia. She nodded grimly but said nothing.

Sophia was the first one to spot the ship. "I see it. I see the ship." The thick beach grass had been gradually replaced by a forest of dense spiky trees with long dagger shaped orange leaves. Sophia pointed through the trees to sparkling sunlight glinting off a gleaming metallic surface.

They slipped silently between the trees, finally approaching the wide clearing which held the silver ship. Neither of them spoke, their eyes scanning the area, afraid of what they might find. Sophia shook her head. "I don't see anything. We should look inside."

"You wait here. I'll check." Orville stepped over to the ship and tapped the violet disk next to the outer hatch. The door whirred open and Orville stepped inside, glancing anxiously into the control room, then into the two cabins and the propulsion room. He saw nothing which would indicate an act of violence had occurred inside the ship. He stepped out through the hatch and waved to Sophia. "Nothing. Everything looks normal. It looks as though the ship was simply abandoned."

Sophia nodded. "I want to search the ship before we use the time goggles."

Ten minutes later Sophia was sitting alone in one of the small cabins. She had her paws over her face and Orville could hear her crying. He waited outside the ship until she came out.

"It's the right ship. I found a photo of Papa and me that he always took with him." Orville watched as she carefully tucked the photo into her pack. Sophia turned to face Orville. "We need to use the time goggles and find out what happened."

Orville pulled the cap and goggles out of the brass box. He slipped them both on and connected the two cables. "I'm going to stand back so I'll have a wider view." When he was in position Sophia dialed the time goggles to three hundred and ninety-eight, the day of the ship's arrival. Orville pushed the small silver tabs and began rotating the brass time dial.

"I see it. I'm running it forward now. I can see the ship coming down. They're landing." He twisted the dial forward slightly. "They're standing outside the ship talking. It's your papa. Your papa and Draken Mouse." Orville paws were shaking. "They're leaving now, both wearing packs. They must be going out to search for the monastery."

Orville continued turning the dial until he finally saw the two mice return to the ship. There was no sign they had found anything but it looked as though they were arguing. A few minutes later they emerged from the ship. Sophia's papa was gesturing with both his paws, trying to convince Draken Mouse of something, perhaps persuade him to do something. Draken Mouse abruptly and violently pushed Sophia's papa away from him. Draken appeared furious and was shouting. Rowland held up both paws and backed away from Draken, then turned, heading off toward the trees.

Without warning Draken held out his paw and a brilliant blast of focused purple light shot out, hitting Sophia's Papa directly in the back. Orville watched in horror as Rowland Mouse toppled over a small ledge into the dense underbrush. Draken turned away with a scowl and headed back toward the beach. Orville turned to Sophia, the look on his face telling her everything she needed to know.

"Draken killed Papa?"

Orville nodded mutely.

"We need tangible proof. We have to be able to prove it happened just as you saw it."

Proto poked his head out of Orville's pack. "This is what glowbirds are for. Let me look through the time goggles. I can make a record of it – a record we can show on a display panel to the Metaphysical Adventurers."

Twenty minutes later Proto had the record of Draken's murderous crime safely stored on a crystalline memory cube.

Orville put his paw gently on Sophia's arm. "You wait here. I'll be right back." Orville walked over into the dense brush where he had seen Sophia's Papa fall. It only took a minute to find him. Orville felt sick, but this was something he had to do. He gently removed Rowland Mouse's silver Metaphysical Adventurers ring and searched his coat pockets, finding only a gold pocket watch and a wrinkled piece of folded paper. He stood up, bowing his head for a moment before heading back to Sophia. He handed her the ring and put his paw on her shoulder. "I'm sorry. I'm so sorry." Sophia put her arms around him and held him for a long time.

Finally she broke away and he handed her the gold watch and the folded paper. "This is all I found."

"Mum gave him this watch. It's Mintarian, very old. It was his most prized possession." She unfolded the piece of paper, scanned it quickly, then read it aloud to Orville.

Dearest Sophia,

If this letter has found its way to you then you know something has happened to me. Things have not gone well on this trip. Draken Mouse is far more dangerous than I had previously thought. I suspect him to be quite an evil fellow. He has attempted to convince me again and again that Metaphysical Adventurers should be able to use lethal force as they see fit. He also has the delusional idea that the Metaphysical Adventurers should be transformed into a military force, using their combined shaping powers to take control of Symoca, then invade our neighboring countries Lapinor and Grymmore. It is sheer insanity, and also the reason I have not been entirely forthcoming with him regarding our mission here on Periculum.

Sophia, I know more about the lost monastery than I first told you. At the time, I felt such knowledge would put your life in jeopardy, but I no longer have the luxury of protecting you. This is what I know. There have been rumors for centuries about a monastery on Periculum which contains the secret to unlimited power. I always assumed this was a myth, a tall tale, but during my research on ancient Anarkkian communication crystals I discovered the Anarkkians were searching for the lost monastery during the war. I also learned they had narrowed their search area to the western coastline of the Senyph Ocean. I made the mistake of telling Draken what I knew and he immediately volunteered to help me look for the monastery. It's very clear to me now that he craves power beyond all else, and in my estimation he is the last mouse in this world who should have access to such power as the monastery might hold. We searched up and down the coastline for the monastery but found nothing. At least that's what I told Draken. Draken was studying some old charts while I piloted the scout ship, scanning the ground below. Sophia, I believe I have found the monastery, which appears to be in ruins. But things are seldom as they appear, which is why it is important that someone carefully investigates this area. There is no one I trust more than you, Sophia, and I know if you do find a source of unlimited power you will use it wisely and with great compassion. I have sketched a small map on the reverse side of this letter showing the location of the ruins. Sophia, always remember we are far more than our physical bodies. We shall see each other again, just as a dropped marble must fall to the ground.

With all my love,
Papa

Orville and Sophia buried her Papa on Periculum, but she knew he had left the planet over a year ago, off to the next world, off to his next adventure. She would see her Papa again. It was only a matter of time.

The next morning Sophia found Orville gazing thoughtfully at the scout ship. "There's no way we can fly this across the Senyph Ocean?"

Sophia shook her head. "No, I checked. The CDETS is missing and I have no idea how to shape one. There's auxiliary power but that's not enough to fly it. Draken did not want this ship to go anywhere."

"You're right about that. He said the CDETS had failed and the craft had been destroyed in the crash, so if someone brought the ship back to Earth he would be exposed as a liar and a murderer." Orville furrowed his brow. "Wait, what about your Papa's map? Should we look for the monastery?"

"Absolutely. Remember what I was saying about the secret purposes hidden within our adventures? The universe has placed this map in our hands for a reason. We need to listen to what it is telling us and then follow the truth of our inner voice."

"Do you think when I first noticed the clockwork glowbirds, the universe was laying down a trail of breadcrumbs which would lead us to the monastery?"

"Well, I suppose the short answer is yes, although none of that really matters. We don't need to know the grand plan, we just have to listen carefully to the universe and do what our hearts tell us. My heart is telling me we need to find that monastery. Every event on this adventure has been leading us in that direction."

Sophia unfolded the map her Papa had drawn and studied it carefully. "This is where we are, right here at the landing sight. We have to head south along the coastline for over a hundred miles, then move inland for three or four miles. There's a drawing of a big tree right next–."

Orville interrupted Sophia. "Wait, a big tree? Do you think this has anything to do with my dream about the huge tree with the round blue leaves? And that mouse in the blue robe?"

"It wouldn't surprise me at all if your orange grove dream was connected to this. Dreams often reveal the invisible strings that connect seemingly unrelated events."

They closed up the scout ship after Proto had made a

detailed record of the gleaming craft, showing clearly it had not been in a crash and that someone had carefully removed the CDETS. They now had more than enough proof to bring Draken Mouse's mad scheme to a sudden and ignominious end. Orville slung his pack onto his shoulder and the two adventurers headed south along the Senyph coastline.

Proto was having a marvelous time flying above the ocean and making records of the frightful beasts that leaped out from the depths. The scarier they were, the louder Proto squawked and the more he liked it. "Oh, my, did you see that one, Orville?? Hideous beyond measure!"

Other than the occasional dreadful beast leaping out of the ocean, their journey south was quite relaxing, and now that they had proof of Draken's guilt there was no longer a dire sense of urgency. They stopped to pick up seashells and oddly shaped pieces of driftwood. Orville shaped campfires on the beach and they took turns preparing their meals, often with very exacting instruction from Proto. The days were sunny and lazy and seemed to roll by without effort. Orville was learning a lot from Sophia about shaping and a lot about her former life on Quintari. The more stories she told, the more he wanted to visit the planet and see it for himself.

"You could visit, Orville. It would be so much fun to show you Quintari. I have a lot of family and friends there, and once Draken Mouse is out of the picture, Master Marloh could open a spectral door for us. I think you'd love it, especially all the advanced technology we have."

The sunsets along the Senyph Ocean were glorious

to behold, and marked the time of day when Sophia would shape sleeping bags and Orville would shape the cots. If it looked like rain he would also shape a waterproof canopy to keep them dry. Their long daily treks along the sandy beaches agreed with Orville and also assured he would fall into a deep sleep the moment his head hit the pillow.

Chapter 27

The Forest Wolf

The first thing Orville noticed was the double bladed axe. He had split a fair amount of firewood over the years to heat their home in Muridaan Falls, but a broad double bladed axe wasn't something he normally dreamed about. Then there were his clothes – heavy canvas trousers, a thick woolen shirt and stout leather boots with more than a little wear to them, all topped off with a dark blue woolen cap.

Orville was quite aware he was dreaming. Sophia had taught him how to focus on his paws during a dream until they became sharp and clear. Once his paws had become real, the rest of the dream followed suit. The dream became as real as his world of Muridaan Falls. A rush of awareness would fill him, and in less than a second he would be fully present and fully aware in his dream.

He had awakened in this particular dream to find himself strolling through a dark forest, a heavy axe resting on his shoulder. The sun had not yet risen, but a golden glow from the horizon was reflecting off the branches high overhead.

"What is this place? What an odd dream. Why in the

204

world would I be dressed as a woodcutter? Hmm... I must admit it's quite lovely in this forest, quite peaceful really. A little dark, but the sun is coming up. I suppose I should just keep walking and see where this path takes me."

Orville strolled on through the forest, admiring the trees and watching with interest as the morning sun rose higher into the azure blue sky. He had been walking for a little over a mile when he heard the piercing scream.

"What was that? It sounded like a mouseling! Creekers, I have to find them!"

Orville dashed forward through the forest toward the sound of the scream. The forest path veered sharply to the right and after fifty feet opened up into a small sunlit meadow. The first thing Orville noticed was the beautiful yellow wildflowers. The second thing he noticed was the enormous growling forest wolf facing a cowering little mouseling wearing a red cloak. The mouseling was terrified, her arms and legs shaking, tears streaming down her face.

"Oh, no, I hate forest wolves! Why am I dreaming about one?"

The wolf whirled around at the sound of Orville's voice. It's eyes narrowed to two small glowing red slits. Orville felt every muscle in his body tighten. "Red glowing eyes. This can't be good."

A low guttural growl rolled out of the wolf's throat. Its ears were flattened back against its head as it slowly crept toward Orville.

A sudden thought popped into Orville's head. He was a rough and tumble woodcutter. Woodcutters didn't put up with nonsense like this, and besides, this was his dream. He could do whatever he wanted to. He could even fly. He would teach that wolf a lesson it would not soon forget. With a roar that shook the forest Orville shot up into the air high above the forest floor, raising the huge double bladed axe above his head, then flashed down toward the wolf.

The wolf gave a ferocious snarl and leaped toward Orville, his deadly sharp fangs glinting in the early morning sun.

"Stop." The mouseling was holding up her paw. The huge wolf halted instantly, looking back at the mouseling. With a whimper the enormous forest wolf sauntered back to the mouseling, and then with a great yawn it lay down next to her. The mouseling smiled sweetly, gently scratching the top of the wolf's head. Moments later the wolf was sound asleep.

Orville had landed and was standing in the middle of the meadow with the double bladed axe still raised high over his head. He lowered the axe, his eyes fixed on the mouseling.

The mouseling said nothing, but sat down next to the wolf and leaned back against it, her head resting on his thick coat of fur.

Orville was, of course, quite confused. He caught a quick movement from the deep shadows behind the mouseling and the wolf. A mouse stepped out into the clearing. It was the mouse from the orange grove, the mouse with the blue robe, the mouse who had asked Orville who was having the dream.

Orville's axe fell to the forest floor with a dull thud. His eyes were on the plump old mouse wearing the blue robe. "Who are you? Why do you keep showing up in my dreams? Do I know you?"

The huge wolf rose slowly to its feet and gazed at

Orville, then turned to the mouse in the blue robe. "Does he see?"

The mouse studied Orville carefully, then replied to the wolf. "He sees, but does not yet understand."

"That is to be expected. I will speak with him when he arrives."

Orville felt something grab his shoulder and shake it.

"Wake up, sleepy bones! Time to get moving. We should reach the lost monastery by late afternoon."

Chapter 28

A Monastery in Ruins

Orville told Sophia about his puzzling woodcutter dream but she found it just as confusing as he did. "He said he would speak with you when you arrive? Arrive where?"

"I don't know, he didn't say. Maybe when we arrive at the lost monastery?"

"Well, that doesn't make much sense, but neither did big green rolling ball creatures who like tasty cakes. I guess we'll find out this afternoon."

Orville felt Proto rustling about in his backpack and a moment later Proto's head poked out from under the flap. "Good morning, adventurers. I trust you had a lovely sleep? While you were sleeping I was strolling along through Pavorak Gorge. Quite lovely there in the late afternoon with the low light illuminating the colorful cavern walls. As it happens, while I was admiring the lovely scenery, I realized something. More precisely, I realized two things. First, I was not thinking about tasty snacks, and second, I was not worrying about being attacked and torn to pieces by a gigantic silver autonomous Anarkkian Attack Spider. In fact, I had quite a pleasant walk and I believe I shall do it again tomorrow, after I have completed a little project I'm working on."

"That's wonderful! It looks like your idea of safely experiencing adventure through the eyes of the glowbird has been very successful. What is the project you're working on? Something to do with Anarkkian history?"

"No, nothing to do with those dastardly Anarkkians. Something else entirely, but it's a surprise, so you'll just have to wait." Proto gave a loud chuckle. "And if you think it has anything to do with tasty snacks, I'm afraid you would be quite mistaken." With a great flap of his wings Proto shot off into the sky, heading south.

Orville watched as Proto grew smaller and smaller. "That's rather mysterious. I wonder what he's up to?"

"Maybe he's raising a giant carnivorous centipede to be your pet."

"You really are so cruel."

Several hours later when they stopped for lunch Sophia held her Papa's map out for Orville to see. "We're getting close. Look, you can see this big rock that looks like a bird just down the beach about half a mile. That's where we turn and head inland. We should reach the monastery after about a two mile hike. Well, we should reach the *ruins* of a monastery. I'm not completely certain why Papa said things aren't as they appear to be, but he definitely wanted us to explore it. Maybe we'll find some stone carvings or hieroglyphs or something like that."

Later that afternoon they were standing next to what Orville had named Bird Rock, the huge granite outcropping which bore some resemblance to a Gnorli bird.

"We head inland through there." Orville pointed to a dense stand of trees and headed toward them, pushing his way through the heavy beach grass. The thicket of trees turned out to be a mile wide forest and was unfortunately filled with tangled, thorny underbrush. Before long Orville and Sophia were swatting at clouds of annoying buzzing insects stirred up by their passage through the dense spiny undergrowth. Finally the trees came to an end and the two adventurers stepped out into the bright summer sunlight.

Orville could not move. He was looking at the very last thing he had expected to see. Sophia stepped out behind him and put her paw over her mouth.

"I don't believe it." It was the most picturesque, pastoral orange grove they had ever seen, a gentle breeze carrying the delicate fragrance of ten thousand newly bloomed orange blossoms across the balmy summer air.

"This is it, Sophia. This is my dream. This is where I was. This is where we were."

The two adventurers stepped into the grove, walking slowly through the long rows of blossoming orange trees, the delicious scent filling their nostrils. "How can this be?"

"I don't know. The only thing I know is I will never truly comprehend the depth of this world."

Orville pointed past the end of the grove. "There it is."

Sophia halted, her eyes on the gigantic blue tree. "How can a tree be that big? How old do you think it is? It has to be thousands of years. The leaves are so bright, brighter even than in your dream. I'm feeling something, Orville. It's... I don't know... some kind of force. It's not something bad, it's something very, very good, but it's like nothing I've ever sensed before."

"I feel it too. There's a feeling of absolute joy. It's deep and it's old. How very strange."

Sophia and Orville strolled past the last orange tree, heading toward the astonishingly large blue tree. "It must be five hundred feet wide. And so tall. I don't know how it could be so tall." Orville walked over to one of the gigantic branches which was almost sweeping the ground. He plucked off one of the blue leaves and held it out for Sophia to see. "It's beautiful, a perfect circle. Do you think it might be from another world?"

Orville was waiting for Sophia's answer when he heard the voice of the forest wolf from his woodcutter dream.

"Is he true?" Orville whirled around to see the now familiar blue robed mouse step out from behind the tree's gargantuan trunk. Sophia stopped in her tracks, staring at the mouse with wide eyes.

"Is that him, Orville?"

"Yes, it's him, the mouse from my dreams."

The old mouse in the blue robe walked slowly toward them with an odd shuffling gait, coming to a halt about ten feet away from Orville.

Orville heard a second voice. It was coming from the mouse who stood facing him.

"I believe him to be true."

"Does he see?"

"He sees, but does not understand."

"That is to be expected. He is young still. I will speak with him now."

The blue robed mouse motioned for Sophia and

Orville to follow him, then turned, slowly making his way around the perimeter of the enormous tree. When they had reached the other side of the tree Orville spotted the ancient stone ruins. He whispered to Sophia. "Look! It's the ruins your Papa wrote about. He was right, it's old collapsed walls and piles of rubble."

As they drew closer to the ruins Orville studied the old stones for ancient carvings or hieroglyphs which might give him a clue as to the creators of the monastery, but he was having a difficult time focusing on the walls. The ruins were vibrating, moving, changing. The walls were slightly taller than they had been, the piles of rubble were smaller, stones were missing, new stones were forming, doorways were appearing, roofs were blinking into existence. Orville watched as a mammoth wall of stone seemed to form out of nothing, quickly winding its way around the monastery. A pair of massive thirty foot tall wooden doors lined with heavy wrought iron bands rippled into the world before his eyes. Orville could scarcely breathe. The monastery looked as though it had been built yesterday. He turned to Sophia. She shook her head. There were no words.

The blue robed mouse reached up and raised the heavy iron ring on the door. He let it fall and a deep echoing gong rang out when it collided with the heavy wrought iron band. The mouse took several steps back and waited. The massively heavy wooden doors slowly groaned open, giving the adventurers just enough room to enter. The blue robed mouse stepped through first, followed closely by Sophia and Orville. The doors rumbled shut behind them.

The first thing Sophia noticed was the immense sprawling garden. It was lovely beyond imagination, filled with thousands of magnificent multicolored blooms in all shapes and sizes. A dozen red robed mice were tending the garden, digging and planting, watering and weeding. They continued working as though Sophia and Orville were not there. In the center of the vast garden stood a massive square stone building thirty feet tall and a hundred feet wide. The blue robed mouse led them down a wide curving garden path made from thousands of colorful, artfully arranged river stones. The path looked ancient, worn smooth by a thousand years of wear. Orville could see no windows in the stone building and spotted only one entrance, a single sky blue door with a golden eye embedded in the center. Orville recognized the symbol instantly. It was the same symbol used by the Shapers Guild.

The blue robed mouse turned to face Sophia and Orville. "Sophia, you will sit here on the stone bench while Orville goes inside. I'm uncertain how long he will be."

"You know my name?"

The blue robed mouse smiled kindly at Sophia. "We will speak of this later."

He turned back toward the blue door and sang three crisp and clear exquisite notes that seemed to linger and echo through the garden, finally becoming part of the monastery. The door swung open, revealing only shadows within. The mouse in the blue robe motioned for Orville to enter. "He will speak with you now."

Orville looked back at Sophia, who gave him a reassuring smile. He took a deep breath and stepped into the darkened building.

Chapter 29

Monks of the
Blue Robe

Sophia watched as the door closed behind Orville. She couldn't wait to find out what he would learn inside the monastery. The blue robed mouse took a seat on the stone bench next to Sophia. He sat quietly, his paws resting in his lap, his eyes on the beautiful blooms of the garden.

"It's beautiful. I've never seen a garden as lovely as this one." Sophia smiled brightly, hoping the mouse would reply. She wanted to find out who these strange mice were.

"Yes. Lovely and very old. This garden has been tended by the Red Monks for millennia. The flowers come and go, but the garden is eternal."

Sophia nodded. "As it is with mice. The mice come and go but the village remains."

The mouse smiled, his eyes wrinkling. "I know your name because I knew your father. Rowland Mouse was a dear friend of the Blue Monks."

"What? I think you must be mistaken. My Papa was looking for this monastery but never found it. He thought it was only a ruins. He's the one who asked us investigate the site."

"Sophia, I am the Fourth Monk, a member of an ancient order of monks known as the Monks of the Blue Robe. There are always thirteen of us. I am the Fourth, and Orville will be speaking with the Thirteenth Monk, the most senior of our order. Your confusion is understandable. Your father did not know us on Periculum, but he did know us on Nirriim, on the Island of Blue Monks. He visited us there on many occasions and was always a welcomed guest. He was true, but it was not the proper time for him to understand. That will come later, as it shall for you. It is quite clear to me that you are true also. You follow the truth from within. Many mice call it the truth that is found in your heart. While that is indeed quite lyrical, the truth really comes from your deeper self, a vast consciousness most mice are unaware of. You are a raindrop, your deeper self is the ocean."

"I do understand what you're saying, but I'm still confused. How could my father know you on Nirriim? Do you travel back and forth between the two worlds?"

The Fourth Monk smiled again. "No. This monastery, as you may have noticed during your arrival, is not an ordinary one. Think of worlds as pages in a book. When you poke a sharp stick through the book, the stick will touch all the pages simultaneously. So it is with our monastery. It exists simultaneously in many worlds. Two of those worlds are Periculum and Nirriim. Your father knew us as the Blue Monks of Nirriim, but not as the Blue Monks of Periculum."

"Oh. That seems quite extraordinary."

"The world is filled with extraordinary things. You

215

only have to look for them."

"Orville is good at that. He always finds puzzles. That's how we found you here on Periculum. He noticed a group of clockwork glowbirds back in Muridaan Falls and it was our search for the truth behind them which eventually led us here."

"A most fortunate series of events, wouldn't you agree?"

"I think there was more to it than that. I think the universe wanted us to find you. There is a very evil mouse with terrible plans for the Metaphysical Adventurers."

"Yes, Draken Mouse. We are quite aware of him. You may be assured that all is as it should be. It is often said that beneath apparently chaotic events you will find order and perfection. A dear friend of ours named Bartholomew the Adventurer used a handful of glass marbles to clearly illustrate this concept. He said if you throw the glass marbles at a wall, it first appears to be a scene of total chaos, marbles flying and bouncing every which way, clattering across the table tops and floor. If you look more deeply, however, you become aware that every marble is following precisely the laws of physical motion. Each marble is exactly where it should be at every moment in time. It can be no other way. That is why you are sitting here next to me on this bench. It can be no other way. All is as it should be."

"That's lovely. Thank you for teaching me that."

"I quite suspect you already knew it, but perhaps you were looking at it from a slightly different perspective. I do apologize, Sophia, but I must leave you now. Orville will more than likely be out within the hour. You may both stay with us as long as you wish, and our doors shall always be open to you."

The Fourth Monk patted Sophia gently on her shoulder, then sang three short notes. The blue door swung open and he disappeared into the monastery, the door closing softly behind him.

While Sophia had been outside talking with the Fourth Monk, Orville was having his own extraordinary experience inside the stone building.

The first thing he noticed was the sweet smell of incense mixed with the musty scent of ages gone by. The room was nearly one hundred feet square with ceilings that stood twenty or more feet tall. The floor was of the same design as the garden path, made from beautifully arranged river stones worn smooth by the feet of uncountable mice.

The room was empty and almost dark, illuminated only by a slight glow from the stone ceiling high overhead. He squinted his eyes, peering out into the darkness. Who was he supposed to talk to? There was no one here.

A slight movement at the back of the room caught his attention. There was a flash of blue, then he noticed a robe, then a mouse wearing the blue robe. Orville blinked, trying to focus. There were thirteen mice all wearing blue robes. Orville stepped back. What was this place? Who were these mice, and what in the world was he doing here?

One of the mice stepped forward, making his way across the stone floor toward Orville. Orville could hear the sound of the mouse's feet sliding over the smooth stones. The other twelve mice faded away, leaving only the mouse who was walking toward him.

The blue robed mouse stopped when he was six feet

away from Orville. He paused, his eyes focused on Orville.

"Orville, I am the Thirteenth Monk, the senior monk of our order, the Monks of the Blue Robe. I welcome you to our monastery. I understand you have traveled a great distance to find us."

"Well, umm... to be very honest I wasn't really looking for you until recently."

The Thirteenth Monk laughed, inexplicably amused by Orville's reply. He hummed a few short notes then said, "Please, have a seat." Orville looked behind him and saw a large green chair which had not been there before.

Orville looked with surprise at the Thirteenth Monk. "You're a shaper?"

"Something like that. The Blue Monks manipulate energy as shapers do, but we do it with song, with sound. I am speaking to you with words now, but the original language of the Blue Monks is song. It is quite an effective method of communication if you think about it. It's quite expressive, allowing for a transfer-ence of deep emotions and feeling. Orville, why do you think you're here?"

"Well, Sophia thinks the universe was leading us here."

"She is quite right, of course. You are here for the same reason a coin falls to the floor when we release it from our grasp."

"We were drawn here by some kind of force?"

"Orville, is the purpose of your visit to find the fabled source of unlimited power?"

"Well, I don't exactly know what the *real* purpose is. Sophia's Papa wasn't sure if there really was a source of unlimited power, but he said if there was one he didn't want it to fall into the wrong paws."

"I see. That does indeed sound like our dear friend Rowland Mouse. I can tell you that there *is* a source of unlimited power, but I can also tell you that the wrong paws would be unable to hold it. The wrong paws may as well be grasping at the empty air around them."

"You're saying only a good mouse is capable of using this power?"

"Are you a good mouse?"

"Umm... I hope so. Sometimes my Mum says I dream too much and don't spend enough time trying to make the world a better place."

A green chair rippled into view behind the Thirteenth Monk. He sat down with a long sigh. "Ahhh. That's better. I'm not as young as I used to be." This also seemed to greatly amuse him. "Green is a lovely color for comfy chairs, don't you think?"

Orville stared at him blankly. Did he know about Proto and the comfy green chair he had chosen? "Well, yes, green is my favorite color."

"We shall begin now. Your Mum says you dream too much. Do you happen to remember a dream you once had where you played the part of a woodcutter?"

Orville's eyes widened. "Yes, I just had it on the way here. There was a Blue Monk in it. I didn't know if it was my dream or his."

"That was the Fourth Monk you saw. I asked him to orchestrate a particular dream scenario for you. Your woodcutter dream was a test, Orville – a test which you passed with, as they say, flying colors."

"A test? What kind of test?"

The Thirteenth Monk closed his eyes. "Orville, let

me ask you a question. In your dream about the woodcutter, who were you?"

"Oh, I was the woodcutter."

"I see. And who was the terrified little mouseling?"

"I don't know what you mean. She was just part of the dream."

"She was just part of the dream. And tell me again whose dream it was?"

"Well, it was my dream."

"So the mouseling was..."

"Me? I was the mouseling *and* the woodcutter?"

The Thirteenth Monk clapped his paws together and sat up straight in his chair. "Now we're getting somewhere. Orville, who was the ferocious forest wolf?"

"I was?"

"Who was the trees? Who was the sky? Who was the sunlight reflecting off the trees? Who was stars in the night sky? Who was the forest floor? Who was the leaves? Who was the heavy two bladed axe?"

"I was all those things. I was everything in the dream."

"Excellent. You were everything in the dream. You have awakened from that dream now, and you have realized you were everything in the dream. You now clearly see that the apparent separateness of all the elements in your dream was only an illusion. There was only one consciousness in the woodcutter dream, and it was yours, Orville. Now, when you realized the forest wolf meant to harm the helpless little mouseling, your first thought was to save her. You were aware it was a dream, and you realized you could do anything you wanted to. You had access to unlimited power, did you not?"

"Well, I guess I did. It was just a dream though."

"So. In this 'just a dream' you flew toward the ferocious wolf with your axe held high, but something happened. Can you tell me what happened?"

"The mouseling said to stop."

"And remind me again who the mouseling was?"

"It was me. I said stop."

"Now we're *really* getting somewhere. You said stop. And what happened then?"

"The wolf lay down next to the mouseling and she scratched the top of his head and then he fell asleep, and the mouseling lay down and rested her head on him."

"Do you understand the test now?"

"I think so. You wanted to see what I would do if I had access to unlimited power. And instead of killing the wolf, part of me stopped and resolved the problem with kindness."

"With love, Orville. You resolved the conflict with love."

"Well, what does all that mean exactly? I still don't really know why I'm here."

"We will discuss that tomorrow. I would like you to stay here at the monastery for three days. Then I will send you back to Muridaan Falls. For now, I would like you to think about the deeper implications of everything we have discussed today."

"Wait, you can send us back to Muridaan Falls? Don't we have to go through the World Doors?"

"No, there is no need to cross the Senyph Ocean. I will send you home through a spectral doorway. I will also send you and Sophia back in time so you will arrive the morning after Master Marloh sent you here through his spectral door. If I were you I would run home and get the letter you wrote to your Mum before she reads it. It might simplify matters a great deal if she did not learn just yet you are a Metaphysical Adventurer who travels to other dimensions and does battle with gigantic carnivorous centipedes. You know how Mums tend to worry about that sort of thing." The Thirteenth Monk gave a hearty laugh, a laugh that filled Orville with the deepest and most profound sense of joy he had ever experienced.

Chapter 30

Orville's Dilemma

Orville leaned back on the stone bench and watched the Red Monks tending their glorious garden. He turned to Sophia and said, "Your Papa was really friends with the Blue Monks?"

"That's what the Fourth Monk said. The monastery exists in many worlds simultaneously and Papa knew the Blue Monks on Nirriim, but he never knew the monastery he was looking for on Periculum belonged to the Blue Monks."

"Why do you think they hide the building on Periculum but not on Nirriim?"

"I don't know, maybe Nirriim is a safer planet. You know, not so many carnivorous centipedes and giant flying scaly worm things jumping out of the ocean."

"That makes sense."

"What did the Thirteenth Monk say to you?"

"Well, he said my woodcutter dream was a test, and I passed it because I didn't kill the wolf even though I could have. Oh, and he made a big point of telling me I was everyone and everything in the dream, not just the woodcutter. That the separateness of all the dream elements was just an illusion."

"That's interesting. He wants to talk to you again?"

"This afternoon. He told me I was supposed to think about all the things he said before he sees me again. I don't really understand what he's trying to tell me. It sounds like he thinks I would use power wisely if I had it, but I have no idea how I would ever get it. Maybe he'll explain it today."

"Maybe so. I must say these Blue Monks are pretty mysterious. I know they're really good mice and they're wise beyond my understanding, but they're a little bit unnerving."

"I know what you mean. When I'm talking to the Thirteenth Monk I feel like I'm a one year old mouseling learning to tie my shoes."

Sophia snickered. "I heard a rumor that your Mum still does tie your shoes."

"So beautiful and yet so cruel."

"Did you just say I was beautiful?" Sophia raised both her eyebrows.

"What? Well, it's just kind of an expression... um, you know."

"Oh, an *expression*. Well, if the Thirteenth Monk asked you if your friend Sophia was beautiful, and he said you had to tell him the truth, what would you say?"

"He's the Thirteenth Monk, he's not going to ask me something silly like that."

"But if he did ask it and you *had* to answer it."

"Okay, I guess you're sort of beautiful, in a best friend kind of way."

Sophia snorted and pounded Orville's arm. "Ha! I knew I could get you to say it! Orville thinks I'm

224

beeeyooootiful!"

Orville made a gagging noise. "I wish I'd known how mean you were before I picked you for my best friend."

Orville felt a tap on his shoulder and turned to see the Fourth Monk standing behind them. "Good afternoon, Orville. I hope you and your very beautiful friend Sophia are enjoying this lovely day. The Thirteenth Monk would like to speak with you now. If you would please follow me I will open the blue door for you."

Sophia was trying not to laugh at Orville's embarrassment.

As he was walking away Orville turned back and stuck his tongue out at Sophia, who burst out laughing.

Five minutes later Orville stepped through the open doorway into the main building. He'd forgotten how dark and how quiet it was in there. He looked around the huge shadowy room, waiting for his eyes to grow accustomed to the dim light. Finally he spotted a slight movement at the back of the room, then realized all thirteen Blue Monks were standing in a row facing him.

"Creekers, it's spooky how they do that." The Thirteenth Monk stepped forward and made his way across the room. He approached Orville, then stopped and sang five short notes. It was the most beautiful tune Orville had ever heard and for some inexplicable reason made him think of Proto. Two comfy green chairs appeared out of nowhere and the Thirteenth Monk motioned for Orville to take a seat.

"Did those notes you just sang shape those chairs?"

"Yes. It's not as difficult as you might think, although I have been doing this for a very long time."

225

"Why did it make me think of Proto?"

"The song was about comfy green chairs."

"So you can make me think of something just by singing notes like that?"

"Think of it as a foreign language. If someone is speaking to you in Muroidian, you might have no idea what the words mean, but you can tell if they're angry or happy or sad by the tone of their voice. It's a little like that. It helps if you're very intuitive, as you are."

"Oh. Could you sing something else for me?"

"Very well." The Thirteenth Monk thought for a moment then sang a short wordless song. The power of the song swept through Orville like a hurricane, whirling his thoughts into what felt like long brightly colored threads, carrying them far away. He felt his body evaporating, the atoms and molecules spreading out across the universe, becoming infinitesimal specks of ancient stardust. He was in his kitchen back in Muridaan Falls. He was sitting at the breakfast table. Mum was putting a plate of warm snapberry flapcakes on the table when Papa walked into the room and put his arm around Mum, kissing her on the cheek. "I'll be back in three days." He kissed Orville on the top of his head. "Be good for your Mum. Remember I love you always."

Orville was back in the comfy green chair, tears streaming down his face. "I saw Papa. I was a mouseling. It was the day he left and didn't come back."

The Thirteenth Monk nodded. "It is a song draws on your mouseling memories. Sometimes they are happy memories, sometimes they are impossibly sad ones."

"I didn't mean to cry like that."

226

"There is no need to apologize, Orville. In the center of dark and overwhelming grief lies a radiant star of pure love. Your tears have proven to me we were not mistaken about you. You are true, and that is all that can be asked of any mouse."

The Thirteenth Monk waited silently until Orville was ready, then continued. "Orville, I would like to talk more about your woodcutter dream. Would that be all right?"

"Sure. It was kind of a weird dream."

"Let me ask you this. Suppose in the dream, besides being awake, you were also fully aware that everyone and everything in the dream was you. Suppose when you saw the wolf getting ready to snap at the helpless little mouseling you held up your paw and told the wolf to stop. You told the wolf that he was not separate from the mouseling, he was not separate from you. He was not separate from the trees and sky and the stars, that this separateness was only an illusion, that you were really all one consciousness named Orville. If he bit the mouseling he would really be biting himself. What do you think he would have said to you?"

"Umm... I think he'd say, 'All this talk is giving me a headache. I'm going to eat both of you.'"

The Thirteenth Monk gave a great laugh. "You might be right, Orville. All right, suppose I were to say to you right now that the separateness you feel as Orville Wellington Mouse is only an illusion. You and I and Sophia and all the Blue Monks, the trees, the stars, and the galaxies are all part of a great consciousness and in reality are all one mind, just as they all were in your dream about the woodcutter."

Orville's head was spinning, but he tried to answer.

"Well, Sophia is always saying all things are connected, and things happen for a reason even if we don't know what that reason is. But this world is real, it's not just a dream. Dreams are different, they're all in your head."

"These are simply things for you to think about, Orville. You are the one who will decide the deeper truth to be found within them. No one else can do it for you. All I ask is that you think about them. Tomorrow will be your last day here. Tomorrow I will tell you the secret to limitless power, the power to change the universe in any way you choose."

Orville felt a rush of fear wash through him. "I'm not sure I want to know that. I might do something wrong or make things worse."

The Thirteenth Monk rose to his feet and stepped over to Orville. He placed his paw on Orville's arm. "The mouse who does not seek power is the one who should wield it. You are much more than you think you are, Orville, and far, far older than you think you are."

"What?"

"I will see you tomorrow." The Thirteenth Monk turned and walked toward the back of the room. Orville kept his eyes on him until he realized he was staring at empty space. The Thirteenth Monk had faded away into the darkness. Orville sat alone in the silence of the monastery for almost an hour thinking about his conversation with the Thirteenth Monk. He had a feeling everything he needed to know was there, but he couldn't quite put all the parts together in the proper order. What would he do if he did have unlimited power? What would he change? He sighed. Maybe Sophia would have some good ideas.

Twenty minutes later he was sitting next to Sophia

beneath the gigantic tree with the round blue leaves. "Orville, I asked the Fourth Monk about this tree and he said it was here when the monastery was built, almost two thousand years ago. I got the feeling he knew more about it but he didn't want to tell me."

"They sure have a lot of secrets. Maybe it's some kind of magic tree or something."

"Magic? Really?"

"Well, maybe it has some weird shaping powers or something that we don't understand."

"Or it could just be a really big old tree."

"Sophia, if you had the power to change anything in the universe, what would you change? If the Thirteenth Monk is going to give me the secret to unlimited power I need to think about that."

"Well, you *could* make yourself a little taller and really handsome. Maybe make your ears just a little bit smaller."

"Sophia!"

"Oh, I don't know. Papa always said the universe is perfect the way it is even though it's not always how we want it to be. We might not like giant carnivorous centipedes, but they teach us valuable lessons, like how to overcome our fears."

"Hmmm... that's kind of what I was thinking. What about mice like Draken? If I had unlimited power I could just make him vanish and we'd be done with him."

"You could, but that doesn't seem right to me. He's greedy and horribly evil and only cares about power, and he killed Papa, but in the end he's still a mouse who used to be a little mouseling. There's always a chance he could change, even after the horrible, unforgivable things he's done, and if you killed him you would take away that chance."

"You're right. Mum says every mouse is here for a reason. I can't just go around picking out ones I don't like and making them vanish because they did something I don't agree with. Creekers, I don't even know why the Thirteenth Monk wants to give me this dumb power."

"Let's go walk through the orange grove. It's a beautiful sunny day, and those orange blossoms smell sooo good."

"Good idea, I'm tired of thinking about limitless power." Orville got to his feet and looked up at the gigantic tree. "Look at those leaves. I wouldn't want to be the one who had to rake up all the–" Orville stopped, looking at the ground around the tree. "Does it seem odd to you that there's not a single blue leaf on the ground anywhere?"

Sophia studied the ground beneath the tree. "You're right, that's very odd indeed. I don't think we should pick any more leaves off the tree. You really are the best at finding puzzles."

"I wish I was as good at solving them. I have a whole notebook filled with unsolved puzzles back in Muridaan Falls. I guess I'll just add this tree to my list."

Chapter 31

The Secret

Orville had a hard time falling asleep that night. He couldn't stop wondering about the secret to unlimited power, and wasn't even sure he wanted to know what it was. He liked things the way they were and he didn't want to turn into some kind of scary powerful mouse everyone was afraid of. Finally he drifted off to sleep. It seemed like only moments later when he was awakened by a gentle rapping on his door.

He heard the voice of the Fourth Monk. "Orville, the Thirteenth Monk is ready to see you."

"Okay." Orville jumped out of bed and threw on his clothes. Ten minutes later he was standing in front of the blue door with the Fourth Monk, and then he was sitting in his comfy green chair facing the Thirteenth Monk.

"You seem nervous, Orville. Are you worried about something?"

"Well, I'm kind of worried that my friends might be afraid of me if I have so much power. Maybe Sophia won't want to be my best friend any more."

"Ahh, I see. I assure you that all your friends will still like you. If I thought differently you would not be sitting here in front of me. I am going to tell you the secret to unlimited power, but it may not become clear until later on exactly how this secret allows you to access that power. What I say may not make sense to you right now, but the time will come when it does make sense. When you need it most is when you will understand."

The Thirteenth Monk leaned forward in his chair and whispered, "Every dream is real until you wake up."

Orville stared at him blankly. "What?"

"Repeat it, please."

"Every dream is real until you wake up."

"Excellent. Let the Fourth Monk know when you and Sophia are ready to return to Muridaan Falls. You may stay here as long as you wish. When you return you will arrive outside the Book Emporium the morning after Master Marloh sent you through his spectral door to Periculum." Before Orville could say a word the Thirteenth Monk faded away into nothingness.

Orville was more confused than ever. The Thirteenth Monk's whispered secret had not made the slightest bit of sense to him. "I don't understand what dreams have to do with unlimited power. Dreams aren't real, they're just in your head."

Sophia was equally as puzzled by the Thirteenth Monk's riddle as Orville was. "It doesn't make sense to me either. But he did say you won't understand it until you really need to, so I wouldn't worry about it. When the time comes you will understand it. Anyway, we can stay here as long as we want. Let's walk down to the ocean and skip a few stones. Whoever makes the biggest monster pop out of the water wins."

"Creekers! That sounds scary but fun. Proto can be

the judge – you know how much he loves those big scary monsters. Let's go!"

Sophia and Orville spent two lazy weeks at the monastery, strolling through the orange grove, having long conversations beneath the mysterious blue tree, and taking relaxing walks along the coastline. Sophia had ultimately won the stone skipping contest when an immense worm creature covered with long purple spikes had burst out of the water and snatched her stone out of the air. The creature's enormous yellow glowing eyes had focused on Orville and it let out a terrible piercing shriek. Sophia grabbed Orville just as he was toppling over. He adamantly insisted he had not fainted, but had simply tripped over a large rock. Proto declared Sophia the winner since she had attracted such a terrifying creature that it caused Orville to 'trip over a rock'.

Finally the day came when they decided it was time to return to Muridaan Falls. Orville found the Fourth Monk sitting in the garden and told him they were ready to go home.

"The Thirteenth Monk would like you and Sophia to wait in the main monastery building. The Blue Monks will sing for you."

"They'll sing for us? I don't understand."

"Their song will carry you back through the Void to Muridaan Falls. The Thirteenth Monk will explain this more fully to you before they sing."

After one final stroll through the glorious orange grove, Orville and Sophia headed to the monastery. As they approached the main building the Fourth Monk appeared, opening the blue door for them. "You may enter. Please stand in the center of the room."

This was Sophia's first glimpse at the interior of the building. "Orville, this is amazing. It's so old, and I feel such enormous power emanating from the stones, as though they have a life of their own."

"Perhaps they do." Sophia whirled around to see the Thirteenth Monk standing behind her. He smiled brightly and took her paw. "It is a pleasure to meet you, Sophia. Your father Rowland was a wonderful friend of ours, offering his kind assistance to us on numerous occasions. You should be very proud of him."

"Thank you, I am very proud of him."

"Wonderful. Orville, don't worry yourself about the secret to unlimited power. When you come to understand my words you will see it's really not much of a secret after all. When you gain this power you will be exactly the same mouse you are now, but your perspective of the universe will have taken a rather unexpected turn. Now, if you are both ready, I will join the other Blue Monks and we will sing for you. In some ways our songs are similar to shaping, in some ways they are not. We will be singing a song known as the *Ocean's Wordless Song of Incomparable Beauty*. All the elements of our world have their own song, but it is the ocean's song which will carry you home. You will both enter the Void, the space between all worlds. Once you are in the Void all worlds are only steps away. I will create a tear in the Void opening to the precise time and place of your arrival on Earth. When you see a sliver of light in the distance, simply will yourselves toward it and you will be there. Jump through the rift and you will be safely home. Oh, one last thing before you go." The Thirteenth Monk held out a round blue leaf. "Please take this. If you ever wish to return to Per-

234

iculum, hold this leaf and ask for my assistance. You will soon find yourself within the Void and on your way back to our monastery."

Orville couldn't help himself. "What kind of tree is that? There are no leaves on the ground anywhere around it."

The Thirteenth Monk smiled. "You are quite perceptive, Orville Wellington Mouse. I suspect you will make an excellent Metaphysical Adventurer and one day you will discover the answer to this marvelous puzzle. Please give my best regards to Master Marloh when you see him. We will sing for you now. It will help if you hold paws."

The Thirteenth Monk turned and walked slowly to the far end of the huge stone room.

Orville took Sophia's paw. They waited silently for the Blue Monks to begin.

Sophia saw the line of thirteen Blue Monks appear out of nothingness. She gripped Orville's paw tightly. "I'm kind of nervous."

When the first monk sang it was not at all what Orville and Sophia had been expecting. It was a clear and perfect sound, soft and smooth and full, and though it was barely audible it seemed to echo through the room for an eternity. Sophia gave a slight gasp. "Oh, this is so beautiful."

Two more Blue Monks joined in the song, forming a complex and exquisite melody, swirling and soaring through the echo of the first monk's voice. The resplendent harmony seemed to flow through Orville and Sophia, flow through the walls and floors of the monastery, flow through the vast empty spaces between all things. A thought popped into Orville's mind. "I am no different from the stones that form this building, I am a field of flowing energy just as the stones are, just as the song is that passes through us all."

Nine more voices joined in and Sophia and Orville were lost, carried away by the whirling joy of the song. They were the song now, they were the stones, they were the air, part of the vast and infinite universe. They swirled and flowed within the racing harmony of the song, flowing into a warm infinite darkness filled with the ocean's wordless song of incomparable beauty. It had become the song of the sky, the song of the trees, the song of life. Orville felt Sophia's presence but couldn't tell if they were still holding paws, or even if they still had paws. He had no voice, but her thoughts whirled about within him. "Orville, what is this place?"

"He said it was called the Void, the space between all worlds."

"It's so strange, I can't tell where I begin or where I end. I feel as though we are moving a thousand miles an hour, and yet standing perfectly still in absolute silence."

The Thirteenth Monk's voice entered the song, its sound filling Sophia and Orville with a deep and profound joy, the voice merging with their essence, carrying them forward through the infinite darkness of the Void. A sliver of light appeared in the distance.

Orville sent his thoughts to Sophia. "We just have to will ourselves toward the light." Before they had even begun, they were already there, gazing down into a crevasse of brilliant blinding light. Orville could see beautiful sunlit grass gleaming through the light.

"Sophia, we're home."

They tumbled down through the tear in the Void,

landing gently on the soft green grass of a small meadow only a few hundred feet away from the Book Emporium.

Orville jumped to his feet, grabbing Sophia's paw and pulling her up.

"We need to get to my house as soon as we can. I have to get the letter I wrote to Mum before she reads it!"

Chapter 32

Home Again

The two adventurers took off across the pasture, hopping over a wooden rail fence and dashing through streets and alleys until they reached Orville's home. Orville ran up the steps and into the house. He heard his Mum's footsteps coming down the stairs as he darted into the kitchen.

"It's still here!" Orville grabbed the letter and stuffed it into his pocket just as his Mum walked into the kitchen.

"Orville, if you don't want to be late for work you'd better get going. Hello, Sophia. Any news on your application to the Institute of Mechanistic Studies?"

"Oh, nothing yet, I'm afraid. Hopefully I'll hear from them soon."

"You must be a bundle of nerves waiting to hear what they say. It must be quite stressful."

"Yes, I'm kind of nervous, but I'm also hopeful."

"I don't think you have a thing to worry about. Orville tells me you're the smartest mouse he's ever met."

"Really? Is that true? I'm the smartest mouse you've ever met?" She gave Orville a wide smirky grin.

Orville snorted. "I don't recall saying any such thing. I guess you're a little bit clever though. Sometimes."

Orville's Mum laughed, waving them out of the kitchen.

"Off to work! You need to earn lots of money so you can support me when I'm old."

"I will, Mum. I promise." He headed for the front door with Sophia right behind him. The moment his house was out of sight they dashed into a nearby grove of trees.

"Whew, that was close! She was just coming down the stairs. How do you think the Thirteenth Monk sent us back in time like that?"

"I'm not sure, but I think it has to do with the Void. If the Void is outside of time and space, maybe you can enter it and then come back out at any place and any time. I think the hard part is entering the Void. That's what the Blue Monks' song was for, but it's way beyond anything I understand now."

Orville felt Proto moving around in his pack and unbuckled the flap. Proto poked his head out and looked around.

"Ahh, I see we're safely back on Earth. While you two have been gallivanting about I have been quite busy in the Cube working on my project. It's nearly complete, only another day or two and it will be done. Very exciting, I must say."

"You can't give us even a hint about what you're doing?"

"Oh, dear, I think not. That would ruin everything. Are you off to put a stop to the dastardly schemes of that dreadful scalawag, Draken Mouse? I would offer my services but I'm otherwise occupied at the moment."

Orville heard a loud whining noise coming from the glowbird. "Proto, what's that whining noise I hear?"

"Whining noise? Oh, nothing to be concerned about, I assure you. Well, I'd best be off now. Do give that horrible Draken Mouse a piece of my mind when you see him."

Orville felt the glowbird slump down into his pack.

Orville gave Sophia a puzzled look.

"What is Proto up to?"

Sophia grinned. "Whatever it is, he's having fun, and I'm happy to see that. I'm glad our friend Proto is spending less time on tasty snacks and has moved on to more enjoyable endeavors."

"He's right though, it's time to put a stop to Draken Mouse. Now that we have proof of his guilt, how do we go about this?"

"Let's go visit Master Marloh first. He'll know the best way to handle it."

"It's too bad we can't change our appearance with shaping so Draken Mouse won't recognize us. What's that called again?"

"It's called formshifting. It's a really advanced shaping skill. The concept is simple but it's difficult and very dangerous. You understand what blinking is, right?"

"Yes, the shaper converts their body to a thought cloud, then wills it to travel at enormous speed to another location where he converts the thought cloud back to his body again."

"Right, but the shaper can't stay in thought cloud form for more than two or three seconds or his consciousness enters a different state and he can't convert back to his physical self again."

"Yikes. That sounds scary."

"It is scary. That's why only the most advanced shapers can blink places. Formshifting is basically the same thing except you don't travel anywhere, and when you convert your thought cloud back to its physical form you create a new form that doesn't look like you at all."

"Huh? So I could turn myself into a rabbit?"

"Exactly. If we could formshift we could turn into any creature we wanted to. Master Marloh told me that Bartholomew the Adventurer once formshifted into a fly so he could sneak into the Fortress of Elders when evil King Oberon was still in power."

"Creekers. I don't think I'd want to be a fly."

"It might be fun to be a bird and soar over the mountains."

"That does sound fun. We could both be birds and fly to Pavorak Gorge to visit Proto."

"I guess we'd better go find Master Marloh. We can't formshift, but we could make some disguises, like big floppy hats and dark goggles or something."

"I think maybe two mice wearing big floppy hats and dark goggles might attract more attention than just wearing our normal clothes. The only mouse we have to really watch out for is Draken Mouse, and he thinks we're inside the belly of a carnivorous centipede on Periculum."

"You're right. We'll go in through the back door of the Book Emporium and find Master Marloh. We'll have to scout it out first to make certain Draken Mouse isn't there."

After a twenty minute walk Sophia and Orville reached the old barn behind the Book Emporium. They slipped into the barn and Orville peered out through a crack in the wood at the back door of the Emporium.

"I don't see any movement. Maybe we should sneak–" He let out a small gasp. "It's him! It's Draken Mouse! He's coming out the back door!" Sophia dashed over and peeked through the crack.

"He's leaving. This is perfect. Now we know for certain he's not here and we can talk to Master Marloh."

The pair of adventurers waited until Draken Mouse was out of sight then slipped out of the barn and over to the back door of the Book Emporium. Orville lifted the iron latch and they entered the shop.

Master Marloh was standing next to the blue door, a look of grave concern on his face. He looked up when he heard the back door open, his jaw dropping with stunned surprise at the sight of Sophia and Orville. He had sent them to Periculum only hours ago and there they were, standing in front of him.

"How did... how could you..." He stopped, quickly looking around to see who else was in the store, then waved them forward.

"Come with me, both of you, right now!" He dashed over to the blue door and opened it with his ring paw. He slammed the door shut behind them and they hurried down the long stone staircase.

"Master Marloh, we did it! We have proof that Draken Mouse killed Papa."

"I knew it! I knew he was behind it. Sophia, this is wonderful news, and your timing couldn't be better. In two days the High Council and all the members of the

Metaphysical Adventurers will meet to elect the new Supreme Counselor. Draken Mouse persuaded the council to hold the election, an election he is confident he will win. If he is elected he will make the use of lethal force an option for all members. That's the beginning of the end, the first step toward war and the ultimate destruction of Symoca. He must be stopped, no matter what the cost."

Safely down in the Metaphysical Adventurers Headquarters, Sophia showed Master Marloh the evidence they had against Draken Mouse and told him about their meeting with the Blue Monks. Proto projected onto a wall the moving images of Draken killing Rowland Mouse with the deadly beam of light. Orville had never seen Master Marloh so enraged, his paws clenched tightly as he watched the projection, his face grim and taut.

It took almost a full minute for Master Marloh to regain his composure.

"Your father Rowland was one of my dearest friends, Sophia, and Draken Mouse shall pay dearly for this horrific act of treason. We must be careful however, for he does have a following among the members of the Metaphysical Adventurers. He has lied and cajoled and blackmailed many members into promising him their support and their vote in the election. The timing of our revelation will be absolutely critical. It must be done in front of the entire membership and Draken must not be allowed to interrupt the projection. He is a powerful shaper and the full weight of his fury will be unleashed when he realizes what is happening. He is capable of anything, and he would kill either one of you without hesitation if it would save even one hair of his own fur. We need to formulate a foolproof plan. The election is in two days and that is when we must present the evidence against him. I must admit I am at a loss as to how we can prevent him from interfering with the glowbird's projection. Your friend Proto is familiar with the glowbirds. Do you think he might have any ideas?"

"He might. He's busy working on some kind of secret project, but I will talk to him. I'm certain he will help us any way he can."

"Excellent. Both of you must remain in hiding until the election. It's vital that Draken does not know you have returned from Periculum. He would kill you both in an instant."

"Master Marloh, what about formshifting? Could you formshift us into something else?"

"Just what I was thinking. I can change your faces quite easily, and make you both a little taller. That way you could move about freely, and if Draken did happen to see you at the Book Emporium his suspicions would not be aroused."

Orville said, "I'll tell Mum I'm going on a book hunting trip for three days and then hide out down here in the headquarters until the High Council meeting."

Sophia nodded. "I'll stay here with you, Orville. Together we can come up with a good plan. Let's talk to Proto tonight and see if he has any ideas. He knows a lot more about the glowbird's projection system than we do."

Master Marloh nodded. "Hurry back, we need to get you and Sophia safely formshifted as soon as possible."

Sophia grinned. "Any chance you could make Orville's big ears a little smaller?"

Chapter 33

A Beautiful Lesson

Orville was back in less than an hour, having told his Mum he was going to be visiting book stores in northern Symoca for three days. Master Marloh was waiting for him at the counter and they hurried down the stone stairway to the Metaphysical Adventurers Headquarters.

"Orville, I've talked to a few of the members here who I know to be trustworthy. They will keep their eyes and ears open for any sign of Draken Mouse or his followers. We are well aware who supports him and who does not."

"Are you going to formshift us now?"

"Yes, it won't take long. I will introduce you as two initiate members from western Opar. That should be a safe bet, as few Symocans have ever been to Opar. Just be aware that the land there was completely devastated during the Anarkkian War by cloud bombs and all manner of mechanical beasts released by the Anarkki-ans. The great silver attack spiders with their dreadful force beams were the worst, I am told."

"We saw those spiders, Master Marloh! Proto showed us the old Anarkkian records on moving image panels back at the Cube."

"Perfect, that will work in your favor in the event anyone asks you questions about Opar. Now, what do you want to look like? Wait, don't answer that. I believe I have a solution which will provide a rather enlightening lesson while still concealing your true identity." Master Marloh grinned. "Let's go find Sophia."

They found Sophia talking to a Metaphysical Adventurer about spectral doorways and their creation. He was demonstrating to her an old Anarkkian device officially designated the *Model M1 Portable Spectral Field Actualizer*, a device capable of producing a small spectral doorway to other worlds.

"This was used by the Anarkkian Secret Forces to infiltrate behind enemy lines. The troopers nicknamed it Death's Door, not for any sort of unreliability, but because very few of the troopers returned from these inherently dangerous missions. Quite a remarkable machine, and a reminder to us that shaping is not magic, but is based in deep physics and science."

Sophia glanced up from the device and saw Orville approaching.

"Hi, Orville, are you ready to get formshifted?"

"I guess so. Master Marloh says he's going to change us into something that will be enlightening, whatever that means."

Sophia gave a frown. "Enlightening events usually aren't very much fun."

Master Marloh looked extremely amused.

"Oh, I think this one will be fun. You two follow me."

Master Marloh found a quiet practice room which

offered complete privacy. "I'm probably being overly cautious, but I want to make certain none of Draken's followers witness your formshifting. Who's first?"

Sophia raised her paw. "I volunteer Orville to be first."

"Huh?"

Master Marloh laughed. "Orville it is then. Now, let me see... ah, I have it. This should work nicely."

He raised both paws and Orville glowed with a brilliant blue light then abruptly vanished.

"And now, the new Orville." He flicked his paws and a mouse appeared where Orville had been standing.

Sophia gave a loud gasp. "Creekers! Look at him!"

Orville looked down at his formshifted body with concern. "What?? Why are you saying creekers? Am I scary looking?"

Sophia shook her head emphatically.

"No, you're the most handsome mouse I have ever seen in my entire life. You are ridiculously handsome. I can't take my eyes off you. Creekers. Double creekers."

"I'm handsome? I've always wanted to be handsome." He raised one eyebrow with a grin and gazed deeply into Sophia's eyes.

"Creeeekers... you are so handsome. I think I'm going to melt."

"Now it's your turn, Sophia." Sophia was bathed in the brilliant blue light, vanishing an instant later. With a bright flash of blue light a new mouse appeared where she had been standing.

It was Orville's turn to gasp. "Whoa! You are beautiful! You're so beautiful it hurts my eyes to look at you, but I can't stop looking."

"I'm beautiful? Thanks, Orville. No one has ever

said that to me before."

"I said it to you once, remember?"

"Oh, after I practically had to pull it out of you with a big pair of pliers."

Sophia found herself gazing into Orville's eyes, realizing she had completely lost her train of thought.

"What was I saying? You are *so* handsome. I could just sit here all day staring at you." Sophia gave a long sigh, resting her chin on her paw as she gazed at Orville.

"I can't take my eyes off you, Sophia. I've never seen a mouse as stunningly beautiful as you. I could spend the rest of my life just looking into your eyes."

Master Marloh had an enormous grin on his face.

"All right, you two, it's safe to go out in public now. Would you mind running down to the general store and getting me a large ball of green twine?"

"I could shape one for you. I'm a little busy looking at Sophia right now."

"No, they have a very special green twine at the general store. Nothing else will do, I'm afraid."

"Master Marloh, isn't Sophia beautiful?"

"Yes, quite beautiful, Orville."

"You're so much more handsome than I am beautiful, Orville."

"Thanks, Sophia, but I'm quite certain your beauty is unsurpassed in this world or any other."

Master Marloh interrupted them. "The twine? You were going to get me some twine?"

"Oh, of course. Let's go."

Soon Orville and Sophia were strolling down the street toward the general store. Orville was finding it impossible to take his eyes off Sophia. "Your face is like an exquisite painting, your eyes the deepest blue green color I–"

Orville never finished his sentence. He never finished it because he walked into a low hanging branch.

"OWWW! My head! I knocked my head on that dumb tree!"

Sophia looked at him with concern. "Are you all right? You... you... you're *sooo* handsome. Your fur is so smooth, so perfect, and your eyes... I can't seem to..."

"Stop saying how handsome I am! I just walked into a tree and almost bashed my brains out because I couldn't stop looking at you."

"Oh, sorry. This is not exactly what I thought being beautiful would be like. It's just that you're *so* handsome..."

Sophia noticed two mice approaching them and stepped out their way. One of mice nodded his thanks, glancing over at Sophia.

"Creekers, you're a beauty! Where have you been all my life? Would you mind if I just stood here forever and gazed at you? Your eyes, so green... your fur is so smooth and the color of honey, with..."

Sophia found herself suddenly very embarrassed.

"Stop saying that, please. You don't even know me, you can't just say things like that to someone you don't know."

The mouse stopped, giving Sophia an irritated look.

"Oh, I get it, too beautiful for the likes of us? Just want to be with your ridiculously handsome friend? Fine with me, you two belong together, a pair of snooty little beautiful mice."

The two mice turned and walked away, laughing

loudly for the benefit of Sophia and Orville.

"Was I being snooty?"

"Not at all, Sophia. He shouldn't have said those things to you when he doesn't even know you... even though your beauty overwhelms my senses, your eyes, so green, your fur so..."

"Stop! Stop that right now. Stop saying how beautiful I am! This is going to drive me mad. I can't walk down the street without mice stopping me, and I can't take my eyes off you because you're so handsome. How are we supposed to get anything done? We have to figure out how to keep Draken from disrupting Proto's projection during the meeting."

"Oh, I forgot about that. We also need to get the green twine for Master Marloh."

"Master Marloh doesn't need any twine. He just wanted us to walk around in public so we'd see what it was like to be amazingly beautiful. Nobody cares who we really are, all they see is how beautiful we are. They don't care how smart I am or how good you are at finding puzzles. They don't care how cute it is that you faint at the sight of giant centipedes."

"You think that's cute? I hate it that I faint."

"I love it that you faint. It makes you special. Papa used to tell me it's our flaws that make us lovable. He used to laugh and say our flaws make us perfect."

"He might be right. I like it that you're so bossy and always think you know everything."

"What did you just say??"

"Umm, well, just a little bit bossy... sometimes. Not really very much at all when I think about it, though."

Sophia laughed. "Papa used to say that about me too. I know I'm really smart and I guess I like to show off sometimes, and I do like to be in charge."

"We should go back. I want Master Marloh to formshift us again into not so beautiful mice."

They turned around and headed back to the Book Emporium, crossing the street several times to avoid approaching mice.

"Whew, I'm glad I don't have to do this every day."

Master Marloh could not stop grinning when he saw them step back through the door after only fifteen minutes. "Back so soon? How was your walk?"

"Please make us not quite so beautiful. It caused far more trouble than I ever imagined it would."

"Congratulations, you two have learned a valuable lesson in a very short amount of time. It doesn't mean much if a mouse only finds value in your physical self. True friendship begins when another mouse appreciates you for who you really are."

Chapter 34

Back in a Blink

"This is much better, now I can concentrate again. Orville, do you still think I'm beeeyoootiful?"

"Creekers, don't ever ask me that again."

Orville opened the flap on his pack and took Proto out, setting him on a nearby table.

"Proto, we're here in the Metaphysical Adventurers Headquarters below the Book Emporium. Are you there? Proto? Proto?"

The glowbird abruptly moved its head, then stood up.

"I'm here, Orville. My apologies, I was just putting the final touches on my special project. I'll be testing it tonight. If you see a gigantic orange explosion on the horizon you'll know it was less than successful."

"What? Proto, whatever you're doing, please be careful."

"I am quite indestructible, I assure you. Now, what did you need to know?"

"We need your help, Proto. We're planning to reveal the truth about Draken Mouse at the Metaphysical

Adventurers High Council meeting two nights from now. Draken Mouse will be there, and we're afraid if the glowbird is projecting the images onto a wall Draken will simply blast the glowbird to pieces and that will be the end of it."

"Quite a quandary indeed. Hmmm... one moment while I check something. Hmmm hmmm... mmm... yes, that should work... transferring data now... mmm hmm... that does it. Yes, quite humorous, this should work. Ha ha ha ha! Orville, I believe I have just this moment concocted a foolproof plan to deter any action taken by Draken Mouse. I will take care of everything, as always. I've transferred all the data from the glowbird to a crystalline storage cube. You need not worry about a single thing. It will be Proto to the rescue, once again! I do have one question, however. Which do you believe mice would perceive to be funnier, a joke about my mother-in-law or a joke about my very unlikeable first wife?"

"Proto, what are you talking about? You don't have a mother-in-law or a first wife. Why are you asking me this?"

"Very well, one mother-in-law joke and one first wife joke."

"Proto, the sort of jokes you're talking about don't sound appropriate for a meeting like this. I really think you should tell us what you're planning, so we know what to expect."

"What to expect? You may expect a surprise! Ha ha ha ha! Rest assured, I have everything under control. Nothing can possibly go wrong, my plan is quite foolproof. Just relax and have a pleasant evening with your lovely friend Sophia. You said the meeting is in three days?"

"*Two* days, Proto! The meeting is in *two* days at the Metaphysical Adventurers Headquarters below the Book Emporium. It starts at eight o'clock in the evening. Members will be blinking in from all over."

"Very well, I have calculated precisely the necessary space-time coordinates. We're set to go. I'd better get busy, as I have dozens of tests to run before I'm ready."

The glowbird slumped down on the table and closed its eyes.

"Proto? Are you still there?"

Orville looked up at Sophia. "What should we do? I know Proto means well, but I'm not certain about this plan of his. I have no idea why he's asking about jokes."

"Well... I can't think of anything else we can do. Draken is far too powerful a shaper for us to confront head on. Perhaps we should have faith in our good friend Proto. Maybe he was introduced to us for just this reason."

Orville did not look entirely convinced, but nodded.

"I suppose there's nothing else we can do. At least we know he has a copy of Draken's glowbird record safely stored in the Cube. That's something, I guess. Now we just sit and wait for two days?"

"No, Master Marloh wants us to practice blinking. Given our current predicament he thinks we need to become proficient in it."

"I thought you said it was only for advanced shapers?"

"Master Marloh thinks we're ready. I've already blinked a few times, and he said you'll pick it up right away. He's certain we'll do fine. He said we need to practice it until we can blink without thinking."

"Well, if he thinks we can do it, I guess it should be all right."

The following morning Orville rose early and found Sophia out on the main floor of the headquarters. She was having her breakfast while watching one of the advanced members creating a spectral door.

"Hi, Orville! Here's some breakfast for you. You should see him open these spectral doors. It's amazing."

"Thanks."

Orville watched with fascination as a mouse wearing a long dark cloak cupped his paws together, a small vaporous glowing sphere appearing above them. The sphere grew in substance, turning a marvelous shade of blue green, tiny bolts of lightning flashing around its periphery, then expanded rapidly to a diameter of fifteen feet, floating ten feet above the mouse's head. Dark clouds were swirling wildly inside it, sharp claps of thunder echoing through the main room. Great flashes of lightning created dancing light and shadows across the floor.

Orville's breakfast tray tumbled to the floor with a great crash when the enormous creature wriggled out of the spectral door. Orville's first thought was of the beasts in the Senyph Ocean, but this particular mon-strosity had legs, not fins. In fact, it had a dozen legs, and attached to each leg was a set of six frightfully long glowing green claws. Orville wasn't certain if the creature actually had a face, but there were six yellow orbs on the end of long waving tentacles which may have been eyes, and something resembling a snake's blue forked tongue flicking in and out of a round aperture filled with hundreds of small pointy teeth. The creature hit the floor with a horrible wet smack, the yellow orbs whirling about on their sinewy blue tentacles. The orbs were now all pointing toward Orville, and with a great howl the hideous monstrosity began clawing its way across the floor toward him.

Three things happened in rapid succession. First, Orville's legs gave out from under him and he began to fall. Second, Sophia lunged forward and grabbed him before he could hit the floor. Third, the mouse in the dark cloak shot out a brilliant beam of blue light and the hideous creature vanished, blinked back to its own world.

"Sorry! Is your friend okay? Must be his first en-counter with a Plindorian Swamp Hornet. Kind of scary looking, aren't they?"

Orville was still groggy but sitting up. "Is that thing gone? What happened?"

"I think you tripped on your chair when you were jumping up to save me from that awful beast."

Orville studied Sophia's face. "You really think it's cute when I faint?"

"I think it's adorable."

"Well, I guess it's okay then. Maybe Master Marloh can help me with it."

"Speaking of Master Marloh, we're supposed to meet him in the second practice room right after breakfast."

Orville made a wide detour around the flashing spectral doorway and they headed toward the practice room where Master Marloh was waiting for them.

"Ah, there you are. Ready to learn about blinking? We have a lot to cover in a short time, so lets begin. You are both fully capable of creating objects from thought clouds by compressing the energy fields into physical matter. You are also able to convert physical matter back into energy fields again. Blinking is simply the process of converting your own physical body into an energy field, willing it to travel a certain distance, and then converting the energy field back into your physical body again. Sophia, you have done this a number of times. What was the most difficult part of the process for you?"

"Being an energy field without a body was very strange, even though it lasted for less than a second. It felt dreamlike, as though I was just floating conscious-ness. I didn't want it to end, but I knew if I stayed in that form for more than two or three seconds I would not be able to convert back again."

"Precisely. You have to be able to convert back and forth almost instantly. Go ahead and demonstrate blinking for Orville."

Sophia held one paw out and glowed with a brilliant blue light, vanishing a split second later. She reap-peared almost instantly across the room.

"Creekers, that was amazing."

"Thanks. It's not too hard once you get used to the feeling of being a cloud of energy."

Master Marloh pointed to the wooden chair sitting next to Orville. "Orville, convert that chair to an energy field and back again, over and over as quickly as you can."

Orville held out his paw and a bright blue light flashed out. Sophia watched as the chair rapidly blinked in and out of existence.

"Excellent job. Now, instead of the chair, I want you to blink me across the room. No need to worry, if for some reason you are taking too long I will convert myself back to physical form. Just pretend I'm a chair."

Orville nodded and the blue beam of light flashed again. Master Marloh vanished, almost instantly reappearing across the room.

"Wonderful. It's almost as if you've done this before. Now, I want you to blink yourself into a thought cloud and back again. If you're taking too long I will take over."

"When I'm an energy field with no body I can still think?"

"Of course. Your mind is separate from your physical body. You will not have a body but you will still have the consciousness and awareness you are used to."

"Well, here goes." Orville glowed a brilliant blue and vanished. Less than a second later he blinked back again. "Creekers, that was amazing! You're right, Sophia, I didn't want it to end. I was just a cloud of energy and I could move around anywhere I wanted."

Master Marloh stepped over and clapped Orville on the back. "Well done, both of you. You have both successfully blinked, something which many shapers never do even after a lifetime of practice. That being said, you still have much to learn. You need to blink without thinking about it." A long gleaming dagger appeared on the chair next to Orville. "Orville, I want you to throw that knife at me as hard as you can."

"Huh?"

"Throw it at me, but don't tell me when you're going to throw it. Don't worry, you won't be able to hit me with it."

Orville reached down and picked up the knife. Without warning he hurled the deadly dagger at Master

Marloh. Before the dagger had even left his paw Master Marloh was standing next to Orville.

"See how fast I moved? I could have used a sphere of defense, but by blinking next to you I now hold the advantage of surprise. Both of you need to practice your speed. When you're comfortable with it, I want you to throw a ball at each other and blink before the ball hits you. We have two days left until the High Council meets. You must be completely proficient in the art of blinking by then. Do not underestimate the shaping skills of Draken Mouse, or his willingness to use deadly force against you. The instant he realizes the significance of Proto's projection he will react, and I know you are well aware of how a vicious beast reacts when cornered."

Chapter 35

Stop.

Orville cracked the door open, peering anxiously out onto the main floor of the Metaphysical Adventurers Headquarters.

"They're starting to arrive!" He watched as blue lights blinked across the room like fireflies on a warm summer night, each flash heralding the arrival of a mouse, rabbit, or muroidian. The main room, once filled with practice areas, work stations, and laboratories was now a sea of chairs, all facing a solitary raised podium on a wide stage.

Sophia squeezed in next to Orville and peeked out. "How do you think Proto is going to do it? There's not much time left. Once all the members are here Draken Mouse will be introduced, make his grand entrance, and then give his speech. There will be a show of paws and the election will be over."

Orville studied Sophia's face. He had never seen her so tense.

"He'll do something, I know he will. Proto would never let us down."

"Not on purpose. But if something goes wrong I will go out there myself and tell them everything I know."

Master Marloh stepped across the small practice room toward them. "I don't believe it will come to that, Sophia. I'm getting a good feeling about tonight."

With a brilliant flash two long green cloaks appeared in his paw.

"Put these cloaks on when you go out there. Green cloaks are worn by initiate members of the Metaphysical Adventurers. With these cloaks on, your unfamiliar faces won't arouse any suspicion. Sit as close to the podium as you can. We have no idea what Proto is going to do, but we must be ready for anything. Don't forget there are a lot of members who support Draken, so no talking. Use thought clouds if you need to communicate. Ready?"

Master Marloh pushed the door open and stepped out into the main room, Sophia and Orville trailing behind him. "Come on, Sophia, let's go find seats near the front of the room."

The room was filling rapidly, the blue lights of arriving members flashing almost continuously, the room echoing with the dull drone of a hundred different conversations. Sophia and Orville were just in time and found two empty seats in the third row.

The blue flashes finally dwindled and then stopped. The room grew quiet as a distinguished elderly mouse slowly made his way up to the podium. A gavel blinked into his paw and he rapped the podium three times.

"I bring this meeting of the High Council of Metaphysical Adventurers to order, and offer my heartfelt thanks for your presence here this evening. You all know why we are here. Draken Mouse has presented us

261

with the requisite number of signatures for a show of paws to determine whether or not he is to be our new Supreme Counselor. I understand there are strong feelings on both sides regarding this matter, and perhaps even more so regarding the potential use of lethal force by our members. Please remain silent during Draken Mouse's presentation. If you must communicate with other members, have the courtesy to use thought clouds." The old mouse gazed slowly across the sea of members. "Above all, listen to your inner voice, listen to your heart. I now present to you the candidate for the position of Supreme Counselor of the Metaphysical Adventurers, Master Draken Mouse."

There was a brilliant flash of golden light and a mouse appeared near the podium. He was wearing a long formal blue cloak and approached the elderly mouse, firmly shaking his paw. He gave a friendly wave to the crowd of members.

"Thank you, thank you all for being here on this very auspicious occasion. I know I have many support-ers in this room, but I also know there are many members who are uncertain about what they may perceive as a radical new proposal regarding the use of deadly force. Let me assure you I am not suggesting the Metaphysical Adventurers go on a mad killing spree, destroying any mouse or rabbit or muroidian who disagrees with our views. What I am suggesting is that in the very rare instance when a member's life is in jeopardy and there is absolutely no alternative, that he or she may be allowed to save their own life or the life of a loved one through the use of lethal force. There are no secret hidden agendas, simply a deep hope that opening this new option will save the precious lives of some of our members."

Draken look out across the crowd, his face a picture of deep sincerity and concern.

"Liar!" The word popped out of Sophia's mouth before she even realized she had said it. There were a few murmurs in the crowd.

Draken Mouse frowned, trying to spot the source of the interruption. He was about to say something when he was interrupted by a sudden cry from the other side of the room.

"Spectral door!"

A mouse leaped to his feet and pointed up to an enormous black swirling spectral doorway, bolts of white lightning flashing wildly within the dark churning clouds. Hundreds of spheres of defense popped up across the room as the members leaped to their feet.

"What is it? Where it is from?"

Draken Mouse popped up a powerful sphere of defense, his eyes blazing with fury. He had the crowd eating out of his paw and someone had dared to interrupt him. Whoever was responsible would pay dearly.

The members cried out in unison as a large blue sphere shot out from the spectral door and hovered silently above the crowd. The roiling spectral door vanished, leaving behind the mysterious metallic sphere.

"What is that thing? What is it doing here? Is that an old blinker ship?" They watched with concern as the sphere descended until it was floating only ten feet above the main floor. A voice boomed out from the craft.

"Oh my, this is quite thrilling indeed! So many

shapers and adventurers all in one big room. I'm sad to say I don't have a single tasty snack or beverage to offer you, but do feel free to shape any manner of refreshments you choose. I thought this would be the perfect time to begin my presentation. Our talk today will be on the dreadfully frightening and hideously brutal creatures found on the planet known as Periculum. If you think you would be able to survive on Periculum without using lethal force, I'm afraid you would be quite mistaken. Good heavens, just feast your eyes on these frightful gigantic carnivorous centipedes!"

Draken Mouse had no idea what was happening. This was not part of the show, but it certainly couldn't hurt. Whoever this was obviously supported the use of lethal force. This could work to his advantage. Draken called out, "Everyone take their seats please! It's all just a bit of theatrics to help make my point."

Orville shot a thought cloud to Sophia. "It's Proto! That's Proto's voice!"

"What is he doing? He's supposed to be exposing Draken as a murdering fiend, not supporting him!" Sophia looked furious.

"Just wait. I know he won't let us down."

A wide beam of light shot out from the blue sphere and spread across the expansive wall behind the podium. Draken Mouse gave a sudden start when he saw the gigantic mass of writhing centipedes, then laughed to himself, knowing that Orville Mouse and his little friend Sophia were probably inside one of them.

Proto's voice rang out again. "Just look at those beasts! They'd be the perfect pet for my mother-in-law – if they weren't too frightened of her!"

The crowd roared with laughter. Draken Mouse was thrilled. He rubbed his paws together with glee. What a stroke of good luck this was.

"Look out, here's one of those terrifying Gnorli birds, the only beast alive feared by the great carnivorous centipedes of Periculum. Who wouldn't consider using lethal force if this brute was screaming down from the sky toward you or a cherished loved one? Simply dreadful, but nothing at all compared to *this* hideous monstrosity!"

A moving image of the rolling Senyph Ocean now covered the front wall. Without warning a huge glistening orange wormlike creature resembling a centipede with six wings and a mouth filled with razor sharp teeth flashed out of the water. Cries erupted from the crowd, followed by clapping and cheering.

Proto's voice rang out again. "I think I just found the perfect vacation spot for my first wife! Come on in, the water's fine!" Again the crowd roared with laughter.

A second beast leaped out of the water, a ghastly creature with two green heads and a long wriggling scaly body covered with sharp yellow spikes. It opened its gaping mouth, revealing row after row of horrifically long curved teeth.

"If that's not a good enough reason to use lethal force, I don't know what is."

Proto paused for effect, then continued. "Except perhaps for this terrifying beast! Hold on to your adventuring hats and take a look at this monstrous creation!"

The image of the Senyph Ocean vanished, replaced by a close up view of a sparkling silver scout ship.

"Whoops, where did this come from? One moment

please while I adjust this storage crystal!"

The group watched as a mouse stepped into view. They recognized him immediately as Sophia's Papa, Rowland Mouse. So did Draken Mouse. He froze, a look of terror washing across his face.

"No. No! This is impossible! Stop this right now!!"

The crowd gave a unified gasp as the huge image of Draken Mouse appeared on the wall, obviously angry at Rowland Mouse. They watched as the two mice argued, Draken Mouse suddenly shoving Rowland away from him. They watched as Rowland held up his paws and backed away from Draken. They watched as Draken Mouse snarled and shot out a brilliant beam of purple light that hit Rowland square in the back. They watched as Rowland tumbled lifelessly to the ground. There was a terrible silence, then a furious roar of anger erupted from the members, so loud it shook the entire building. Rowland Mouse had been a trusted and beloved friend to many, and as one, the group shouted out their protest against Draken Mouse.

Draken Mouse shrieked, "LIES! Nothing but lies! It's a trick! Who is responsible for this?? Tell me right now who is behind this vicious plot to destroy my good name?? Stand up now and show your face, you sniveling coward!!"

Before Orville realized what was happening Sophia had shifted back to her true form and stood up to face Draken Mouse.

"I am responsible for this! Rowland Mouse was my father and I have irrefutable proof that you ruthlessly murdered him for your own personal gain. You murdered my father so you could have his job!"

Sophia pulled a sheet of paper from her cloak and

waved it in the air.

"This is a letter written to me by my father exposing you for the fiendish creature you are. We know about your plans to start a war and invade Lapinor and Grymmore, we know about your plans to turn the Metaphysical Adventurers into a brutal militaristic force under your evil control!"

Every member of the Metaphysical Adventurers leaped to their feet. A tall, red cloaked rabbit bellowed, "Draken's not fit to be a member of the Metaphysical Adventurers! Throw the murderer in Malgraven Prison!" Cheers rang out from the crowd.

Draken Mouse looked as though he might explode. His paws were tightly clenched, his face seething with a horrific burning anger. Sophia had never seen such rage in a mouse. His eyes were red and bulging, his fury focused directly at Sophia. Draken's mind was gone. He shrieked, "You! You're supposed to be dead, along with your friend Orville Mouse! Well, you'll be dead soon enough!" He gave a maniacal screech and held out both paws, an inconceivably brilliant purple light blasting out across the room aimed with deadly intent at Sophia.

An odd thing happened when Orville saw the purple light flashing across the room toward Sophia. It wasn't something he had planned, and to be truthful it wasn't even on his mental list of things which might possibly happen. But, nevertheless, out of Orville's mouth popped a single word.

"Stop."

There was something about the way he said it that rang familiar. Then he remembered it was exactly the same word the little mouseling in his woodcutter dream had spoken. Much to Orville's surprise, the instant he said the word, everything around him stopped. The brilliant beam of purple light stopped, frozen in mid air. Orville glanced about the room in wonder. His dear friend Sophia, along with every other member of the Metaphysical Adventurers, had been transformed into living statues. He looked across the room at Draken Mouse, his frozen face twisted and contorted with a monstrous rage. He wondered how a mouse could be filled with so much hatred and burning anger.

Orville was surprised and yet not surprised when the Thirteenth Monk blinked into view on the podium next to Draken Mouse. He studied Draken's face curiously, then blinked down next to Orville.

"Good evening, Orville Wellington Mouse. You've been quite busy, I see. I don't know of many mice who are capable of stopping time with a single word. Tell me what you've learned today."

The words of the Thirteenth Monk jarred Orville's memory. He realized he had changed profoundly in the fraction of a second before he had uttered the word, "Stop."

The transformation had occurred so quickly he could barely comprehend it, never mind putting it into coherent words for the Thirteenth Monk.

Orville put one paw over his eyes, trying to think, trying to remember. "I heard your voice in my head. I heard the words you said to me in the monastery. *Every dream is real until you wake up.* Somehow, in that split second I realized that the woodcutter dream seemed absolutely real until I woke up inside the dream. The dream was real until I woke up, and once I woke up I could do anything, even destroy the ferocious forest

268

wolf. I simultaneously realized that the world I live in, the world of Muridaan Falls, the world of everything and everyone I am familiar with has always seemed absolutely real to me. Until that fraction of a second when I woke up in this world, just as I woke up in my dream. I understood clearly then the source of unlimited power. Just as the woodcutter and the wolf and the trees and the stars shared a single consciousness in my dream, so does every mouse and rabbit and every tree and star and galaxy in this world that I call my home. There were no limitations for me now. I could access the shared power of every shaper in this room, of every shaper on every planet in the universe. I could access the power of a billion stars, a trillion galaxies. And I could use the power of an entire universe against one angry little mouse who took the life of another mouse simply for his own personal gain."

The Thirteenth Monk motioned for Orville to take a seat. "What will you do now? What will you do with this infinite source of power?"

Orville shook his head. "I don't know. Draken Mouse tried to kill Sophia, and he succeeded in killing Sophia's Papa."

"So you will kill him?"

"No. I can't do that. If I killed him I would become just another Draken Mouse, become the very thing I am fighting against."

"This is a good start. Just because you possess un-limited power doesn't mean you are obligated to use it. Draken Mouse is a villainous, brutal, egotistical, murdering fiend. But he is still a mouse, and as you well know, he shares a consciousness with you, just as the wolf and the little mouseling shared a consciousness in your dream. They are one. If the wolf kills the mouseling he is killing part of himself, and if you kill Draken Mouse you would be killing part of yourself. So, I ask you again, what will you do?"

"The world needs to be protected from mice like him. I will take away his shaping powers and he will be placed in Malgraven Prison. After that, it is up to him and him alone. He must choose between hatred and love."

The Thirteenth Monk nodded. "As it should be. We are all exactly where we should be at every moment in time. We are all connected and we are all here to help each other awaken to the true wonder of this world. Even a creature as despicable as Draken Mouse serves a purpose. Perhaps he has taught you the greatest lesson of your life, Orville Wellington Mouse. You can be grateful to him at least for that."

"Do you think I should tell Sophia about... this waking up business?"

"That's up to you, but do remember every mouse is learning exactly what they need to learn at this moment, nothing more. When Sophia is ready you will know it."

"I think I understand. Well, now that I've stopped time, I guess I need to figure out how to start it again. I also need to do something about that purple beam of light shooting toward Sophia."

"I imagine you'll think of something." With a smile and a quick wave the Thirteenth Monk vanished. Orville found himself standing alone in the vast silent sea of living statues. He studied Sophia's face and saw the beginning of fear in her eyes. She had realized the purple beam was heading toward her.

Orville put his arms around Sophia and gently lifted

her out of the beam's path. "That should do it."

He walked across the room to the podium and stepped up onto the stage. He gazed at Draken Mouse's snarling face.

"You are such an angry mouse. We certainly don't want you shooting deadly beams of purple light at anyone else." Orville held out one paw and streams of colored light flowed out of Draken Mouse and up through the ceiling. A pair of heavy iron manacles blinked onto Draken's outstretched wrists.

"And that, as they say, is that." Orville walked back across the room and stood next to Sophia. He whispered a single word.

"Start."

The room was chaos, two hundred screaming mice popping up spheres of defense while pointing to the beam of deadly light Draken had shot across the room toward Sophia. The two best friends were standing a safe distance away when the beam vaporized both their chairs.

Draken Mouse screeched with rage when he realized he had not harmed Sophia. He spotted Orville and Sophia and tried to shoot another beam, but much to his dismay discovered his arms were tightly manacled. When he tried to blink away the manacles, he could not. When he tried to blink himself out of the room, he could not. His shaping powers were gone, sent up into the starry night sky by Orville Wellington Mouse.

Sophia cried out, "The beam missed us! We need to stop him!"

Orville grabbed her arm. "It's all right! He can't hurt anyone now."

Sophia looked up at the podium and saw Draken

Mouse surrounded by a group of burly Metaphysical Adventurers, heavy iron manacles on his wrists. He was screeching wildly at them, threatening to vaporize them all.

Sophia looked puzzled. "Why doesn't he blink off the manacles?"

Orville grinned. "You and I need to have a talk."

Sophia nodded absently, watching as the Metaphysical Adventurers trundled Draken Mouse over to a swirling spectral doorway. Sophia could sense that this particular spectral doorway led to the dark and infamous Malgraven Prison. She also knew Orville was right. Draken Mouse would never harm another living creature. She reached into her cloak and withdrew her Papa's silver Metaphysical Adventurers ring, clutching it tightly in her paw until Draken Mouse had disappeared through the spectral doorway.

Chapter 36

The Scream

Two days later Sophia and Orville were sitting comfortably under the large shade tree behind Orville's home.

"I told you Proto wouldn't let us down."

It was the first time Orville had ever seen Sophia give a look of chagrin.

"I should never have doubted him. I guess I was so worried that Draken Mouse would get away with murdering Papa that I didn't want to give up control, but I have to admit Proto's tactics were truly brilliant. I think he surprised me even more than he surprised Draken Mouse. His jokes were a little bit rude but also kind of funny. Who would have guessed a Rabbiton could have a sense of humor and understand what makes mice laugh? As long as I live I will never forget the look on Draken Mouse's face when he realized he had been exposed. It's hard to believe one mouse could be filled with so much rage and hatred."

"Would you like another little cake? Every since I gave Mum the recipe there's been no shortage of them in our house."

Sophia was opening her mouth to reply when they

heard the scream. It was a shrill piercing scream that carried with it a sense of unbridled terror, and it had come from the front of Orville's house. An image of the little mouseling in his woodcutter dream popped into Orville's mind. The two friends leaped to their feet and blinked into the front yard. Orville spotted a mouseling pointing up at the sky, her face a mask of fear.

Orville was the first to see it, a large pale blue metallic sphere descending from the sky. Sophia ran over and picked up the mouseling.

"It's all right, little one, the big blue ball won't hurt you. I think it just wants to talk to us. Isn't it funny that a big blue ball from the sky could talk to us?"

The little mouseling snuggled closer to Sophia, not looking entirely convinced that a huge talking blue ball coming down from the sky was something to laugh about.

With a soft humming noise the gleaming sphere settled gently on the ground in front of Orville's house. Neighbors were peering out from their windows, some rushing outside and calling their mouselings home while gazing fearfully at the sphere.

A curved rectangular panel on the side of the craft hissed open, folding downward to create a stairway. There was a collective gasp from the dozens of anxious spectators as a ten foot tall silver Rabbiton strode out of the ship and down the stairs. The only sound was the whispering breeze as every mouse present waited to see what this astonishing creature would do.

"Oh my, this is not at all as scary as I thought it would be, and even better, there's not a single Anarkkian Attack Spider in sight. Everyone looks so friendly, as if we've been dear neighbors for a hundred years.

274

What a lovely little village. Quite peaceful and utterly picturesque."

Proto smiled and waved to the crowd of wide eyed mice.

Sophia ran over and threw her arms around Proto. "Proto! Thank you from the bottom of my heart! Your plan worked perfectly! Draken Mouse is in Malgraven Prison, exposed for the murdering beast that he is. Thank you dear Proto, for all your wonderful help."

"You're ever so welcome. I quite enjoy being thanked for something besides a tasty snack or a warm beverage. I quite like it, indeed. Speaking of tasty snacks, I almost forgot the lovely gift tray I have for all your charming neighbors."

Proto dashed up the stairs into the ship, returning moments later with an enormous tray laden down with several hundred tasty little cakes, freshly baked cookies of every size and shape, and dozens of little white boxes filled with delicious chocolate creams. He carried the tray over to the growing crowd of mice, some who backed away nervously at his approach.

"Would anyone care for a light snack? I have tasty little cakes, an assortment of freshly baked cookies, and a wide variety of delicious chocolate creams. I've been told with some authority by Orville Wellington Mouse that the lemon creams are quite delightful."

Five minutes later Proto was surrounded by almost a hundred mice clamoring for tasty snacks.

"Oh my, you're all so hungry! How wonderful!"

Sophia could not stop smiling.

"How does he do it, Orville? I've never seen anyone make friends faster than Proto does. It's hard to comprehend how much he has changed since we first met him at the Cube. Somewhere he found the courage to step outside of the Cube and fly an old restored blinker ship all the way to Muridaan Falls. In five minutes those mice lost their fear of him despite his size and appearance. Look, there's even a mouseling sitting on his shoulders!"

"I think he should make Muridaan Falls his new home. He could stay with me and Mum. Do you think my Mum would mind having a ten foot tall silver robotic rabbit living in her house?" Orville grinned, trying to imagine the expression on his Mum's face when he introduced her to Proto.

"Knowing Proto, I have a feeling it wouldn't be long before he and your Mum were the very best of friends."

When Proto's tray was empty he waved goodbye to the mice and made his way through the crowd to Sophia and Orville. A mouseling called out, "Bye, Proto! Can you come back tomorrow and play?"

Proto was almost giddy. "Did you hear that, Orville? That little mouseling would like me to come back tomorrow and play."

"I had a thought, Proto. What would you think about making Muridaan Falls your new home? You could live with me and Mum and make tasty snacks whenever you like, if that's what you want to do. You saw how much the mice love them. And even better, you could go on adventures with me and Sophia."

"Oh my, that does sound enticing. I would see the world firsthand, not just through the eyes of a glowbird. Think of all the delightfully ferocious creatures I would encounter! Imagine standing face to face with a deadly poisonous Plindorian Swamp Hornet, its hideous stinger only inches from my nose! Oh my, how thrilling that would be! You have convinced me, Orville Wellington Mouse. I'll do it. I shall move to Muridaan Falls."

Orville was genuinely surprised by how quickly his Mum accepted Proto, and how readily she had agreed to let Proto stay with them.

"Well, he seems friendly enough, and we could use a little help around the house. I've been working so many extra hours I've barely had a moment for housecleaning. Proto, would you mind helping out with the chores if you live with us?"

"I would be quite delighted, I assure you. I have already taken it upon myself to plan our menus for the next three months. Leave the grocery shopping to me, along with the preparation of all meals. Dinner will be served promptly at six o'clock every night, so please do try to be on time."

Orville's Mum took a step back, looking at Proto with new eyes. "Orville, clear out the spare room for our guest. My new friend Proto is more than welcome to stay with us as long as he wishes."

Chapter 37

Sophia's News

Orville was not surprised when Sophia told him she had been accepted at the Symocan Institute of Mechanistic Studies, but he was also not entirely happy about this turn of events. She had done so well on her entrance exams that not only was she granted a full scholarship, but the school was providing her room and board at no cost.

"Isn't that amazing? There's so much I want to learn there. Mirus Mouse says it's an excellent school, and even though Quintari's technology is far more advanced than Earth's, I still need to learn all the basic mechanistic theories and their practical applications first. After I graduate I can advance to a more specialized school if that's what I want to do."

"That's great. I'm really happy for you."

"You don't sound very happy for me."

"Well, to be really honest, you're my best friend and you're going away. I won't see you very much."

"You're forgetting about blinking. The Institute is only fifty miles north of Muridaan Falls on the other side of the mountains. I can blink back here in less than a minute, and you can blink up to the school in less than a minute. Don't forget you're my best friend too, and I want to see you just as much as you want to see me."

"I forgot about blinking. Maybe this won't be as bad as I thought."

"That's not all, Orville. The headmistress of the school is an old friend of Mirus Mouse and used to be a Metaphysical Adventurer. She told Mirus I could take time off from school if Master Marloh needs us, as long as I make up the work. That means we can still go on adventures together!"

"Now I really feel like celebrating. Why don't you come over for dinner tonight? Proto has a delicious meal planned and I know Mum would love to hear the good news about your school."

Orville hurried home to clear out the spare room and found Proto standing beside the blinker ship next to a mound of wooden crates and boxes. "What's all this stuff, Proto?"

"Good afternoon, Orville. I dashed back to the Cube for a few items I thought might come in handy on our adventures. I'll just set everything up in the spare room. Do you think our mum would mind if I installed a small duplonium powered electro-temporal optical synthesizer?"

"Wait, you said *our* mum?"

"Quite so. I've never had a mum before, so this will be a wonderful new experience for me. I will be relying on you to teach me the necessary protocols involved when addressing our mum. So, a duplonium powered optical synthesizer would be all right?"

"It won't explode will it?"

Proto threw back his head with a great laugh.

"Ha ha ha ha! I assure you, the odds of some cata-

279

strophic event such as that occurring are relatively small. Now, if you would give me a hand with some of these boxes, it would be most appreciated. Oh dear, do be careful with that one! If you drop it, a good portion of Muridaan Falls will be relocated to a most inhospitable environment filled with dreadful green fog, simply dreadful. If you think the creatures in Periculum are scary, you should see what's creeping around in that deadly green fog. Quite frightful, I assure you. Perhaps I should carry that for you."

Three nerve-racking hours later Orville was sitting at the kitchen table breathing in the delightful aroma of Proto's culinary creations.

"Mmmm... that smells wonderful, Proto. Mum, did Sophia tell you her good news?"

"She did indeed. I had no doubts at all she would be accepted by SIMS. Sophia is quite brilliant, as you yourself have said many times."

"You think I'm smart?" Sophia beamed brightly at Orville, a wide grin on her face.

"Yes, I've only said that about five hundred times now. You're very, very smart. Happy now?"

"I guess so. Oh, I almost forgot, Master Marloh wanted me to give you this note." Sophia pulled a crumpled piece of yellow paper from her pocket and set it down next to Orville.

"What is it?"

"I don't know. I'm not the kind of mouse who goes around snooping in other people's business."

Orville was about to mention the clockwork glow-birds but remembered his Mum was there. He unfolded the note and scanned it. "That's odd, Master Marloh wants to see me tomorrow afternoon, but the store is closed tomorrow. I wonder what he wants? Probably a bunch of new books arriving or something." He glanced over to Sophia, sending her a thought cloud. "Do you know anything about this? Is he sending us out on another mission already?"

A blue thought cloud floated out of Sophia's ear and over to Orville. "I don't know anything about it. He just asked me to give you the note."

Orville read the note again. He was getting a strange feeling about this. He glanced up to his Mum, who gave him a bright smile. "More snapberry pie, Orville?"

Chapter 38

The Ring

Orville found himself becoming more and more anxious about his meeting with Master Marloh. He knew it didn't have anything to do with new books. It was something far more important than that, but what that was Orville had no idea. He sat at the kitchen table absently poking his fork into a plate of snapberry flapcakes.

"Our mum seemed a little worried about you this morning, Orville. She said she heard you get up several times during the night. Are you all right?"

"Oh, thanks for asking Proto, I'm fine. I'm just a little nervous wondering why Master Marloh wants to see me."

"Oh my, I'm sure it's nothing at all. Perhaps he wants us to go fetch him one of those dreadful centipedes from Periculum. Ha ha ha ha!"

Orville smiled, but his apprehension was growing even stronger. There was much more to this than was readily apparent. He went to his room and attempted a short nap but couldn't sleep. He was still wide awake when it was time to go. He threw on some clean clothes, hurried downstairs and out the front door.

Twenty minutes later he was standing in front of the Book Emporium. He had to force himself to open the front door of the shop, stepping into the darkened building.

Master Marloh popped up from behind the counter when he heard Orville enter. "Ah, there you are, on time as always. Thank you for coming on your day off."

"Oh, I don't mind, Master Marloh. Umm... are there new books or something?" Orville knew there were no new books.

"No, nothing like that, but there is something I need to show you in the library. It's something you should see."

Master Marloh was studying Orville's face carefully. Orville had a feeling his world was about to change.

Master Marloh swung the blue door open and Orville took a deep breath, then followed him in. What he saw in the library was not what he was expecting to see in the library. He thought he had run through every possible scenario during his long sleepless night, but this was not one of them. He stood facing three mice he never thought he would see standing next to each other. He stood facing Sophia, the Thirteenth Monk, and his Mum.

"Hi, Orville. Surprise!" Sophia was trying her best to smile brightly, but Orville could see the anxious look in her eyes.

"Uhhh... Mum... what are you doing here?"

Orville's Mum stepped over to him and gave him a hug.

"I never thought I would see this day, but here we are. I have something for you."

His mum removed a small gold box from her coat

pocket and pressed it tightly into Orville's paws. "This is for you."

Orville's heart was pounding. He looked at Sophia and saw tears welling up in her eyes. He unlatched the small gleaming box and flipped it open. There was a ring inside. It was a Metaphysical Adventurers ring.

Orville looked up at his Mum in bewilderment. "You know about the Metaphysical Adventurers? I don't understand."

"That ring belonged to your Papa. He was not a fishermouse, he was a Metaphysical Adventurer. This was his ring, and I want you to have it." Orville could tell his Mum was trying not to cry.

"Papa was a Metaphysical Adventurer? That doesn't make sense. Why didn't he ever tell me? I thought he was a fishermouse."

Orville's Mum brushed her paw across his cheek.

"He loved you more than life. He didn't want to keep the truth from you, but he didn't want you following in his footsteps. He didn't want you to face the dangers he had to face every time he went out on a mission. He hid the truth from you even when you showed such an intuitive understanding of the meta-physical world."

"He wasn't lost at sea, was he?"

"No, he wasn't lost at sea. That was the story we both agreed on if something should happen to him."

"Sophia, did you know about this?"

"I just found out today. I can't believe our Papas were both Metaphysical Adventurers."

Orville turned a questioning eye to the Thirteenth Monk.

"You're wondering why I'm here?"

"You knew my Papa?"

"I did indeed, and that is part of the reason for my presence here, and part of the reason why your mum decided to give you the ring." The Thirteenth Monk's gaze moved to Orville's Mum.

She nodded. "You should be the one to tell him."

"Your papa was a true and cherished friend of mine. I have never met a kinder, more generous soul than your papa." The Thirteenth Monk paused. "Your Mum has been in possession of the ring you now hold for only two days. It was given to me by an old friend who found it while searching for ancient technology. There's far more to the story of course, but all that can wait. Orville, there is a chance your Papa might still be alive."

Chapter 39

Best Friends

A gentle breeze carried the delicate fragrance of ten thousand newly bloomed orange blossoms across the balmy summer air. It was far too early in the season for the trees to be bearing fruit, but the intoxicating scent of the blossoms floating through the grove was more than enough to satisfy Orville Wellington Mouse. Besides, strolling alongside Orville beneath a gloriously radiant summer sun was his best friend in the world, Sophia Mouse, and that alone made him supremely happy.

"I like this dream, Sophia. I'm glad we share it."

"I like it too, Orville. You know, I think we've been best friends for a very long time, a lot longer than you think."

"What do you mean?"

"Well, Papa always told me that if someone you love dies, you will find them again. You are drawn to the mice you love, no matter where they are or when they are. Your love for each other creates a connection that acts sort of like gravity. The universe warps the world around you and you just roll through life toward each other until you meet again."

"Kind of like those big green ball creatures who tried to eat me?"

Sophia snorted. "Well, not exactly like that, but maybe a little."

"Are you saying you love me, and that's why we met?"

"Of course I love you, Orville. Just don't ask me to say it when we're awake or I'll pound your arm till it turns purple."

"I promise I won't ask. I love you too. I feel as though I've known you forever."

"Do you really think someone as smart as I am didn't already know that about five minutes after I met you?"

"Unnggh! You think you know everything!"

"Maybe I do know everything. Hey, let's go climb that tree with the blue leaves and see how high we can go."

"Sophia, we can't climb that tree! It's a special mystical tree with perfectly round blue leaves. The Thirteenth Monk gave us one of its leaves and said we could use it to visit Periculum. We can't climb a tree that does weird things like that."

"Why not? Did the Thirteenth Monk tell you not to climb it? It's almost a thousand feet tall. Think how fun it would be."

"Well, I guess he didn't exactly say NOT to climb it."

"So let's go, then."

"Suppose I fall?"

"Orville, have you forgotten everything?? This is a dream, remember?" Sophia held her arms out and floated up into the air. "We can do anything we want in

a dream, if we know it's a dream. It's only when we don't know it's a dream that things get tricky."

"Who told you that?"

"Nobody told me that, I just figured it out."

"Oh, well in that case..." Orville floated up next to Sophia. "We could just fly to the top of the tree and take a quick look."

"What fun is that? The fun part is climbing the tree, not being at the top."

"You make a very good point, Sophia Mouse, and that is why, I, Orville Wellington Mouse do solemnly declare that the last mouse to reach the top of the giant mystical blue tree shall be known for all time as THE BIG PURPLE MONKEY BUTT!"

Orville flashed across the orange grove to the base of the gigantic tree and began scrambling up a low hanging branch. Sophia was only scant feet behind him, hollering, "Orville Wellington Mouse, you are the most immature mouse I have ever met, and I guarantee before this dream is over I will be calling you by your lovely new name, ORVILLE THE BIG PURPLE MONKEY BUTT!"

If you enjoyed reading
Orville Mouse and the Puzzle of the
Clockwork Glowbirds
please leave a short review or rating
on Amazon.com or on Goodreads.com
Reviews are the lifeblood of indie publishers –
we can't survive without them!

If you have any comments or suggestions
or would like to be notified of upcoming book
releases and Free Kindle book day promotions,
please email me at
BartholomewtheAdventurer@gmail.com

Best wishes until we meet again,

Tom Hoffman

ABOUT THE AUTHOR

Tom Hoffman received a B.S. in psychology from Georgetown University in 1972 and a B.A. in 1980 from the now-defunct Oregon College of Art. He has lived in Alaska with his wife since 1973. They have two adult children and two adorable grandchildren. Tom has been a graphic designer and artist for over 35 years. Redirecting his imagination from art to writing, he wrote his first novel, *The Eleventh Ring*, at age 63.

www.ingramcontent.com/pod-product-compliance
Lightning Source LLC
Chambersburg PA
CBHW071252170626
46809CB00001B/183